Envisioning the Americas:
Latina/o Theatre & Performance
a NoPassport Press Plays Sampler

Preface: "Who We Are"
By José Rivera

Cigarettes and Moby-Dick by Migdalia Cruz
Liz One by John Jesurun
Dias y Flores by Oliver Mayer
Marea by Alejandro Morales
and
Land of Benjamin Franklin
by Anne García-Romero

Introduced and Edited by Caridad Svich

NoPassport Press

Dreaming the Americas Series

Envisioning the Americas: Latina/o Theatre &
Performance Volume Copyright 2011.

Cigarettes and Moby-Dick © 1996 by Migdalia Cruz

Liz One © 2009 by John Jesurun

Dias y Flores © 2009 by Oliver Mayer

Marea © 2011 (revised) by Alejandro Morales

Land of Benajmin Franklin © 2007 by Anne García-
Romero

"Considering Utopia" © 2010 by Caridad Svich

"Who We Are" © 2011 by José Rivera

NoPassport Press, First edition 2011 by NoPassport Press, PO
Box 1786, South Gate, CA 90280 USA;
NoPassportPress@aol.com, **ISBN: 978-0-578-08274-5**

Book Design:

All scripts in this volume have been formatted for publication by Patrick Danner.

Spanish text formatted by Meghan Walker.

Additional formatting and overall book design by Caridad Svich

Cover image: from the world premiere of John Jesurun's <u>Liz One</u>. Photo credit: Paula Court.

Considering Utopia

Find yourself in a hotel room in Utopia, Texas
overlooking the cypress-lined Sabinal River.
Consider the expanse of sky and the relative
ease of the river's current. An image of a
perfect society emerges in your mind, where
the metaphysical space that encompasses
language, history, morality and sexuality is in
harmonious, hopeful balance. Here in the
small room in the middle of seeming
nowhere, considerations of beauty, love and
social change dance on an open stage
liberated from the concerns of globalization,
neo-liberalism and terror. Today, you think, is
beauteous pretend and play. Tomorrow will
be another day. But the more you look out of
your hotel room and scan the limits of Utopia,
the more the Texas sky calls you to action, to,
in effect, give up pretend, and get on with the
reality of life. And yet, what if your job is to
pretend, and indeed, to play?

In the collective no-space shared between
audience and practitioners, expressions of
utopian desire abound when we walk into and
take part in the theater laboratory. In the Here
of shared literal and metaphorical space,
dreams of new societies are imagined,
constructed and dismantled, liberated from
the constraints outside the demarcated space
of deep play. Theater and live performance
retains its dangerous potentiality, in part,

because it posits a shared space of dreaming for society. Running counter to theater's multidimensional, utopian impulse are the anti-utopian modes of hierarchy and exclusivity inscribed in its economics, forms and institutions (especially of bourgeois theater). Thus, if you are committed to a utopian practice after the onset of late capitalism, where do you go to dream?

In Utopia, Texas, the modest Main Street runs through the center of town, and talk of fishing, hunting, gardening, cycling and swimming tends to dominate the conversations overheard on the street. There is some talk of art and occasionally of photography, but very rarely, if ever, of live performance, unless the subject is of a local or national pop, country, or roots band playing in a town or two nearby. Theater, in other words, is something of a curiosity and best left to the local kindergarten or high school play. How odd it is to pretend to be someone else? Odder still to want to do that for a life's journey.

I've been writing plays and theatre pieces for nearly twenty years. Sometimes I can't even imagine what compelled me to consider the strange utopia of the stage as the most exciting embodiment for my stories. I often ask students to describe the first live performance they say that truly made an impact on them. Most of them speak of moments when they were on stage for the first time in their local kindergarten, elementary, middle or high school and often how they delighted in singing, dancing or some combination thereof. Occasionally, some of my writing students will talk about a show their parents took them to see for a special birthday or graduation. Often, the show was a Broadway musical or a touring production of a Broadway musical. One of my students said to me the other day without the least bit of facetiousness that the Disney Corporation probably had had the greatest impact on his imagination.

If you write for the theater, invariably, you know you're writing for what is likely a limited audience. The collective no-space of play rarely can accommodate thousands or even millions, unlike the non-collective space of film, which doesn't even require an audience to complete its experience. A piece of film runs on a loop and it matters not whether someone is watching, but a play really cannot truly exist and vibrate in the resonant space of performance without the presence of the audience, even if it is an audience of one.

What happens, then, when you build a dream in virtuality? In 2002 I wanted to expand some of the experiments I'd been conducting through the creation of online texts with multiple authors into something less tangible and yet hopefully as utopian as the making of a theater piece. I reached out to a band of twelve colleagues in the field to see if they'd like to be part of a virtual, national collective called NoPassport. I said "Let's play with words and music. Let's see what mind of word-songs we can share in the free digital utopia of e-mail and the internet. The space we inhabited for about a year was mutable, quirky, offbeat, passionate, adventurous, bold and intimate. We posted pieces for live performance, we wrote texts together, and we performed live in venues such as Tonic and the Bric and even wrote a manifesto entitled "Dirty Thoughts About Money." In 2003, I curated a symposium at INTAR Theatre in New York City about the state of U.S. Latino/a playwriting. My goal was then to simply gather voices from across generations and also from across the country. Not just the Nuyorican voice, but the Southwestern, Chicano, Afro-Caribbean, Cuban, Western, Southern and hybrid voices that make up the vast, complex, multivalent shelf where U.S. Latino/a writing is placed within the larger American voice. A symposium turned into a jam session and the jam session turned into a call for a hub, a network, a virtual place where we could always meet, jam, riff, rant, advocate, mentor, debate, and play. Suddenly, the band of 12 became a band of 500 and counting and NoPassport theater alliance was in action.

Since 2003, we've staged roundtables at universities and theaters across the country, convened for five national conferences (2007-2011) - the first three hosted by Frank Hentschker and the Martin E. Segal Theater Center at the CUNY Graduate Center in New York City, and the last two hosted by Daniel Gallant and the Nuyorican Poets Café in new York City - published fifteen titles of new plays and translations, and sprung a spoken word arm mischievously called Hibernating Rattlesnakes, that has performed at the Nuyorican Poets Café and INTAR, respectively, over the last two years. I can't even imagine what kind of utopian dream was being conjured when I put out the invitation to play back in 2002, but I do know that a virtual space was transformed by the living, breathing, thinking bodies and minds of a critical mass of practitioners, scholars, and fellow dreamers. How does one prepare to build and confront a dream? How does one enter a space of Utopia?

As a playwright (and in my parallel careers as translator and editor), I find myself constantly negotiating the difficult, complex terrain of utopian desire(s). Much of my writing for the stage in particular addresses the shifting political and emotional geographies of characters left behind by their societies or caught in the rigid hierarchies of non-utopian states. I write hybrid, Latina/o, Anglo, Black, Creole, Asian, Indigenous, transgender, bi, queer, straight figures who often are not labeled or categorized, and do not want to be either. I've always thought the most amazing thing about writing is the fact that you can enter any Body, that are you always as a writer Another at one and the same, and that the political freedom of writing is charged with the profound borderless-ness that the creative act requires and demands. In effect, the lack of passport, the No Passport, where the bounteous beauty and chaos of creation lives, regardless of the kind of story (genre) you're writing or its subject matter.

As founder of NoPassport theater alliance & press, I'm also negotiating my role as citizen of the Americas and the world with my role as an artist. A speech I wrote, for example, on legacy and revolution at the 2009 NoPassport theatre alliance conference at the Martin E. Segal Theatre Center at the CUNY Graduate Center in New York City made me think about how I was going to then actually put forth some of the ideas and challenges I presented in the speech in my own work for the stage and in addition, the kind of dialogue I wanted to sustain and nurture with my ongoing, unofficial band of collaborators.

What does it truly mean to dream a space of radical utopia, for example, when you're creating work within an institution that has its own set of hierarchies and boundaries?

I find the utopian desire and the shared experience of live performance and the space of possibility and transformation that it calls forth, at its best, to be as honest, flawed, raw, strange and beautiful as life itself. I recognize the deeply collaborative, intertwined nature of the work we all do in the theater, and how community is and can be sustained with simple acts of grace and the joy of playing, despite the considerable hardships that can pose themselves financially on those of us, many of us, in the starving class. I'm invariably surprised by the imprint left on a shared experience long after the experience itself has become worn into memory, how, in effect, the spaces of play invite us to re-consider our daily lives and our interactions with our fellow citizens on this planet.

The following five plays written by dramatists who have been part of the NoPassport Press imprint since 2008 represent five distinct visions of a new America and a renewed perspective of and on the Americas. Playwrights Migdalia Cruz, John Jesurun, Oliver Mayer, Alejandro Morales, Anne Garcia-Romero bear witness in joyful and profound ways to the deep mysteries alive in our communal soil, and how these mysteries make us more wakeful citizens in and out of the theatre. José Rivera's preface "Who We Are" opens the window of inspiration for the present and next generation of theatre-makers and teaches all of us in the field to embrace the beauty and promise of the imagination.

As the Texan sky bears down on a hotel room deep in the heart of Utopia, I wonder at the fact that when we Pretend and Play, real things, real transformation, can happen.

Caridad Svich

Playwright and founder of NoPassport

Who We Are

This is who we are.

We're partisans in a great struggle that may seem holy to some and crazy to others, but is wildly quixotic even at the best of times.

We're all veterans of hope, sergeants and captains of an idealism and courage that seem anachronistic and beautifully, dolefully, painfully antique.

Because what we do, what we are trained to do, is to keep an ancient and sullied and disrespected and much maligned and amazing tradition alive.

We together keep the spoken word from going silent, spectacle from disappearing in the ones and zeros of forgetfulness, great life-and-death themes from dying of malnutrition, enormous characters and souls from the purgatory of indifference and ignorance.

Together we keep the The House of Atreus from foreclosure and the Skryker from extinction and Kent and Salem from dying of cancer and Pozzo from getting too lucky.

We are apostles of language, dreamers in blank verse, aristocrats of sight gags, archeologists of gesture and dance and sword battles and mask wearing and mythic games of tragic and comic consequences.

We bring Falstaff to the party and hope he doesn't get too drunk and pinch too many butts even as we enter through the back door and try to deliver dream-worlds to the wary and the post-modern and the unsuspecting.

We traffic in awe and metaphors and are impatient with the ordinary and expected.

We fight the inertia of silence and talk too loud in polite locations and there is no Ritalin for us.

We don't succumb to psychoanalysis and the voodoo of easy answers.

We thrive on complexity and ask that our monsters truly terrify us, that our lovers truly slay us with their passion, that our magicians truly make something out of nothing and hand it to us with smoke and a rakish smile.

We seek connections with the strange and communion with brave souls seeking the truth – not the entire truth, just a piece of it will do – a coin of truth we can keep in a pocket near our valuables, that we can spend in those frightening moments when we don't know ourselves, when we're in too deep and some clarity would help, some beauty that could redeem and enliven the night.

We turn awful experience and bad relationships and murdering office jobs and loveless parents and poverty and addictions and angst and loss and death itself into the fearsome gold of art.

We are alchemists and con artists, acrobats and used car salesmen, liars and enlighteners, and we are here to do the earth's bidding because the earth is screaming out its stories and begging for us to write them down, and act them out, and draw her pretty pictures on the face of the clouds.

Here are some of the highs and lows of this amazing journey.

There's joy as you travel to wonderful places and receive the smiles and affection of new friends made in the crucible of performance, in front of raging armies of critics and prove-it-to-me, I've-paid-too-much-for-these-tickets, I-saw-it-last-year-in-London audiences and a perfect stranger comes up to you after the show to say they never felt so transported in the theatre before and they understand something about life they never understood until tonight and how you captured her parents' pain and nobility so beautifully.

Fatigue as you give it everything you have, every single day, every muscle engaged in a marathon that doesn't end until you end.

Pain because you tell yourself it's just a gig, just a job, but then you fall in love with it anyway.

Discovery of your limits and appreciation for the breathless power of your mastery.

Bliss when you've written that one good sentence; or you delivered that one perfect moment when the lights are on you and only you; or you discover in the text an idea or an image or a parable so true that it makes your audience weep with recognition; or you put out into the world a rendering of a staircase or a costume or a throne of gold in three brilliant dimensions that just last week existed in none.

Awe when you sit backstage, a moment before your entrance and realize you're about to give the greatest soliloquy in our language.

Gratitude when it dawns on you that you make a living from the honey and perspiration of your mind.

Excitement when you write Act One, Scene One on the top of the first page; and you sit along the wall on the afternoon of your third call-back for your favorite play; and you stand in the back of the house and that moment you worked on for fourteen hours with that actor who never seemed to get it gets the biggest laugh of the night.

Amazement when your lights reflect in the physics of time and space exactly what's happening in the unlit chambers and labyrinths of the hero's soul.

Even more amazement when your project, which you put together with faith, spit, and favors, turns a remarkable profit in actual U.S. currency.

Humility when you look around and everyone else seems more successful, or richer, or quicker, or better reviewed or living on both coasts and are equally familiar with Silver Lake and Williamsburg.

Relief when you figure out that, like all great cyclical events in nature, your long career will rise and fall and you'll be hot, then forgotten, then hot, then forgotten, then hot again.

Anger when the words won't cooperate and the costume's too tight and you made a grave error in casting the world premiere, or passion seems to be ebbing, or you'd rather have a baby, or the grant goes to your rival, or that barbarian in the second row keeps texting his lawyer, or ten people show up to your reading in a theatre with three empty hundred seats, or you can't stand Bushwick anymore, or the McArthur people overlooked you – again – or the sitcom's too tempting, or your favorite actor's not available, or the culture's going south while you're going north.

Or maybe you've forgotten something – you forgot the joy and the magic and the purpose and the need for it all.

But then you remember and come back anyway.

That's the amazing part.

You come back the next day because even when the words don't come and the costume's cutting off the blood to your legs, this activity connects you to your most authentic and naked self, to the child who told sweeping sock puppet sagas and imitated your dad's big laugh and drew pictures of avenging super heroes, to the adolescent who fell in love with the smell of opening night flowers, to the mature artist who became enthralled with the great blank space, that enchanted oval, on which battles determine the course of history and lovers learned the key expressions of the heart and men and women modeled heroism and humanity and Estragon lost his way and colored girls considered suicide and Proctor wouldn't sign his name and Arial was free to go and a wicked Moon under a Lorca sky betrayed the idea of love.

You come back to balance art and family, and sometimes your checkbook, because nothing feels as good as the act of acting.

You endure the indifference of agents and literary managers because nothing sounds as nice as the click of that perfect metaphor falling into place.

You put off children, or you put off real estate, or you put off the thousand intangible compromises of the spirit because nothing frees you from the dark enchantments of gravity like this.

You stay up to three in the morning memorizing those sides for your best friend's new play even though she wrote the part for you and the producers insist you have to audition anyway, because nothing brings you closer to Creation that this.

So why do you do these things?

Why come back when it hurts so much?

What kind of people are we?

How crazy do we have to be to put up with this?

Let's face it, given the speed of today's run-away clocks, given the accumulation of power and money in the hands of the very few and all the injustice that flows from that, given the complexity of social intercourse in an age of instant talk and delayed reflection, you're a member of a different species entirely.

You age differently than the rest of the population.

You try hard not to succumb to the common theories and manias of the crowd.

You speak in tongues when everyone else is speaking in fortune cookies.

You make one-of-a-kind little miracles with your bare and blistered hands for below minimum wage as stock markets soar and die and soar and die.

You write about your existential pain in unsentimental words for sentimental audiences.

Your curiosity is so vast and out of control you don't know boundaries and you annoy your lovers with your constant need to analyze their every nuance and no answer is ever good enough because each answer leads to ten new questions.

You dream in such vivid colors, you wonder if you can market your sleep as the next cool drug.

Your sensitivity to the pain and joy of others is so acute you might as well have multiple personalities.

You and failure are so intimate with each other you could birth one another's bawling babies.

You are gifted and cursed with a love of words so intense few other pleasures can move you like Lopahin's declaration that he bought the cherry orchard, or what Li'l Bit had to do to learn to drive, or what devils of self-doubt whispered to a beautiful and wounded soul in a psychosis at 4:48 am.

For all this and more you went school and sacrificed, and worked your ass off, and delayed some big life decisions, and dreamed exceptional dreams, and fertilized your mind, and kept important promises you made to yourself.

That's the important part: you kept the promises you made to yourself to stay in it and work.

You, the fighter and hero of this morning's tale are primed and ready to unpack your Heiner Muller and your tap shoes and your colored pencils and are brimming with ideas and full of courage and full of fight and you know the obstacles and laugh in their faces and the dragons you fight are windmills and the windmills you fight are straw and the time to talk about doing it is over.

It's time to do it.

So let's go out now, you and I, lets go out and make some art.

■ José Rivera

José Rivera is the author of many plays, including <u>Marisol</u> and <u>Boleros for the Disenchanted</u>, the screenplay for "The Motercycle Diaries," the forthcoming novel <u>Love Makes the City Crumble</u>, and is the writer-director of the film "Celestina." This text was originally written as the 2010 USC School of Theatre Commencement Speech, and was revised for this publication by the author.

CIGARETTES AND MOBY-DICK

A play

by

Migdalia Cruz

About the Playwright:

MIGDALIA CRUZ is an award-winning playwright who has written more than forty plays, operas, screenplays and musicals including: Fur, Miriam's Flowers, and Another Part of the House. Her work has been produced in venues as diverse as the National Theater of Greece in Athens, Old Red Lion in London, the Houston Grand Opera, Ateneo Puertoriqueño, and the Latino Chicago Theater Company where she was writer-in-residence from 1991 to 1998. She is an alumna of New Dramatists, was mentored by Maria Irene Fornés at INTAR, and her latest play, El Grito Del Bronx, was performed at NYU, at Milagro Theater in Portland, OR, and opened in Chicago at the Goodman Theater in a co-production of Teatro Vista and CollaborAction. TWO ROBERTS: A Pirate-Blues Project, commissioned by the Lark with an NYSCA grant is slated for a studio workshop in February 2011. Her 2010 collection of plays published by NoPassport Press, entitled El Grito Del Bronx, features: Yellow Eyes, Salt, Da Bronx Rocks, a portion of Song For New York: What Women DO While Men Sit Knitting presented by Mabou Mines, and El Grito Del Bronx.

For all performance rights to Migdalia Cruz's work Contact the author c/o Peregrine Whittlesey Agency, 279 CPW, NY, NY 10024, 212-787-1802, e-mail: pwwagy@aol.com

CAST OF CHARACTERS

MIRANDA - a woman in her 20s, assimilated, downtown Puerto Rican; sexy and self-destructive

LILA - a woman in her 20s; an accent from somewhere in Eastern Europe; pretty but doesn't know it; likes to talk to things that don't talk back

MARILYN - a woman in her 30s; the image of Marilyn Monroe from AndyWarhol's lithograph

JOHN 1 - a sailor in his 20s; white, earnest, affectionate

JOHN 2 - a sailor in his 20s; Latino, lusty, abusive in a pragmatic way

JOHN 3 - a sailor in his 20s; black, quiet, intellectual

TIME: The near future.

PLACE: One summer to fall in New York City.

CIGARETTES AND MOBY-DICK

PROLOGUE:

Lights up dimly on MIRANDA curled into a ball on the red velvet couch,clutching a stuffed white whale, at Loew's Paradise Movie Theater in the Bronx. We hear the sound of a scene from the movie "Gentlemen Prefer Blondes," this segues into crashing waves and seabirds. A flashlight follows the edge of the wall and finally rests on MIRANDA. The light of the flashlight freezes on her face. MIRANDA wakes up suddenly, and holds her head for a moment, then begins to hit herself on the forehead repeatedly. The lights cross to three sailors, the JOHNs, who enter around her. MIRANDA reaches for her book, a copy of Herman Melville's "Moby-Dick". We hear the sound of a subway mixed with the sound from the intro to "Detour Ahead" as MIRANDA crosses to a pier in Manhattan.

ACT ONE:

Chapter One

(MIRANDA is alone on a pier in Manhattan. JOHNs 1, 2, & 3 watch her and describe her actions.)

JOHN 3: The serious girl with black braids streaked too early by gray, takes out a pair of scissors and cuts the middle out of a thick book...

MIRANDA: Good place to hide cigarettes.

JOHN 2: She tucks five cigarettes into the hole and closes the book...Herman Melville's Moby-Dick. Her wet fingers search her pocket for the last of her pack...

MIRANDA: Better light up before it rains again. It keeps raining again.

JOHN 1: The cigarette lights with a flash of orange showing the moonlight off her painted pearly coral fingernails...

MIRANDA: People don't look out for the details like I do. I got all the ammunition in myself to fight most anything. I got the smell of peaches on my brain so I won't ever go hungry. I got the feeling of a telephone in my hand so I can call anybody I want to—so I'm never lonely. I got the taste of uncooked meat in my mouth so I know when I'm bleeding.

JOHN 3: She takes a deep drag that she can feel in her toes...

MIRANDA: It's a red feeling. Deeper than I thought there was room to go. I feel long now. I can touch the top of anything.

JOHN 2: She keeps filling herself up with smoke.

JOHN 1: And silence.

(As MIRANDA speaks, the MEN act like they're friends at sea, JOHN 2 is the object of desire for the other two. A fight breaks out. The two suitors tear the clothes off the object of desire, who runs from them and tears the American flag off a flagpole and wraps it around his naked body. JOHNs 1 & 3 push him to the ground and JOHN 2 rocks on the floor, crying softly, as JOHNs 1 & 3 watch and cheer. It's timed to coincide with MIRANDA's telling of the events.)

MIRANDA: I almost finished reading this book, but it made me sad. Men almost always make me sad, when it's just them alone— without women. They always do crazy things when they're all together like that. Like pirates. I bet they did weird shit on the ocean. In the middle of the great big like that...they probably ate too much fish. I bet that did something bad to them. I bet they started to smell like fish and I bet a lot of fights broke out. Who stinks more than who and shit like that. I bet most of the fights were about smells...I bet there was one guy who smelled like a woman...He was a really busy guy. He drove all the other men nuts for his smell. They rubbed up against him, trying to steal his sweat, cop his smell. They put out long pieces of fabric for him to roll up in, naked. And leave his body stains there for them to raise like a flag. That was no ordinary Jolly Rogers on this pirate ship—this ship floated on the fluids of a man who smelled like a woman. It was a slow ship. Languid. It liked to take naps in the afternoon and make love for many hours at a time...I'm a pirate too.

(MIRANDA takes a cigarette from the inside of her copy of Moby-Dick,tears off the filter, sticks it roughly in her mouth and lights it.)

MIRANDA: I think I better buy another copy and finish reading it though. Commit it to memory. I have a feeling it's gonna have my life.

JOHN 3: Books can do that—for some of us they're the only way.

JOHN 1, 2, 3: Call me John.

(We hear Jackie Moore's "This Time Baby" as the lights follow MIRANDA as SHE crosses the deck of the Staten Island Ferry. LILA joins her.)

Chapter Two

(LILA & MIRANDA are on the Staten Island Ferry. John 2 watches.)

JOHN 2: Two women alone could get up to all sorts of things. My sisters glued my head to my pillow once—so I could get good dreams.

MIRANDA: Want a dog?

LILA: I hate those things.

MIRANDA: But they taste better on these boats. They taste like dogs are supposed to taste. And the mustard here is real good.

LILA: Gulden's.

MIRANDA: A classic.

LILA: Just plain old Gulden's...I hear there's a great French restaurant on Staten Island.

MIRANDA: Get outta here!

LILA: No, really. A fabulous—like four-star restaurant.

MIRANDA: Why would a fabulous four star restaurant be on Staten Island. It could be in Manhattan or Paris or Milan. But Staten Island? Like my Papi used to say, "Somebody was grabbing your leg." I can't believe you'd fall for such a lie. It's not possible.

LILA: Why not? Sometimes you just start a restaurant where the rent is cheap. Maybe they were poor French immigrants who had to buy cheap and grew to love the little hamlet of Staten Island.

MIRANDA: I hate French food.

LILA: Nobody with a tongue hates French food.

MIRANDA: It's too delicate. It doesn't even seem like food. I like food that stays around for a while—Spanish food or Italian food.

LILA: How about German food?

MIRANDA: Franks, yes, but not those wurst things—they're too big.

LILA: Not delicate enough for you.

MIRANDA: It's got nothing to do with delicacy. It's style. Wursts have no style.

LILA: But you sleep with men.

MIRANDA: Men are not wursts. They are more than wursts. They best one are more like franks.

LILA: I wouldn't know.

MIRANDA: It's true.

LILA: Uh, huh. Can we go to this French restaurant?

MIRANDA: You got an address?

LILA: Of course.

MIRANDA: I'm only going because I love you. I might make a scene.

LILA: What kind of scene?

MIRANDA: A big one—with big people. I'll get every overweight person in the place to throw up at the same time so I can get a free meal.

LILA: You're not overweight.

MIRANDA: I know. But you are.

(LILA throws her soda at MIRANDA who laughs and runs away from her. LILA catches up to her. THEY kiss.)

I never kissed a girl in public before.

LILA: It was time. (LILA takes out a small wrapped box.) Here little girl.

MIRANDA: You remembered!

LILA: Of course. Our 30th day of being fully aware of each other—how could I ever forget such a date?

MIRANDA: I did.

(MIRANDA opens the box, it's a ring.)

Wow! That's serious gold. It's so—dykey.

LILA: Yeah, well. You're supposed to say, "Darling, it's beautiful! I'm so glad you gave up two months of your nurses' salary from the hospital from hell to buy it for me!"

MIRANDA: You still want me to move in, don't you?

LILA: Second thoughts? Cold feet?

MIRANDA: Maybe... If I was a car, what would I be?

LILA: A Volkswagen... beetle.

MIRANDA: Bitch!

(LILA laughs and beings to exit and MIRANDA follows her.)

JOHN 2: —and for a moment they stop and listen and hum the same song of love...each remembering the other's taste and feeling heavy with it—unable to move anything but their lips...but then they move on.

(We hear a reprise of Jackie Moore's "This Time Baby" as lights cross to MIRANDA and LILA in bed.)

Chapter Three

(MIRANDA & LILA in bed, smoking a joint. JOHN 2 watches.)

JOHN 2: It's enough sometimes—just to watch. Let your eyes do the walking. No awkward conversation. No declarations or false romance. Just melt into someone else's skin. But feel no pain. Just burn. Just skin.

LILA: What do you think?

MIRANDA: Comfy. Definitely better than the Martha Washington Hotel for Hard-up Women. I think my bed had crabs in it.

LILA: Don't give them to me!

MIRANDA: Don't worry. I escaped in time.

LILA: Damn! How could you stay there?

MIRANDA: No choice. No place else to go.

LILA: You got a place now, baby. Right here. I want you here.

MIRANDA: Really? I want you too... only you. Only my arms, Lila.

(THEY kiss sweetly.)

You sure?

LILA: If you ask me one more time, I'll fucking kill you.

MIRANDA: No, you wouldn't.

LILA: How do you know?

MIRANDA: You got that kind of face. And your hands... the hands of an angel.

LILA: My father used to say, "A devil's just an angel that's human."

MIRANDA: Don't spoil it.

LILA: What?

MIRANDA: Don't.

LILA: What? (No response; re-lighting the joint.) Want some more?

MIRANDA: Yeah... I always want some more.

(THEY share the joint, each inhaling deeply.)

The U.S.S. Governor's in town. Sailors everywhere. My friend Michael, an ex-marine says to call 'em "squids"—that's what you do he says. He says "they called us jarheads and we called 'em squids." Marines are tougher. He says an exotic dancer once had her snake's head bitten off by a jarhead. "Too bad," he says. "She did the nasty with that snake. That snake made her famous. Kept her warm too..." Anyway, yeah, there's luscious squids everywhere. A sea of white in Times Square. And they're at all my favorite bars. And I'm thinking, yeah...I can smell the heat from the folds of those loose white pants and those pants, man...they hitch up in the most delightful way. I look for the stains in those folds...and I can't stop thinking about it.

LILA: You're such a fucking bitch.

MIRANDA: Rub my back.

LILA: Hell-shit-fuck no.

MIRANDA: Rub it, honey.

LILA: Don't you call me that!

MIRANDA: Baby, sweetie, lamby, poochie?

LILA: I lost it to a man in white pants. He wore 'em like a girl. With a belt real tight, giving him hips. And I thought: Okay. Why not? He plunged into me like a stuffed fucking toilet. One deep, hard, pop. And it was over. And his eyes never left the t.v. set. Staring, hypnotized by the flip in the vertical hold washing over the last show of the evening —"Sermonette..." My Catholic virgin's blood staining his plaid Ralph Lauren sheets—from the country collection...He said he had to throw those sheets out—couldn't wash me off them.

MIRANDA: What kind of white pants?

LILA: What do you mean?

MIRANDA: What were they made of? Cotton, polyester, wool?

LILA: I don't remember—not polyester though. Because you know polyester when you feel it. Your fingernails get all caught in it and shit. And it hurts your teeth.

MIRANDA: Yeah... you can always tell polyester.

(MIRANDA kisses LILA and runs her tongue over LILA's eyes. LILA puts her fingers through MIRANDA's hair.)

JOHN 2: I can smell each strand now. Each hair gently touched, softly tasted. A swift bitter bite on the cheek stinging with love... So much better than being there.

(We hear Marilyn Monroe singing "I Wanna Be Loved By You", as the lights fade on the bedroom and cross to the Circle Line Cruise boat. JOHN 1 reads from a thick book, MIRANDA smokes, and JOHN 2 sits across from her.)

Chapter Four

(On the outside deck of the Circle Line, MIRANDA paces in front of JOHN 3, smoking. JOHN 3 notices her and throws a gold coin condom at his feet. SHE approaches it slowly as JOHN 1 speaks. JOHN 1 reads and watches.)

JOHN 1: (Reading a book.) I have part of this memorized.

(HE puts down the book.)

The Circle Line is a romantic ship. It circles— like the Sun, or a boomerang, or a hole— around the borough of Manhattan. It's a view best seen from the sea. On land there is no hope, but the water makes things beautiful—baptizes the Earth. Even the dirty East River looks more inviting than Tenth Avenue...

(MIRANDA reaches for the gold coin condom as JOHN 3 intercepts her.)

JOHN 3: That's mine.

MIRANDA: Doesn't have your name on it.

JOHN 3: Neither does my behind, but I know its mine.

MIRANDA: What is it anyway?

JOHN 3: A condom. Don't tell me you never seen one before.

MIRANDA: I never seen one like that. It could make a nice earring for somebody.

JOHN 3: This is the great, super-duper, supreme works-like-a-charm condom.

MIRANDA: Really?

JOHN 3: Yeah, really.

MIRANDA: It matches your skin.

JOHN 3: What kind of crack is that?

MIRANDA: Like the one in your beautiful, black butt.

JOHN 3: You don't know nothing about my crack. I don't let women see my crack. If they see my crack, they must be my mama, because she's the only one sees my crack. Understand?

MIRANDA: Yeah, sure... Sorry.

JOHN 3: You make too many jokes. You make me feel stupid with your jokes. Your jokes are stupid.

MIRANDA: I know. But the gold does go good with your skin.

JOHN 3: That's ignorant. That's like me saying to you that pork fat matches your face.

MIRANDA: I do look like a pig—I mean, pink like that. But I'm not really pink—except in the parts that matter.

JOHN 3: Oh?

MIRANDA: No. That's just what I look like... Inside I'm midnight. Like burned steak.

JOHN 3: Who burned you?

MIRANDA: Everybody.

JOHN 3: That's boring. You're boring. You bore me, lady.

MIRANDA: I know—it's my nature. What book is that?

JOHN 3: One you ain't never read. Why do you ask?

MIRANDA: Always looking for something to read. Is it exciting?

JOHN 3: Only to me.

MIRANDA: Those are the best kind. Do you do the five-fingered frug when you read it?

JOHN 3: (With a laugh) You're crazy, lady.

MIRANDA: Must get lonely...all that— reading. By your lonesome. Don't you want someone to suck your dick? While you read, I mean. Wouldn't that give your book new meaning?

JOHN 3: Depends— On who was doing the sucking. A man can't let just anyone suck him off. It's dangerous. You put your life into someone else's mouth—and they can bite it off. I can't think of anything more stupid than that. Listen, why don't you just run on off and

ask somebody else your little questions.
There's no room at this inn, baby.

(JOHN 3 stalks off as MIRANDA calls out
after him.)

MIRANDA: Home is where the hard-on is.
See? I can quote out of context too.

(MIRANDA sees JOHN 2 watching her and
moves directly to him.)

MIRANDA: I love seamen.

JOHN 2: Huh?

MIRANDA: Seamen. Navy men. Men of the
sea. Riding waves. Dreaming, eating, living on
the ocean. No dry land to keep you from the
moist sea mist. Foam. Don't you love foam?

JOHN 2: It's ok. You have nice legs.

MIRANDA: Do you have a nice penis?

JOHN 2: Sure... he's my partner. I don't make
a move without him.

MIRANDA: That's good... If I was a car,
what would I be?

JOHN 2: A jaguar. You have a great face.

MIRANDA: Tell me a dream.

(SHE takes his hand and puts it on her lap. HE pats her.)

JOHN 1: With the right kind of information, she can see down inside you, into all those places you can't reach with soap.

JOHN 2: I don't remember my dreams.

MIRANDA: Why not?

JOHN 2: I dunno, I know I have them, because I wake up like I've been somewhere.

MIRANDA: I dream the same thing all the time... that Moby-Dick eats Ishmael, and then there's no book because there's no one to tell the story.

(JOHN 2 pulls his hand away, like he's been burned.)

JOHN 2: I meant that... about your legs.

MIRANDA: Pull up your pants.

JOHN 2: Nooo... Do you mean it?

MIRANDA: Yeah. I'd love to see your legs.

JOHN 2: Okay.

JOHN 1: Those white trousers peel up so slowly—the gentle tearing of the skin of a ripe fruit. Revelation: lean, smooth legs, hairless, fragile...

MIRANDA: You must have your mother's legs.

JOHN 2: Yeah. The boys tease me about it... you know how boys are.

MIRANDA: I know. Those legs must drive them crazy.

JOHN 2: I dunno... just kidding me I think. I've still got this horse face. Nothing feminine about that.

(SHE takes JOHN 2's hand and puts it on her forehead.)

JOHN 1: His sweaty hand trembles. He knows she's the cause for his heat.

MIRANDA: Do I have a fever?

JOHN 2: No... You're kinda cold to the touch. And wet. Like a dog. Like its nose.

MIRANDA: Want a cigarette?

JOHN 2: Can't smoke yet. Gotta wait till we get... off.

MIRANDA: Not to smoke it. Just hold it. Between your lips. Cradle it in your teeth. Rock it there with your tongue. Taste it. It's my cigarette so it'll taste like me. Hold it in your mouth until it comes apart with your spit and your teeth working it like a virus. Getting to its center. Stopping its heart. Letting the brown bits of it shred in your mouth. Choke you. Drink it down fast. Once it's loose it's gotta go fast like a funeral on a French train. Zip. Zip. Zip. Your spit will never taste the same after that. Double exposure—your spit, my taste.

JOHN 2: Wha-what exactly is in your cigarettes?

MIRANDA: My father's ashes. And my mother's. And some of mine. I burn parts of me—as they come out. Tonsils. Appendix. Thyroid. Cysts—one from my right armpit. One from my right ovary. It's mainly the right that's going.

JOHN 2: Give me one.

(SHE slowly takes one from inside Moby-Dick and licks it from top to bottom.)

JOHN 1: He doesn't know the danger—her spit is a liquid form of love. She tastes like him.

(MIRANDA hands him the cigarette and HE licks it too. Then, with a smile, HE hands it back.)

JOHN 2: Here. I don't smoke.

MIRANDA: There's always a first time.

JOHN 2: Firsts are never any good. I like experience. Your legs are experienced. And your forearms. I like thick forearms on a woman. A good place to tattoo.

MIRANDA: What kind of tattoo?

JOHN 2: A white whale smoking a big, blue cigarette, like mine.

(HE lifts his sleeve and shows her his arm.)

See? When I make a muscle it gets a hard-on. See? Like on the legs of the camel on a pack of Camels.

MIRANDA: I gotta buy a pack.

(SHE stokes his tattoo.)

That's a beauty—but my whale would have a sailor on its back. Do you know how to make one?

JOHN 2: Nah. That's an art, y'know. People with needles and storefronts are the only ones who know.

(SHE takes the licked cigarette, unzips her denim skirt, places the cigarette inside her panties, zips up and crosses her legs.)

Some old guy in the Bronx did mines.

JOHN 1: That's the first time she's thought about where it all started— feels like it's started again.

MIRANDA: I know a few things too.

JOHN 2: I could tell that.

MIRANDA: Where you going?

JOHN 2: Home with you.

MIRANDA: Oh... I was gonna go home with you.

JOHN 2: Oh...

JOHN 1: He points at the place he'd most like to go...

JOHN 2: (Pointing at the cigarette in her panties) You could get a rash from that.

MIRANDA: That's my beauty secret. I burn off all my old skin and young, beautiful skin comes back in its place. It's like magic...or plastic surgery.

(We hear the Pointer Sisters' "How Long (Betcha Got A Chick On The Side)", as the lights cross to LILA at the Museum of Modern Art talking to Andy Warhol's Marilyn silkscreen from his seriograph series.)

Chapter Five

(LILA is at the Museum of Modern Art, talking Andy Warhol's to Marilyn Monroe seriograph.)

LILA: I met Miranda at the movies. She tore my ticket. She took that ticket in her left hand and tore it diagonally in half with her right, looked into my eyes, handed it slowly back to me—and our fingers touched. And for one full minute, I was suspended in my own breath. I could hear the air filling up my lungs. I could feel my lungs and they were dark like a forest in Germany. I mean, I've never been to Germany, but I bet they have those kinds of forests. That kind of blackness. And this breath I took was red. It was a warning. A sign from God.

(Pause.)

But I didn't listen. She's in my lungs now.

(Pause.)

I didn't smoke until I met her. She likes that smell. Especially when I've had too many beers and I've smoked. That's a man's smell. I know it. But I want to please her. So—I do. It's a test.

(Pause.)

Did Jack make you do stuff like that? Did he make you smell like something you weren't? Did you put on perfume to cover up your own smell? And show your breasts so he wouldn't think about your hips? I bet he did. And I bet you did it. That's why you died so young. He was a two-timer too, I bet. Miranda thinks I don't know—but I know that smell. And the stains...

(Pause.)

I'm gonna die tomorrow. It's Saturday. And I was born on a Saturday. Saturday's child is... How does that go? Sunday's grace. Monday's face. Tuesday is woe... Wednesday—far to go...Thursday—I don't remember. Friday—I don't remember. Saturday... Saturday... Oh, no... Saturday is full of fun? Is that right? That couldn't be right... Oh—works hard till it's done. Yeah. That's it.

(Pause.)

You see? It's you in your kind of fat period. I like to keep things in perspective. Anyway, you never grew less beautiful. You were voluptuous. Full. From your lips to your hips. I have dreams about you. I used to keep my bedroom door locked at night so no one would interrupt us. I slept with your picture resting on that place between my crotch and my navel. That's my favorite place to touch. You could tell my temperature from there. And I'm always in a fever.

(SHE takes out a camera with a flash, and takes a photo of the painting. After the flash of a first photo, MARILYN steps out of the painting.)

MARILYN: I hope it comes out...

(LILA and MARILYN approach each other. MARILYN puts her arm around LILA as LILA takes a photo of herself and MARILYN. THEY exit as MIRANDA enters wearing sunglasses and a scarf. SHE's out of breath from running.)

MIRANDA: Shit! I lost her.

(Noticing the painting of Marilyn Monroe.)

Damn, that's Marilyn's blonde! Almost nuclear...

(The three JOHNs enter, also in scarves and sunglasses and follow MIRANDA. The light follows MIRANDA as SHE crosses to the waterfront. We hear a reprise of the Pointer Sisters' "How Long (Betcha Got A Chick On The Side). Lights cross to LILA & MARILYN at a bar in LILA's mind.)

Chapter Six

(LILA & MARILYN sit at a table in a bar.)

MARILYN: This was such a good idea. I'm drier than dust. Can I get you something? A vodka martini—very dry—just walk that vermouth past it— with three little olives, maybe?

LILA: How do you know what I drink?

MARILYN: That's what I drink. And anyway, you got that kind of face. So? What now?

LILA: I thought you knew everything.

MARILYN: No, honey. THat's more than anybody needs to know.

LILA: Not me. I can't know enough.

MARILYN: You should have some Coke. That'll settle your stomach.

LILA: Two Vodka martinis please.

MARILYN: Sure, honey.

(MARILYN gets up and mixes the drinks.)

LILA: Is this your bar?

MARILYN: Yeah. You like it? I wanna do some decorating—get some velvet curtains on the wall. You know, get some ambiance. A bar is nothing without ambiance.

LILA: I figure as long as it's got liquor, it's happening.

MARILYN: It's dangerous to have a thirst, isn't it?

(MARILYN sets down four vodka martinis in front of them. THEY each drink one in one gulp. Then reach for the second as we hear Gladys Knight & The Pips' "Love Overboard", as the lights cross to MIRANDA.)

Chapter Seven

(MIRANDA is sitting and rocking, alone on a
pier. SHE is soaking wet. SHE smokes a
cigarette while holding the ring that LILA
gave her. SHE speaks to the ring. JOHN 3
watches.)

MIRANDA: Women know how to hurt you
the best. They've got fingernails on the veins
to your brain and they're shaped like tongues.
Those tongues are sharp, like razors, like
sticking knives used to puncture the
jugulars of fine young cattle. That's good
eating. Prime beef. When you bleed it just
right, its flesh stays moist... but maybe it's just
organs, protrusions, that are different. Maybe
men and women are exactly the same...
"Dainty shapes equal hairy apes." I think I
read that on a bathroom wall. The bathroom
in Phebe's, where we had our first date. She's
my first lover—without a dick. She says her
name is Lila, but I saw her passport. It's some
wierd thing I can't even pronounce.
Lookiechoona or something. She has a scar
from her neck to her right nipple. Her father
wanted to be able to find her in the dark.
She's very easy to find. You can always smell
her first—even through a Camel Straights
cloud I could pick up her scent. She's very
tough. She hates children. Especially crying
ones. When one starts to cry in the street or in
a restaurant, she turns to the mother and says,

"Shut that fucking kid up or I'll kill it." She's so sexy when she does that. So powerful. I took her to the movies and with the sound of "Gentlemen Prefer Blondes" in the background, I lay her on the red velvet couch—the one with the camelback and the mahogany arms. There's one spot near the left arm that's completely worn away. "Lila lay here," it tells me. I lay Lila here. I sit on that spot sometimes... Sometimes when I'm lonely, and her smell comes up through the springs of the cushion and embraces me. Embraces me. Velvet is like flesh to me. Warm mother's flesh. A mother who loves you. A mother who lets you come home—no matter what. And no matter how long you been away she keeps your nightgown on the bed, so you can just slip in anytime, slip in and be home.

(SHE takes a deep drag on the cigarette.)

I'd like to faint and wake up with a cigarette inside. I want to give birth to cigarettes. Maybe I could. Maybe there's things people don't think can happen that happen all the time, but we just don't know. I don't think she'd want to be the father of a cigarette, but that's okay. I don't feel anything for her anyway. She's not going near any of my little filters. No smoke in her eyes.

(SHE takes a drag on her cigarette and begins to cry.)

JOHN 3: Covered in smoke, she doesn't see her own beauty—her life like a mirror, draped in heavy black silk. Her demons will run when she turns on the right light.

MIRANDA: She goes off without telling me where she's going. Lila doesn't understand danger like I do. Comes home smelling like sweet perfume—like she's been with somebody who spends many hours in the bath. Someone who's not me. Stupid fucking ring.

(SHE takes another drag on the cigarette and throws the butt into the river along with the ring as JOHN 2 enters and watches her. SHE watches him watching her. JOHN 1 enters and puts a Rick James tape into his cassette player. It is the song "Superfreak.")

JOHN 1: (Singing along with the tape; THEY both dance.) "She's a very kinky girl—the kind you don't take home to mother./ She will never let your spirits down, once you get her off the street. Ow! Girl!"

(MIRANDA joins in.)

JOHN 1 & MIRANDA: "She likes the boys in the band—she says that I'm her all-time favorite./ When I make my move to her room it's the right time! She's never hard to please. Ow! No!"

MIRANDA: (Turning off the tape.) Are you following me?

JOHN 1: No. I'm following him.

MIRANDA: Oh. Is he following me?

JOHN 1: Probably. He does that. I don't do that. That's why I keep an eye on him.

MIRANDA: Oh. He's cute.

JOHN 1: Yeah, I guess. But is he your type, really? You seem smarter than that.

MIRANDA: I am smarter than that—I don't go out with Latinos—but I don't mind bringing them in. Know what I mean? I mean, they're good in bed. So some lies are true. But they smell weird. They smell like my mother.

JOHN 2: I don't smell.

MIRANDA: Everybody smells. You smell like despair, Sailor. You smell like too much of the same thing over and over. You smell like death to me.

JOHN 2: And you're one of those jive-ass up-fucking-mobile pretend white bitches who wanna erase their faces and become a fucking ghost, but every time you wipe your face, your hands turn the color of your shit family. Am I right? So you can't hide. Am I right?!

(Silence.)

JOHN 1: I used to tell people I was Protestant when really I was Catholic. That's almost the sa—

MIRANDA: Take me, John. On Pier 45. That's my lucky number.

JOHN 1 & 2: Which one?

MIRANDA: (As SHE walks away from them.) The one who needs me the most.

(SHE exits. JOHNs 1 & 2 follow. We hear Marilyn Monroe singing "My Heart Belongs To Daddy," as the lights cross to LILA & MIRANDA sitting in the living room, legs entwined.)

Chapter Eight

(MIRANDA & LILA sit playing a game of "Truth, Dare, Consequences, Promise or Repeat." MARILYN plays solitaire in one corner of the room as JOHN 3 plays solitaire opposite her. JOHN 2 watches MIRANDA closely. JOHN 1 watches JOHN 2.)

JOHN 1: (Reading from a bible.) "Jonah, Chapter One, Verse Seven: Then the sailors said to each other, 'Come, let us cast lots to find out who is responsible for this calamity.'" They cast lots and the lot fell on

MIRANDA: (Confused.) I thought that was Jonah... must have the wrong book...

LILA: You can't keep doing that.

MIRANDA: What?

LILA: Choose something new. If you keep choosing truth, you know what happens. You find out things you didn't really want to know.

MIRANDA: That's something an old person would say.

LILA: I know. Choose.

MIRANDA: Promise.

LILA: Promise to tell me a story you never told me before—one that makes you cry when you're alone.

MIRANDA: What an awfully long promise...

LILA: Stop stalling.

MIRANDA: Okay. Age ten. I'm at the little Miss America Pageant, Palisades Park, NJ. Just over the bridge, and my father has driven me in his piece of shit Chevrolet and we're parking, and I've been inhaling these fumes— 'cause there's a leak in his gas tank. He comes over to my side, opens my door, and I go flying out in a faint, my sister's one-sizetoo-small turquoise blue dress flying over my head. It was already too tight, but now it's covered with mud from the parking lot floor—and even as my papi put his hand out to help me up—he doubled over in hysterical laughter. Then, I heard the sound of many people laughing—and they were all boys, brothers and fathers and cousins of all those other blonde— they all seemed blonde to me—blonde girls with new dresses bought especially for them. And my dad was laughing the loudest...

LILA: Maybe he was just closer to you, so he sounded louder—sometimes that happens.

MIRANDA: I didn't win...even with my stirring rendition of—

(SHE begins singing "Winchester Cathedral.")

"Winchester Cathedral, doo-roo-roo-roo-roo. I'm something, something, something...since my baby left town."

LILA: Beautiful.

JOHN 2: (Begins to sing the "Borinqueña" softly as MIRANDA continues to speak.) "La tierra de Borinquen, donde he nacido yo, es un jardín florido—de mágico primor. Un cielo siempre nítido—le sirve de dosel, y dan arrullos plácidos, las olas a sus pies. Cuando a su playa llegó Colon
exclamó lleno de admiración. ¡Oh! ¡Oh! ¡Oh! Esta es la linda tierra que busco yo; es Borinquen la hija del mar y el sol."

MIRANDA: But you know what was wierd—not wierd but sad, I guess—is that in my head the song I heard was one my papi taught me—his favorite song.

(SHE joins in singing the "Borinqueña" with JOHN 2 but on the last line SHE forgets the words.)

Es Borinquen la algo, algo, la estrella... estrella...

LILA: (Finishing it for MIRANDA.) La hija del mar y el sol.

MIRANDA: How would you know?

MARILYN, JOHN 3 & LILA: You talk in your sleep.

JOHN 3: Most people have dreams—but Miranda has memories.

MARILYN: (To MIRANDA, but only the JOHNs and LILA can hear her.) Hey, we got that in common, you know, that memory thing. Hey... oh... right. (With a shrug of her shoulders to JOHN 3.) Oh, well... can't blame a girl for trying.

JOHN 3: Memories linger.

(MARILYN & JOHN 3 nod sadly.)

MARILYN: Only if you let them. You can also choose. That's one thing I know now. You have to make choices.

LILA: (Repeating MARILYN's last line under her breath and then beginning to whistle.) You have to make choices.

MIRANDA: Earth to Lila! You're not listening and I'm not finished.

LILA: Sorry.

MIRANDA: So my song didn't win over the judges—and the ripped dress and tear-stained face didn't help either. And they called me Milagros, I don't know why. It's like they saw my name and couldn't believe it and just thought I was another stupid spic who didn't even know how to spell her own name. I'm a lot of things, but not that...

LILA: I wish I could hear by placing my fingers on people's lips. Sometimes I wish there was no sound. The voices you create in your head are always kinder.

MIRANDA: I was 234th out of 600—so what's that? In the top three hundred? (Pause.) Always a bridle path—never a bride...

JOHN 2: ...standing in the light of a new moon. She always wanted to be a moon that no one could see but always was there.

JOHN 3: And maybe sometimes someone could see her light.

LILA: You're the most beautiful woman I've ever met—outside of the movies.

MIRANDA: You met me inside.

LILA: That's not what I meant.

MIRANDA: I know.

MARILYN: Hey, even strong moonlight fades.

(The JOHNs pick up MIRANDA and carry her off. MARILYN picks up a blanket and covers LILA who begins to shiver. MARILYN sings her own version of "Moon River: as a gentle lullabye to LILA.)

MARILYN: "Moon River... wider than a mile, your beauty makes me smile—and say.../ Oh, you old moon river—you old moon river, I wish she could love you and stay..."

(Lights cross to the U.S.S. Governor's below-deck quarters, as MARILYN continues to sing "Moon River.")

Chapter Nine

(Below-deck sleeping quarters of the U.S.S. Governor. MIRANDA pulls her stuffed white whale out of the bag and sits back to watch the JOHNs reclining in their bunks. SHE sits with the whale on her lap. SHE rolls back the whale's eyes at the end of each speech. JOHN 2 speaks first. HE speaks to his penis.)

JOHN 2: It's so easy for women to be intimate. I envy that. Men have so much to prove all the time. It's okay to fuck but not to be fucked. That's a prison rule, I guess, I mean, I've never been to prison, but I know some who have—and I might as well have been... Women are mysterious. They wander the sea of life searching for the right port, never satisfied with the first good one that comes along. Always needing to find a newer, more intense one. Women are stressed out a lot of the time and so I wonder why I find myself needing them. I'd like to have a rainbow of women—different colors, but all slim, with tits and an ass you can sink your teeth in... Yeah... It should just be you and me pal. Why can't it just be you and me??

(JOHN 3 sings the first line of Stevie Wonder's "You and I". After JOHN 2 cums, HE hums along with JOHN 3 as HE gently tucks himself in.)

JOHN 3: "You and I... we'll be together till the end of time..."

(Lights cross to JOHN 3, still humming and then also talking to his penis.)

JOHN 3: Hello, my little sailor. Mr. Blue. Long time no see. I forget to look sometimes. Sometimes I forget and I have to think real hard, what is between my legs? I read a lot of books and they don't prepare you for the real thing. Uhuhn... But you like to read too, don't you? Some people use their finger to help them focus on every line—but I have you. I use my third eye to scan different worlds... new horizons. We've taken some incredible voyages together—through Kant and Thackeray, Nabokov and Chandler. We read it all, huh baby? I know which one you liked the best. It was Poe, wasn't it? The melancholy poetry of Poe is what really gets you off. "Once upon a midnight dreary, while I pondered weak and weary..." Oh, yeah...

(Dinah Washington's "Big Long Slidin' Thing" plays softly in the background as JOHN 3 finishes himself off and cums. Then lights cross to JOHN 1 who is talking to his hat. HE is pretending that the hat is a woman.)

JOHN 1: I just don't have a lot of luck with women... My friend John told me, he said, "John, you are not good with women, because of how much you read the bible." "Oh," I says, "is that why?" But I don't read it that much... Though I have died and been resurrected many times through that book. I mean, I'm not religious or anything, but I had to say, yeah, I'm into that, you know. I'm just on this certain kind of journey. It's hard to explain... The Bible does it best: "I will offer you a sacrifice and do what I have promised. Salvation comes from the Lord! Then the Lord ordered the fish to spit Jonah up on the beach, and it did." Now that's poetry. Who else but God could make vomit so appealing?

(JOHN 1 reads a book. It's a sex toys shop-at-home catalog like "Adam & Eve.")

JOHN 1: Love comes in five magic colors. Exotacondom can give you the thrill of Tahiti with the security of Fort Knox.

(Pause. The text now comes from the book of Micah.)

Hear this, all you nations: The Lord is coming from his holy place; he will come down and walk on top of mountains. Then the mountains will melt under him like wax in a fire; they will pour down into the valleys like water pouring down a hill.

(Pause.)

Wow... what was that?

(Continuing to read.)

Don't forget to order our special video release! Miss Vanessa Del Rio, the Puerto Rican Sexbomb, in Tigress & Euphrates. Her four inch squirting clit tells one story but all is revealed in her eyes. They tell the history of the world. They are deep and dark and sunk into her head like a buried people. You can see yourself in the whites.

(Pause; holding his head.)

Wooh, I think I had too much coffee today.

(HE puts on his hat, and the lights cross to MARILYN and LILA, who has her head on MARILYN's lap, as we hear Rufus w/Chaka Khan's "Tell Me Something Good.")

Chapter Ten

(In the apartment. LILA sits with her head in MARILYN's lap. SHE reads to LILA from a thick book. JOHN 3 sits reading a book to himself, mouthing the words.)

JOHN 3: This is where Lila begins to understand something and Marilyn gets to talk a little about something he loves.

LILA: It's so nice of you to do this.

MARILYN: Oh, I love to read.

LILA: I thought you did. I knew you were more than beautiful...I read all those stupid stories about you—about how you posed once with a book turned upside down. And the photographer had to tell you to turn it around. I didn't believe it though.

MARILIYN: Yeah. I was just nervous. I knew how they were just trying to make fun of me—so I had just picked it up and opened it and then, snap, the picture got taken. That was my favorite book too—"Ulysses". Wooh! Ever read any of his stuff?

LILA: Harry gave me a copy—but I didn't understand it.

MARILYN: I don't think there was anything to understand really. I mean, maybe I missed something, but that book does not have a plot. I mean but that's what I kinda liked about it, it just washed over you like a wave, the rhythms of the language like a great big wave that comes over you and on top of you over and over again. Those Irish guys can be so cute, you know. But they just don't always make sense. I have a weakness for them.

(Pause.)

Who's Harry?

LILA: My father.

MARILYN: Your father? And you called him by his first name? That's so...progressive.

LILA: Yeah, well. His real name was hard for a child to pronounce. I still don't know what it was exactly. He died before I was bold enough to ask him.

MARILYN: Ahhh... that's too bad, honey. But people do die sometimes. They get diseases or—

LILA: He cut me with a razor and then hanged himself in front of me. Read, please.

MARILYN: Oh... well people do that too. What's your pleasure, honey?

LILA: This one.

(LILA hands her MIRANDA's copy of Moby-Dick.)

MARILYN: Oooh! This is a good one too. I liked that cannibal guy.

LILA: Queequeg?

MARILYN: Yeah. (Reads from Moby-Dick.) "Chapter Eighty-nine: Fast-Fish and Loose-Fish. Perhaps the only formal whaling code authorized by legislative enactment, was that of Holland. It was decreed by the States-General in A.D. 1695. Yes, these laws might be engraven on a Queen Anne's farthing, or the barb of a harpoon, and worn round the neck, so small are they."

(JOHN 3 softly reads along with MARILYN.)

"I. A Fast-Fish belongs to the party fast to it.; II. A Loose-Fish is fair game for anybody who can soonest catch it."

LILA: How do you turn a Loose-Fish into a Fast-Fish?

MARILYN: I guess you kill it fist, so it belongs to you and nobody can take it away because it stays by your side because you can tie it to your ship.

LILA: You've read this book before.

MARILYN: Oh, sure... When I used to read. I miss it so much. My real, real, real favorites were Shelley, Whitman, Keats and Rilke—you know them? They're like poets and anyway, so reading them made me feel all in love with myself—not how I was but how I was going to be. You ever feel like that?

LILA: In love with myself? Never. Never used to anyway.

MARILYN: Oh, you will. Just learn your own rhythm and you'll find your emotion, don't you think? Just don't move your lips when you read to yourself—then they might put you away because many crazy people do that. I used to do that—until somebody told me that. So be careful!

(JOHN 3 looks chagrined and pulls up the book to cover his face.)

LILA: Sometimes I just wish she was dead—It hurts so much...

MARILYN: I know. You just want them dead for a little while and in the morning you can get up again and everything will be like normal—but better.

LILA: I daydream about it.

MARILYN: I daydream chiefly about beauty, other people's beauty. A new face I can put on over my own that makes me somebody else—now that would be a gift. My face covered in something...

(MARILYN exits to look in the bathroom mirror. LILA puts on a tape—it's Connie Francis singing "Who's Sorry Now?", picks up a book and begins to read as MIRANDA enters.)

Chapter Eleven

(Lila is sitting engrossed in a book. JOHNs 2 & 3 watch. The stereo is playing Connie Francis songs as MIRANDA enters with a bouquet of flowers. SHE sneaks up on LILA and startles her by kissing her neck from behind.)

MIRANDA: Boo!!

LILA: SHIT!! What's wrong with you?!

MIRANDA: I—

LILA: Shit! Are you trying to give me a heart attack or something? Shit.

MIRANDA: Ahh, baby, baby. Don't be like that. These are for you.

(SHE hands LILA the flowers and turns down the tape player.)

LILA: (With a smile.) So what did you do now?

MIRANDA: What do you mean?

LILA: You never bring me flowers. Something must have happened. Some horrible guilt-making thing—they're beautiful.

MIRANDA: You're welcome. What are you reading?

LILA: A book.

MIRANDA: About what?

LILA: Things. People.

MIRANDA: What kind of things? What sort of people?

LILA: "Couples Who Kill." Have you ever read it? It's incredible. People in love do the strangest things.

MIRANDA: Don't know it—oh, but I did see that movie—with Shirley Stoler, "Honeymoon Killers." Is it like that?

LILA: Yeah. I met her once.

MIRANDA: Yeah?

LILA: Uhhuh. At the Chelsea Place bar. Drinks and laughs a lot. But I could never think of her as anything but that commandant in "Seven Beauties." You know, when she makes Giancarlo Giannini fuck her for food in the death camp. I found myself searching her eyes—for signs. Signs of cruelty, but there weren't any. That's the cruel part though, I think. You can't really see it—in their eyes.

MIRANDA: You should stop reading this stuff at night. It makes you jumpy. I want you to bend back into my lips when I kiss you there. Not scream like a maniac.

LILA: Yeah, well. Come home earlier. Where you been?

MIRANDA: Out. Looking for the perfect flowers, for the perfect woman.

LILA: Yeah. Right. Thank you. They really are beautiful.

MIRANDA: Where were you yesterday?

LILA: Museum.

MIRANDA: New exhibit?

LILA: Same one. I don't like the new ones. What do they mean bringing all this new art around? I mean, what can you do when there's so much to look at? I like the Portrait galleries. Nothing changes. Always perfect. Why go anywhere else?

MIRANDA: Portrait galleries lend out their paintings sometimes. What if you go there and your favorite portrait is gone? What then?

LILA: You're jealous of my trips aren't you? You want me to look only at you, right?

MIRANDA: That would be nice.

LILA: You really don't know how much I love you, do you?

MIRANDA: Would you give up your murder stories for me?

LILA: No.

MIRANDA: Why not?

LILA: That's literature. That's my choice. It has nothing to do with you. You think you can tell me what to read? What's that? Like a fascist or something? No way.

MIRANDA: Would you give up your trips to the museum?

LILA: Hell now.

MIRANDA: Would you run away with me?

LILA: Where to?

MIRANDA: Away.

LILA: Maybe. But just us two, huh. No one else. What are you still looking for?

MIRANDA: Found it. Scared. You know.

LILA: I know.

(She puts her arms around MIRANDA.)

This is know.

MIRANDA: Tell me something I don't know.

LILA: Funny or sad?

MIRANDA: Are you kidding?!

LILA: Okay... The first time I saw my father naked. It was on a morning in December. Cold and gray. And my mother had just died—

MIRANDA: Wait up. This is the funny one, right?

LILA: Just listen. My mother had just died, and dad and I were sitting there crying, and it started to snow again, we already had like ten inches of it—the Sun still out, but this miraculous snowstorm. And dad gets up and goes to the vitrola.

MIRANDA: One of those old wind-up things?

LILA: Yeah—

(We hear a scratchy old recording of "Detour Ahead." MARILYN dances on with JOHN 3 as LILA continues.)

—and he put on this old American record Mother had from I don't know when. Anyway, he puts it on, takes off all his clothes, and then picks her up and dances with her—I mean, she's dead so she's not really dancing, but he holds her and dances... and dances out

76

the door. And I follow them out. And he dances some more and then begins to roll her in the snow. So I help him. We roll her and roll over each other desperately trying to cover her. And dad is trembling. But I know it's not the cold
making him tremble. And when she's one big snowball, we stand her up. But it doesn't look right. And dad dances around her rolling another snowball, and then we give her another—snowball head. And I use pieces of loose brick to make her eyes and nose. And it made us laugh. She loved the snow so. It made us laugh. She was alive again in that snow. Till the first warm day she could be with us.

MIRANDA: That's the wierdest fucking story I ever heard—but so sweet. You're so sweet. When I go, will you roll me too?

LILA: (Kissing her.) Yeah, I'll roll you alright.

MIRANDA: Nasty. You're a nasty girl.

LILA: Two of a kind.

(THEY kiss sweetly. JOHN 1 enters and speaks to the other two JOHNs.)

JOHN 1: Oh, man! I missed it. What happened?

JOHN 3: They—they've remembered why they fell in love.

JOHN 1: Oh.

JOHN 2: They'll forget again soon though.

JOHN 1: Oh...then there's hope for me—I mean us, then.

JOHN 3: Mmhmm. There's always hope.

JOHN 1: Really?

(Lights cross with MIRANDA and JOHN 2 to a pier.)

Chapter Twelve

(On a pier off the Hudson River, MIRANDA and JOHN 2 are having a fight.)

MIRANDA: Is that so?! A man will do it for me, right?!

JOHN 2: Yeah. Right. Once I'm inside you, you'll forget how much you hate me.

MIRANDA: I'd rather go for a swim. In the icy deep. In the dirty sea. Pool for vermin. Water of disease. I'm gonna waste myself in the water. I'm gonna turn into a ghost and I'm gonna come back as a giant dickeater with a big trunk like an elephant, with it I'll be hunting for dicks, big and little. I'll eat them all—when I've got 'em all inside me, I'll vomit them and shit them into the ground. And dick trees will grow. Won't need a man anymore—won't need plastic. Real live dicks, growing on real live trees, hoping for some nice woman to pick him and take him home. And make a pie out of him. But until it's ripe, it can be placed between her thighs, a little warming up, a little forepie. I wanna turn you into mince meat. I wanna feel your erection through rubber gloves, before it's food processed. Before I hand it over to Julia Child. She'll know what to cook with it—that's why she's got that stupid little voice. To throw you off. Throw you off the scent. Think she's harmless? She's superbitch! She's my hero. She's gonna help us make history.

JOHN 2: You really are mad, aren't you?

MIRANDA: Fuck you!

JOHN 3: Miranda dives into the Hudson River wishing that she was someone else. And Somewhere else there is Gershwin music playing...but not for her.

JOHN 1: I don't believe how hard you hit her. I thought her neck would snap.

JOHN 2: Can't let women run away from you like that. Hide in the water. She thought she was gonna win that fight. But all she had to do was come up for air and I was there— waiting.

JOHN 3: And longing... And punching the shit out of her.

(JOHN 2 laughs nervously. John 3 throws down his book in disgust and exits.)

JOHN 1: Why?

JOHN 2: Sometimes it's the only way to make a girl listen.

(As we hear a scene from the movie "Gentlemen Prefer Blondes," lights cross to MIRANDA walking towards the red couch and sitting.)

Chapter Thirteen

(In the lobby of Loew's Paradise movie theater in the Bronx. MIRANDA sits on a red, velvet sofa. There's a deep cut on her nose that has clotted. Her clothing has dried blood on it. SHE rocks for a moment, then sits perfectly still. JOHNs 1, 2, & 3 watch her from dark corners around the room.)

MIRANDA: Now this is a sofa. Red, velvet material wrapped around solid mahogany. Red around brown...I don't care what movie is playing, because it couldn't be as interesting as this sofa. I just come in—pay my way to sit on this couch. I hope sometime...I hope sometime to come on this couch. To wrap my legs around one of the arms and let the velvet rub me up. I want its lint inside me...They don't find me when I'm here. Nobody goes to the Bronx anymore. I escape to the movies.

(Pause.)

Sometimes when I'm sitting here, I'll make up stories. Like I'll think that somebody's gonna sit here. I'll see somebody on the popcorn line and I'll say...

(A light comes up on the JOHNs, LILA & MARILYN on the popcorn line. MIRANDA speaks to them.)

Hey, come over and sit right by me... Yeah, you. The good-looking one.

(THEY all step forward.)

Hold my hand. Hold my hand and we could make love under the stars in the ceiling. They twinkle fiercely—I guess it's because they're trapped— like you'll be when you're between my legs.

(THEY all run off except for LILA, who sits down next to MIRANDA and begins to tend her wounds.)

You're so reliable. You're like a Volvo. Boxy, secure, foreign—

LILA: Boring. I don't hit you nearly enough.

MIRANDA: You never hit me.

LILA: That's what I mean. You like the slap across the face, the fist in the eye, the punch in the back or the ribs. And the kicks...you love those kicks, don't you?

MIRANDA: My mother told me once "que si te hago daño sabes que te quiero."

LILA: My mother told me the same thing. But the difference is that I didn't believe her—not until I met you, because you hurt me all the time and you want to get hurt back. Who was it this time?

MIRANDA: A beautiful angel in white.

LILA: Men are not your salvation, Miranda.

MIRANDA: Are you?

LILA: We have to save ourselves. Each one of us has to save herself. Let's go home...

MIRANDA: (Breaking away from LILA.) No! I wish I was dead.

LILA: I wish you was too...

(Lights crossfade to JOHN 3 reading from a thick novel to the other JOHNs.)

JOHN 3: This is the part where Lila imagines what she would say to Miranda, if Miranda was laying, dead and naked, in front of her.

JOHN 1: And Miranda imagines what it would be like to be dead?

JOHN 2: Of course.

JOHN 3: Lila runs her hands along Miranda's lifeless body...

LILA: There's something missing here. I think it is a heart. I think he took it away with him. He's got it now, in his glove compartment. Maybe this is why. He left no trace. Just Miranda, quiet for once. Her eyes looking up, instead of in. You're so beautiful, Miranda. I could eat you up. There'll be no sweat to mistake for come. He's got it now, in his glove compartment. John's the only person I know, who keeps gloves there. But he didn't use them this time...He wanted to feel it. The warm clotting mess of her. Just Miranda. Quiet for once. You're so beautiful, Miranda. I could eat you up—the cold does things to your eyes. They're like marbles now—the eyes of a China doll. A hot, Szechwan pepper feast. Hot foods always make me sweat. It's white and viscous—cum and pre-cum sweat. It drips out of every hole in my body. My ears are stuffed with it. I can hardly breathe. You're bloating up. Filling up. Your face is full of water. The weight looks good on you. Elizabeth Taylor at forty. Butterfield Eight days. Does she die in that movie? I don't remember. I hope not.

MIRANDA: I'm a marble dropped into a fifty gallon fish tank. Clink, shloosh. Bubbles. From my landing. At home on the bottom. A blue marble, pure blue. Easy to lose on the bottom of the ocean. Or a pool. Or a blue Dodge pick-up. I'm lost at sea now. A pirate at last. I want to be raped by a manatee. Ancient siren. Eat me till I die—again and again. Come sweet sister. Let's roll together on a plain white sheet. Let's draw our birth signs in blood. Where are all the others? Are there other seas to drown in? My sea is everywhere, and in the sea is a place of worship. The church of thieves. Spiritual healing for the cruel and lonely. If I gave a mass, maybe they'll all come back. Come back, Blackbeard. Take my ass in your mouth.

Bite it. Lick it first. Tell me you love me and
fuck me in the ass.

MIRANDA: (Continued.) I hold my breath. I
see how long I can hold it for. To run with
the fish, you gotta breathe through you back.
You gotta learn to filter out the sand or it
blinds you. It turns your brain cells into salt. It
turns your water into wine. My muscles are
jerking, jerking me around, jerking me off.
Can a woman jerk off? It sounds hard. So
hard...I hear violins when I masturbate.
Bartok strings. It's the movie version of death.
I always surprise myself— when it happens. I
think, I couldn't really be doing this, but I am.
I've got my fingers inside me up to the
palm—I'm afraid to go any further. I'm afraid
I'll touch my own heart. It feels like hearts in
there—organ meat I could never swallow. But
it happens. I touch it just right. I always think
I'm touching somebody else. I practiced on
my dolls—when they came I moved their
heads back so their eyes would close.
"Aaahh!" Like that. "Aaahh!" They always
said "Aaahh!" Open wide and say "Ah!"

LILA: You're perfect there. Your skin turning
into glass. I can see through you now.

(LILA exits as MIRANDA curls up on the
couch and sleeps. We hear the intro to
"Detour Ahead" as lights cross to MARILYN
entering the Loew's Paradise movie theater.)

85

Chapter Fourteen

(MARILYN, in dark sunglasses and a scart,
sits on the arm of a red couch, smoking a
cigarette, observing MIRANDA, and talking
to her own reflection in a mirror.)

MARILYN: (Checking her face and redoing
her lipstick.) It's always fun to do a little
spying. Gotta study the animal before you
catch it. Gotta get into the perpetrator's
shoes, so to speak.

(Pause; in an excited whisper.)

And anyways, I just love being back in a
movie theater! This is a really cute one too. All
those stars up there—cut into the ceiling...I
don't think I'd watch the movie with those
stars there, above my head. Astronomy's
something I woulda taken up—if I hadn't
been a movie star. Oh!

(SHE laughs.)

Get it? Stars. Movies. Anyway, it's a pretty
one. A gem of a theater. Too bad it's got all
that de-construction in front of it. I can't
believe they're gonna tear this place down. To
really enjoy a movie, you gotta see it on the
big screen. I hate those multiplex things.

People's noses are right in your face like that. Theaters are so small now. Ick.

(Pause.)

I can see why she'd come here. It's like coming home. A place where you want to spend all your time...I used to spend lots of time in the park. I mean right before I—looking at children. I'd hide sometimes to watch them. And there was a phone there. It was my phone. Couldn't call anymore from my house—cause it wasn't mine anymore—cause people were always watching me. Listening to me. Hunting me...then I died.

(MARILYN lays down next to MIRANDA and sleeps. We hear Russell and Monroe's "Just Two Little Girls From Little Rock" as lights fade to black.)

End of **ACT ONE**

ACT TWO

Chapter Fifteen

(We hear Connie Francis singing "Stupid Cupid." In LILA & MIRANDA's living room, LILA chases MARILYN around the couch. JOHN 3 watches from the shadows.)

MARILYN: Nice place, huh?

LILA: Why are you running from me?

MARILYN: History.

LILA: Whose?

MARILYN: Ours. The history of women...Do you know that Lebanese women are systematically declitorized in order to be good and faithful brides? Did you know that?

LILA: No, I didn't...

MARILYN: And all those missing Chinese baby girls...What do you think that's about?

LILA: They like boys better?

MARILYN: Yes, of course. They will always—they being the people in power—in this particular case the people are men—they always favor their own.

LILA: You're amazing... How come you never showed this side of yourself?

MARILYN: Nobody looked at that part. That's the tragedy of my life.

LILA: Why do you keep disappearing?

MARILYN: Space. I need my space. That's all. Don't overwhelm me with your affection. It's imperialistic. No one owns me, baby. They think this voice, the hair, these tits— make me a stupid, vapid, sex-bunny just looking for someone to fill my hole. It's not that simple...If only life were that simple. (She sighs.) Simple people don't kill themselves.

LILA: So it's true... you're not really here.

MARILYN: I'm here. I'm where you put me. You willed me outside of that painting. So many Marilyns... I should have been the president instead of fucking him. He was cute though... Power's cute to me. I mean it was something I could never have. So I fucked it instead. That's only logical. I was doing the logical thing, that's all. Searching for logic.What's the difference between the divine and the logical? Pure reason and pure lust? Pure pure and stained pure? I'm a blemish, Lila. Don't be jealous over me. I'll just make you break out in a rash. I'm a blister on your heart. I'm burning right through you, to your back, to your spine. I'm disease on your most delicate folds.

LILA: Just get undressed.

MARILYN: Why? I'm dead.

LILA: You don't look very well. We should check for bruises. I always check for bruises on Miranda.

MARILYN: Being dead isn't easy on a woman's body... Hard to exercise. And my skin has been drying for almost thirty years. In a slot in a wall— they call it a crypt but that's so creepy a word, I don't like to use it. But at least I'm not in the ground all covered with soil and the nutrients of earthworms... Hey, do you wanna go fishing? I love fishing... I'm good at it too.

LILA: I bet you are.

MARILYN: Yeah... I dated Hemingway once.

LILA: Really? Now there's a sportsman for you.

(Pause.)

LILA & MARILYN: (Together.) Lousy fucking writer.

LILA: But a true sportsmeister. You know what I wonder about? Those Hemingway girls. They are so tall. I mean, it's nerve-racking to even think of them—like in bed I mean... Damn. I'd feel like a three cent stamp on a thirty pound package. Lint in their navels. Unnatural. Girls so tall with such eyebrows!

MARILYN: Yes, those eyebrows are a problem. And then that younger one goes and gets fake tits... I mean seriously, why? I ask you.

LILA: Ask me.

MARILYN: (Poking LILA in the chest.) Why?
(LILA faints.) Lila! Are you okay?

(A light goes up on JOHN 3; as HE speaks. Marilyn slaps LILA to revive her.)

JOHN 3: Lila gets slapped in the face by a picture in her mind's eye. It really helps.

LILA: I'm sorry! I didn't mean—I don't know what came over me...

MARILYN: Twelve vodka martinis, Honey.

LILA: How'd you know?

MARILYN: I used to follow baseball.

LILA: Yeah? So?

MARILYN: So...one of the lessons any good ballplayer-follower learns is how to revive a drunk. It's different for different types of alcohol. For vodka, a slap always works.

LILA: Incredible... Do you know about everything?

MARILYN: Booze, broads, and baseball. That's it... oh, and I know about pain too.

LILA: I know you do.

MARILYN: You shouldn't drink so much.

LILA: If I stopped drinking, I wouldn't see you anymore, would I?

MARILYN: You wouldn't need to see me then. And I could get some rest. You know how many people call me up?! Out of the grave, I mean. It's like I'm on this forever elevator that someone else is controlling so I never know what floor I'm getting out on. It's exhausting. And the worse part is that I never get to change my clothes... I'd like some new clothes.

LILA: I'll get you some clothes.

MARILYN: You can't. Can't change history, honey. Then things explode.

LILA: Oh.

(MARILYN exits as JOHN 3 speaks.)

JOHN 3: Lila can feel her bottom lip again and she can almost see the mauve and green kitchen from where she's sitting—Miranda chose the colors. Lila is alone again. What does she think about when she's alone and sober?

LILA: Why do I want her so much? Tonight? Maybe tomorrow is the big day. I say it all the time. I say It's going to go like this... pop, pop, pop. A small gun in the right place. A lot of blood. I'll have towels all around me. Red ones. So easy to clean. Not like others. So many others are so hard to clean. Blood everywhere. Brains... bits of tongue and teeth. Where do the gums go? Why doesn't Connie Francis sing about that?

(Singing to the tune of "Where The Boys Are.")

"Where the gums are... someone waits for me..."

(Resumes talking.)

Connie's been so quiet since the rape. I bet she's dead inside. Like me. I have a hard time singing now. And I used to sing all the time. Real slow and low. Like jazz on a bass fiddle.

That was me, my voice. I sang best in the shower of course...

(Pause.)

I heard my mother once in the shower...she was talking to herself—having a real long conversation. The one part I heard real clear went like this: "You have to make choices." and then she whistled, like this—

(Whistles a happy little tune.)

So it went: "You have to make choices."

(Whistles the tune again.)

It was the weirdest fucking thing I ever heard. Then she toweled herself off—still whistling this weird little tune. Whistling away... Weird, huh? Who invented whistling anyway? Somebody fucking weird because it's a weird fucking thing to do. I don't whistle very well. I always wanted to be able to whistle like a man, between my fingers. That would be power — Inserting my index and middle finger into my mouth and blowing.

(Pause.)

I wonder who she'll bring home tonight.

(SHE walks to the kitchen and pours herself a glass of vodka as we hear Connie Francis singing "Where The Boys Are." Lights fade as SHE begins to drink it. Lights cross to MIRANDA at the beach.)

Chapter Sixteen

(MIRANDA standing in sand with waves crashing against the back of her calves, talking to her breasts, as SHE washes them in the water.)

MIRANDA: Listen, I have something to tell you kids and you're not gonna like it one bit. You don't like it when I do these things to us—but I had to. I'm not strong like you, Patria, or, Lydia, as firm as you. So... I moved my bed last night. I moved it and I found three used condoms. I knew they were there. I was just waiting for the right moment. I wanted to see if they were still filled with—it. So I looked at them. I looked a lot. I took the tip of my right foot and poked at it. And they were still alive—moist inside—like the inside lips of another woman. The kind you're not supposed to touch—like your mother's...

(Pause.)

But that wasn't enough. Then I sat on the floor—with my legs straddling them, and ran my right index finger along the edge of one.

The longest one. I wondered who it was who got that hard for me? To make it so long. I couldn't remember... And then I couldn't help it. I picked it up and held it to my lips and drank from it. My tongue darting in and out of that stiff rubber hole. I know you're not supposed to swallow anymore, but I have a thirst for it.

(Pause.)

And it made me smile—tasted so sweet... I knew right away whose it was. There's nothing as sweet as that. Just thinking about it makes my tongue sting. Then, I put that honey on the tips of our fingers and stuck it up inside us. I thought maybe there's something still alive in there and I wanted to catch it. Our baby would be a strong swimmer. I had a dream the other day that all the cums I had ever tasted—washed up under my bed. What a safe feeling that was—to have all that life swimming underneath me... If I lie on my bed with my eyes closed, I can float. It's like sea foam now.

(SHE scoops up some water and drips it onto her nipples.)

How many hours had they lain there? If I could fuck Lila now, I would. If I could strap one on and ride her like a big, fucking wave. And land inside. Mmmhmm... I'd let her swallow all she wanted. And she'd let me come inside her.

(Lights cross to MIRANDA & LILA's apartment as we hear the instrumental part of Liz Torres's "Payback is a Bitch.")

Chapter Seventeen

(In MIRANDA & LILA's apartment. LILA stands by the bedroom door, blasting a recording of Liz Torres's "Payback Is A Bitch" at the door. MIRANDA runs out pulling on her dress, lookin' really hung-over. JOHN 2 watches.)

LILA: Going out?

(MIRANDA puts on her sunglasses, grabs her cigarettes, sees that the pack is empty, and exits. JOHN 1 enters from the bedroom, dressed only in white briefs.)

JOHN 1: Uhh—hi. Uhm, did she go?

(LILA ignores him, plugs in her headphones and continues to listen to Liz Torres's song, as SHE chain smokes and dances. JOHN 1 keeps trying to talk to her.)

Oh...Well, women have secrets. Women wear lipstick so their lips look like vaginas—gaping red holes. Is that red, virgins' blood?

(LILA continues to ignore him and keeps dancing.)

I'm reading this book. It's about being feminine. I love it. It explains all this stuff I never understood before. Like body hair. Men shave to reveal and women shave because men want them revealed. And I said, yeah, that's pretty—you know, right and everything. Because like this girl that I was you know—

(HE makes a motion with his fist meaning "intercourse.")

I mean, it wasn't love right.

LILA: You read?

JOHN 1: Yeah. When I've got the time. I like it.

LILA: Uh, huh.

(SHE turns off the tape.)

What goes around comes around. Payback is a bitch. Bitch, bitch, bitch.

JOHN 1: Yeah...

LILA: Those are the lyrics.

JOHN 1: Oh...

LILA: But the words in Spanish are different. In Spanish, she sings, "You're gonna pay me back, you cheap, stupid son-of-a-bitch. You're gonna pay me back, pay me back, pay me back.

JOHN 1: Oh.

(Pause.)

Right. Spanish let's you do that.

LILA: What?!

JOHN 1: The Spanish know how to say things.

(Pause.)

LILA: How was it?

JOHN 1: Nice.

LILA: Nice?

JOHN 1: Very nice. She's, uhm, incredible.

LILA: Yeah, she's that alright.

JOHN 1: Yeah.

LILA: She sleeps with a lot of men. Not just you. She sleeps with them and puts bite marks on their brains. You think you can forget about her— but you can't. You think you can put her away. File her in a box marked paid. But you can't. She'll be inside you the rest of your life. Her spit will never come out of your hair.

(Pause; a discovery.)

JOHN 1: You're a lesbian, aren't you?!

(MIRANDA enters with a carton of cigarettes.)

LILA: So is she.

JOHN 1: Yeah... New York's like that. I mean, like "Alice's Restaurant" right? Sings. "You can be anything you want at —"

MIRANDA: Don't sing. People who can't sing should never sing. It hurts us. The people who have to listen. It makes our ears bleed.

JOHN 1: I saw a movie like that once.

LILA: I bet you did.

(Pause.)

You're killing me, Randy.

MIRANDA: Don't call me that.

JOHN 1: Randys are dangerous. Miranda's such a romantic name.

LILA: (Handing MIRANDA a straight-edged shaving blade.) Here.

JOHN 2: Lila hands Miranda a pop quiz her dad left her. It still cuts though...

LILA: Here's a razor blade. You do it. You cut me. Don't think I'll let you get away from me without doing it all. Cut away at my heart. Rip it out. I won't fight you. You've been doing it for some time now...

MIRANDA: I don't have time to waste killing you, Lila. I have better things to do. I have a life. I have sunglasses. That's what you need—a new pair of sunglasses.

(LILA cuts her tongue and shows MIRANDA.)

So what!?

(Takes the knife from LILA and cuts her thigh.)

See? Blood is cheap. Everybody has blood.

JOHN 1: That's true. Don't cut anything important, girls. Somes things you can't get back.

LILA & MIRANDA: (Together.) Shut up!

JOHN 1: I need a drink. Anyone wanna—

LILA & MIRANDA: (Together.) Get out!

(Lights cross to MARILYN, JOHN 2 & JOHN 3, LILA & JOHN 1 as we hear the Liz Torres lyric part to "Payback Is A Bitch.")

Chapter Eighteen

(JOHN 2 & JOHN 3 have a drink and talk about movies and other things. MARILYN tends bar. JOHN 1 & LILA watch.)

JOHN 1: Lila imagines what Marilyn wants that she can't give her... (It's chemistry.)

JOHN 2: (As MARILYN pours him a nice, stiff drink.) Hey, don't I know you?

MARILYN: No. I'd remember. I remember everyone I've ever met. Memory's a curse.

JOHN 3: You're a movie star, or something aren't you?

JOHN 2: Yeah! You were in that train movie, right?

MARILYN: You're thinking of Ingrid Bergman.

JOHN 3: That's you, right?

MARILYN: Wrong. What are you drinking?

JOHN 3: Water.

MARILYN: Water? I'd think a sailor might be tired of water.

JOHN 3: I love it.

JOHN 2: I don't.

MARILYN: What do you think about monogamy?

JOHN 2: I don't—think about it.

JOHN 3: I love it.

MARILYN: I don't know... you gotta have a lot of self-esteem to make it work. I mean, it takes courage and will-power and some other things, but especially self-esteem. To think you are complete enough alone that you can make a safe nest for someone else. You know what I mean?

JOHN 3: Please join us. You must be tired, a job like this—on your feet all the time. My mother worked on her feet all the time...

MARILYN: She's dead now?

JOHN 3: No. But her feet are for shit. Always going to lame doctors, who slice off calluses when they know they'll just come back...

MARILYN: Yeah. I know how she feels. I had some husbands like that— like those doctors.

JOHN 2: Maybe I should just go to another table or something. I thought this was gonna be a men's night out, buddy. What d'ya say?

(THEY ignore him.)

MARILYN: I bet your mother was beautiful.

JOHN 3: She sure was... I mean, before the fire.

MARILYN: Oh, no! What she young?

JOHN 3: Yeah... I was just a little boy. I didn't know—I mean how quicklystring catches fire. It was just an experiment. I wanted to be a scientist.

MARILYN: I knew it. When I first saw you I knew you were a man who knew tragedy. It gets drawn on your face like a bad dream.

JOHN 2: I had a really hard life too.

(THEY continue to ignore him.)

JOHN 3: I know exactly what you mean. My name's John.

MARILYN: I'm Norma.

JOHN 3: Such an old name... You must be an old soul.

JOHN 2: My name's John too.

JOHN 3: I hope you don't mind my saying so, but you're a very intelligent woman. Why are you serving drinks?

MARILYN: It gives me something to do. Meet people. Talk a little. Conversation is the greatest aphrodisiac. Don't you agree?

JOHN 2: I love to talk. My middle name is talker. I just keep talking—

JOHN 3: Could you keep it down?

MARILYN: (Handing JOHN 2 a very tall drink.) It's on that house. But you have to

throw it back. On the count of three. Ready?
One, Two, Three!

(JOHN 2 throws back his drink and sits dazed
through the rest of the scene.)

Now where were we? Do you like children,
John?

(MARILYN covers JOHN 3's hand with her
own.)

LILA: Oh... right.

(The lights cross to LILA at a pier
overlooking the East River. We hear Marilyn
Monroe's "River of No Return.")

Chapter Nineteen

(LILA is standing at the end of a pier,
watching the water. JOHN 1 watches her.)

JOHN 1: Lila looks at the gray-green water
and tries to figure it out.

LILA: I've been trying to figure it out.

(LILA sings a song SHE makes up as SHE
goes along. It makes her sad.) "Water,
water...you mesmerize me. You tantalize me.
Oh, sweet water. Mother of the Earth. Sweet
mother, take me. Give me my birth.../ If you

will have me for your own, I will never, ever roam. Oh, mother, take me./ Weeds for my hair. Rocks for my feet. Breath no longer there...

(MIRANDA enters and stands behind LILA. THEY stand in silence for a moment.)

MIRANDA: I always look... and it seems like there's not enough water. As long as you can still see the Bronx, it's not enough. Know what I mean?

LILA: It's so sad.

MIRANDA: It's not that sad.

LILA: I mean the harbor. New York harbor. There's nothing alive in it anymore.

MIRANDA: That's not true. I see people fishing.

LILA: (Beginning to cry.) People fish because they got hope. They're stupid, hopeful people sitting there waiting for something that doesn't exist to come up and bite their lines. Those pathetic little lines. There are no lines strong enough to pull up the heavy shit on the bottom of this river. All those dead people and everything.

MIRANDA: I'm sure I've seen bubbles. There's no bubbles, if there's no breathing.

LILA: Detergent. Toxic waste.

MIRANDA: Don't make me hate you.

LILA: So sensitive today? What happened? Did some guy forget to say what a nice pussy you have?

MIRANDA: If I could strangle you I would.

LILA: If you could strangle me, I'd hang myself.

MIRANDA: If you hanged yourself, I'd leave.

LILA: If you left, I'd burn your sequined slippers, the blue ones with Elvis' head on them.

MIRANDA: No, not those! We had such a great time in Memphis...

LILA: It's my birthday tomorrow.

MIRANDA: Pisces, right?

LILA: Wrong.

MIRANDA: What then?

LILA: Forget it.

MIRANDA: I always do.

LILA: Why won't you hold my hand in public? Or kiss me in Italian restaurants? And even when we're home in bed now, you pull all the shades...Why? So no one can see you fingering an ugly bitch like me?

MIRANDA: You're not so ugly.

(LILA runs away from her.)

Hey, come on! I mean that. Don't you fucking get it? I'm the monster here. I'm always the monster...

(As we hear Edith Piaf's "C'est A Hambourg" lights cross to LILA alone.)

Chapter Twenty

(LILA is alone, standing on the bed, holding a piece of rope.)

LILA: I wish I knew more about knots. Shoulda listened to my father. He knew. It looked fast. I don't think he suffered—much. His eyes were open—and I saw hope there.

(As the lights fade, we hear Edith Piaf continue to sing "C'est A Hambourg." The song plays over the following scene. The lights cross with the JOHNs to the East River. They pull a big fish out of the water with a spear/harpoon sticking out of it.)

Chapter Twenty-one

(The scene is played in silence with Piaf still singing in the background. We see the MEN pose for photos with MIRANDA, who seems to be a very big fish. THEY pose in every configuration possible. Solos, duos & trio. The poses alternate between "proud of the catch" and "sad for the fish." We see the flash but no MARILYN, the photographer, until the last shot is taken.)

MARILYN: Fish cake, cheesecake. Same difference.

(Blackout. Lights slowly up on LILA, her neck bandaged, in the hospital bed.)

Chapter Twenty-two

(LILA in her nurse's uniform, in the hospital where she works. SHE lies in a bed like a patient, her neck wrapped in bandages. JOHN 1 is visiting her. JOHN 2 watches.)

JOHN 2: John brings Lila flowers he found in the cemetery two blocks from the hospital.

LILA: What are you doing here anyway?

JOHN 1: (Hands her the flowers.) Brought you these.

LILA: Lilies? You brought me lilies? Those are for dead people only. And anyway I only like chocolate flowers.

JOHN 1: I didn't know.

LILA: You think because my name is Lila that I just have to love lilies, don't you? But I don't. How did you know where I was?

JOHN 1: I brought you here.

LILA: Oh.

JOHN 1: How's the food here?

LILA: Lousy.

JOHN 1: How's year head?

LILA: Lousy.

(A smoke alarm goes off.)

JOHN 1: Jesus! It's a fire! Get up!

LILA: Naah... this happened five times before. It's that old lady next door. She keeps lighting up by her oxygen tank. Trying to blow herself up.

JOHN 1: What happens when it's a real fire?

LILA: Everybody dies.

JOHN 1: Why don't you get away from her? She's not worth dying over.

LILA: Fuck you! Who asked you?! Who do you think you are anyway? Get out!

JOHN 1: She's leaving you.

LILA: Liar!

JOHN 1: She's moving in with me.

(No response.)

I brought you another present.

(He hands her a bottle of vodka.)

LILA: Leave it on the table and go.

JOHN 1: I didn't mean to hurt you.

(HE exits. SHE takes the bottle and begins to drink. MARILYN enters.)

MARILYN: (Carrying a birthday cake on fire; SHE sings.) "Happy birthday to you! Happy birthday to you... Happy birthday, Ms. Lila... Happy birthday to you..."

LILA: You remembered!

MARILYN: There are some things you just don't forget.

(MARILYN blows LILA a kiss and moves into the shadows to watch, as MIRANDA enters in a turquoise blue dress. JOHN 3 speaks from the shadows.)

JOHN 3: Full of guilt-ripened sadness, she tries to be true—but only shows it in the color of her dress.

(LILA pretends to be asleep. MIRANDA stands over her blowing smoke into her face.)

LILA: This is a fucking hospital, smokehead.

MIRANDA: It's medicinal. I got you outta your coma, didn't I?

LILA: (Grabbing hold of MIRANDA's skirt.) Got a date?

MIRANDA: No... just through I'd dress up a little.

LILA: (With a smile.) For me?

MIRANDA: What do you think?! Yes, for you.

LILA: It almost worked. I got big strong neck muscles though—all that Indonesian dance I took in college, I guess.

MIRANDA: You took dance classes?

LILA: Yeah. But then I got interested in volcanoes—so I switched to geology.

MIRANDA: Practical.

LILA: But then I switched again. Eastern European History.

MIRANDA: I don't believe in history.

LILA: You don't believe in anything, do you?

MIRANDA: No.

LILA: Then why am I the one in the hospital?

MIRANDA: Too much feeling. Too much love... that shit kills you. People say cigarettes kill you—but love does the job quicker. I'd rather spit up blood, than somebody else's body hair. I remember the first time I did that.

A short, blonde one—so there was no mistake.

LILA & MIRANDA: (Together.) It wasn't mine.

(MIRANDA shrugs and exits. MARILYN comes rushing back to LILA.)

MARILYN: I almost forgot! Your present!

(SHE lights LILA's bed on fire with the cake.)

I hope you like it.

(Marilyn continues to talk as LILA gets engulfed in flames.)

I usually hate giving people what they want—especially girlfriends. They always say they want "A" when "B" is what they really want. It's so hard to shop for somebody else. I mean, it's hard enough to figure out what I want. You know what I mean? There's so much to choose from these days. For instance, I was shopping once in this really big store, and I just had to sit myself down and cry. It was too much. Women have to go through so much to find the really good stuff. It's not fair. Men can always go into a shop and pick out what they want in a matter of minutes and have plenty of time left over to go watch a game or have some drinks with the boys. They don't understand what we go through. And this is a rule to live by: Never, ever go shopping with a man if you want to make a reasonable purchase, because they honk the horn if they're in the car, or else they yell at you, or else they look at other women. It's too much. You always make a hasty purchase and then where are you? Nowhere. Square One. I think I better go lie down. Thinking about feminine things always gives me a headache. I hate those people who say Life is a party. It's the kind of party I embarrass myself at by throwing up.

(MARILYN exits, as we hear a short piece of the Trampps singing "Disco Inferno." Lights cross to MIRANDA in bed with JOHN 2.)

Chapter Twenty-three

(In MIRANDA & LILA's apartment. JOHN 2 and MIRANDA are in bed smoking cigarettes. JOHN 1 watches.)

MIRANDA: You really have a great face.

JOHN 2: I do?

MIRANDA: Yeah... great eyes. Great nose. Great cheekbones—I bet you have some Indian in you.

JOHN 2: Maybe.

JOHN 1: She's making such a bad choice... So attracted to the fire—like the fish. She doesn't remember the story of Jonah.

MIRANDA: Yeah, a good, strong Indian face. I love your face.

JOHN 2: Really?

MIRANDA: Yeah—but that's about it.

(HE burns HER with his cigarette.)

Ouch! You asshole!

(SHE burns him with her cigarette.)

JOHN 2: Ouch!

MIRANDA: Now we're even.

JOHN 2: I can't stand that smell.

MIRANDA: You smelled burning flesh before?

JOHN 2: Shut up!

MIRANDA: Did somebody burn you?

JOHN 2: Shut up I said.

MIRANDA: You don't have any scars.

JOHN 2: I'm outta here.

(HE gets up and puts on his clothes.)

MIRANDA: Except around your ass... you got some scars around your ass, don't you? I wouldn't ever have noticed them if I wasn't looking real close. You're so hairy down there... You ever think about shaving?

JOHN 2: You better be careful with other people's memories. They could be your only hope.

(HE begins to exit. SHE stops him.)

MIRANDA: Don't go. Not yet... (SHE smiles.)
Teach me something.

JOHN 2: You first.

MIRANDA: I love to listen to music. It's so alive—always knows what it's about. The only sad part is you know every fucking song has different words. I can never remember all those words.

JOHN 2: Maybe you should learn how to dance. I'll teach you that. Dancing helps you remember the words from the inside.

MIRANDA: Okay. But go slow. I don't like to feel stupid.

(JOHNs 1 & 3 enter with the small tape player. On it plays Celia Cruz's Latinos en los Estados Unidos.)

JOHN 2: Ready? (Jokingly.) You'll play the girl, alright? Just for the lesson.

MIRANDA: Shit! Why not?! Just a fucking dance, right?

JOHN 2: That's right, Miranda.

MIRANDA: I hate my name.

JOHN 2: But it's so beautiful.

MIRANDA: I don't like how it sounds when I say it. It sounds better in your mouth.

JOHN 2: Rule #1: Never let the people watching know how tired you are. Rule #2: Don't get tired—Carry a hard-on for the ladies.

(JOHNs 1 & 3 laugh. MIRANDA and JOHN 2 begin to dance. As SHE listens to the song, SHE begins to cry softly.)

JOHNs 1 & 3: Great song!

JOHN 2 & MIRANDA: (Responding to the lyrics.) What a lying fucking song.

(JOHN 3 looks understanding. JOHN 1 looks like HE's just walked into a Chinese puzzle. THEY exit, leaving JOHN 2 & MIRANDA on stage alone.)

JOHN 2: I had a dream about this book... Tuve un sueño con este libro de mi papabuelo. Y yo tenia ese libro adentro de mi corazon. Este libro me dijo que si yo queria, yo podia ser algo—alguien mas que lo que soy. Algo casi como mi papa, o su papa... pero este libro tenia paginas tan limpias que no podia leerlo. Eran palabras de amor—pero no para mi. Palabras de hombres a hombres. Padre a hijo. En mi sueño mi papabuelo me dijo, "Mijo, tienes que aprender a llorar sin lagrimas o si no los animales del mar te puedan oler y te comen sin cocinarte." But I couldn't stop the tears once I knew they would kill me—in the dream. He knew about that stuff because he was a slave in P.R. Blue eyes, skin like café con leche, and blonde nappy hair. Real tall. He cried a lot the week before he died. He cried a lot because he was married to the same woman for 63 years. And just that week, she first told him that she loved him... "We always pick the right time to die" was the last thing he told me. He was something else. I loved him too.

MIRANDA: It's time for me to stop hating you, sailor. We got the same history.

JOHN 2: What's left of it anyway.

(JOHN 2 & MIRANDA embrace.)

MIRANDA: LIke brother and sister, huh? No more fucking. It gets confusing.

JOHN 2: Good plan. I don't have any sisters.

MIRANDA: I don't have any brothers.

JOHN 2: Funny how things work out.

MIRANDA: You won't remember this tomorrow, will you?

JOHN 2: I never know what I'll remember. Listen, I gotta get back to the ship. That's all I know for sure right now. That's all I know.

(JOHN 2 exits. MIRANDA is left alone. SHE sits in silence for a moment as we hear a reprise of Marilyn Monroe's "I Wanna Be Loved By You," then the lights slowly cross to LILA who is in the apartment, tearing up her lilies.)

Chapter Twenty-four

(In the apartment, LILA tears up her lilies in silence. She is more bandaged than she was in the previous hospital scene. MIRANDA enters, lights a cigarette and sits across from LILA holding a writing pad and a pen. JOHNs 3, 2 & 1 watch.)

JOHN 3: Lila's soul speaks to her when she dreams... but Miranda doesn't listen.

MIRANDA: Tell me another one.

LILA: Why?

MIRANDA: It's good for you. I saw it on Geraldo. You should always keep a record. They tell you a lot.

(MIRANDA writes as LILA speaks.)

JOHN 3: As Lila speaks, Miranda draws pictures of her naked and laughs to herself.

JOHN 2: That's not how a romance should end. There's always music first. Something tragic.

JOHN 1: And dancing.

(JOHNs 2 & 3 give JOHN 1 a look of incredulity.)

I mean—no dancing. Never dancing. Why dance?

LILA: Okay... We're standing in front of a barbed wire fence.

MIRANDA: The one at Alamogordo, New Mexico?

LILA: Yeah. Around the trinity site.

MIRANDA: That nuclear shit scared the shit outta me, until we went and it was like heaven there. Peaceful and still—like death, but sweeter. Everything so white—

LILA: You wanna hear this or not? Because I can stop talking. Talking to me just fills space. Like the sound of no more chocolate or cigarettes. We got a lot of space now.

MIRANDA: What are we wearing?

LILA: We've got on identical outfits, denim pedal pushers, halter tops with polka dots, sky-blue scarves á la Grace Kelly around our heads, and dark sunglasses like Bridgette Bardot would wear.

MIRANDA: Are we touching?

LILA: Yes.

MIRANDA: That's a silly question, isn't it? We always touch in your dreams.

LILA: Suddenly, there's a white, hot flash—

MIRANDA: Cool.

LILA: We're the coldest we've ever been. Our nose hairs freeze and the hair on our arms. I try to pick the ice off your arms, but you scream because it hurts so much, because I'm pulling off the hair too. And then there's a wind that blows us across the street to Lenny's Pancake House.

MIRANDA: Of course.

LILA: Carol Jo, the waitress, opens the door for us. She's got the biggest beehive hairdo I've seen since I left Mentor, Ohio.

MIRANDA: When the hell were you in Ohio? What a place to go.

LILA: People always go somewhere, don't they? Even if they don't really want to go. Anyway, it's blonde with green streaks. "I see you've noticed my hair," she says. "It just keeps growing. I don't gotta wash it anymore or style it or nothing. It just grows newer and cleaner and bigger every night. But not heavier. It still feels like me... from before. So what'll you have?" She waits for us to speak.

All I can say is "The light is burning me." You say, "two over easy with home fries, please."

(Pause.)

You and I stare at each other. We don't speak the same language anymore.

(Pause.)

She comes back with our food. I say, "The light is burning me," but like I'm saying thanks. I smile. I put my fork into my buckwheat pancakes. The heat from my hand moves through the metal, heating it up... it melts my butter. We eat silently, while she smokes Camel Straights. The loose bits of tobacco from her cigarette make their way to the corner of her mouth, building until there's a mole there like Marilyn Monroe has.

MIRANDA: Had.

LILA: I say, "The light is burning me." You say, "I hate buckwheat. That stuff's poison." She says, "Now I got a green streak in my pubic hair too." I think this dream is about freedom.

(MIRANDA lights a cigarette.)

What do you think?

MIRANDA: (Lighting another cigarette and handing it to LILA.) I think you made the whole fucking thing up.

(SHE crumples up the paper she wrote on and throws it in the garbage.)

LILA: People always hear the truth—even when they don't want to.

MIRANDA: What's that supposed to mean?

JOHNs 3, 2 & 1: They both take deep drags on their cigarettes.

(The Johns cough. As we hear a short vocal selection from Patti LaBelle's "New Attitude," lights cross to LILA in the kitchen, holding a pot of boiling water.)

Chapter Twenty-five

(In the apartment kitchen, LILA, unbandaged, looks into a pot of boiling water. JOHN 3 enters and makes a salad. LILA stares at the sun-dried tomatoes she's blanching in the pot.)

LILA: I know what they look like. It suddenly came to me... Sundried tomatoes, only bigger. They're kind of red and kind of brown and they smell like acid. She got that Pearl Drops stuff. And I said fuck it, why bother, you should see if they've got lung drops. Nothing whitens those— takes ten years to clear them.

JOHN 3: My dad smoked his whole life.

LILA: Yeah?

JOHN 3: Yeah. Then he got into a fight. These guys hit him into a concrete wall. There was vomit all around him when I found him. And cigarette butts. I guess they were so drunk, they threw up, and then had a few laughs, a few smokes—right there, by Daddy's cracked open head... There's plenty worse ways to die than smoke.

LILA: But I love her.

JOHN 3: So what? That's your problem. Listen, I've been trying to figure this out. I think love is about power. The person who is loved is powerful, if they acknowledge it, but also, the person who loves and admits to it has power through freedom. You told all you got to tell and, bam, you're free.

LILA: Did you study philosophy or something?

JOHN 3: A little. So?

LILA: So, nothing. You got a lot of interesting theories. What's your theory about me?

JOHN 3: I think you're a self-hating woman with a self-destructive attitude.

(As LILA speaks, JOHN 3 exits and JOHN 2 enters.)

LILA: Do you think I'm suicidal?

JOHN 2: Oh, yeah. But I think everybody is. I mean, why live? What for? You get kicked in the face enough times, you crack.

LILA: You never tried it.

(LILA takes the tomatoes out of the boiling water and drains them as JOHN 2 finishes the salad and puts it on the table.)

JOHN 2: Not exactly—but I did date this Catholic girl once.

LILA: (Sarcastically.) No kidding.

JOHN 2: Yeah. And she tried it a lot. I think it's something about being Catholic. I mean, it's such a sin and everything—it's like a dare. A dare from God and you sniff enough of that incense and your mind gets wacked.

(The doorbell rings. LILA answers it. SHE returns with a bouquet of flowers.)

JOHN 2: Hey, nice. She does love you.

LILA: (Reading the card.) She sent them to both of us.

(SHE hands him the card.)

JOHN 2: (Reading.) "To my favorite assholes..." That's interesting... I never got called an asshole before and felt all goosey about it.

LILA: You've gotta go. Where do you want to go? I'll buy you a ticket. Venice? It's nice this time of year.

JOHN 2: Gotta go back to the ship. And listen—it's nothing to get hyped about. You can keep the flowers. I won't even touch them. Can't smell them anyway. I had this girlfriend once who ate hummus all the time—

LILA: Was she Middle-Eastern?

JOHN 2: Californian. And God, she smelled so much like garlic and I was so into her, you know what I mean? That she ruined my sense of smell.

(JOHN 2 exits and JOHN 1 enters.)

JOHN 1: All I can ever smell is stuff that smells like her.

LILA: Listen. I won't eat another meal with you. Are you listening? I won't have you in my house. Stay away from her. Stay away or I'll rip your pussy pink nipples off. Don't even think about her—if you do I'll hear you and I'll make you bleed from your eyes.

JOHN 1: Wow... well, okay. I'm not that hungry anyway... but you really shouldn't keep loving her like this.

LILA: I know.

JOHN 1: We were almost friends, you an me.

LILA: I like you Sailor. You are a good, honest man. But you're stupid. Stupid people make me sick. They give me fevers. I want to faint when I'm around you. I wanna just slip into a coma. You talk and I don't even know what the fuck you're talking about. You take my soul from me with your tongue. It's like a big, strong wave that lifts up small crafts and drowns them, because you're relentless. You have no relent, Sailor. You talk and talk and talk and I fool you into thinking I'm listening. I'm not. I'm waiting for the full moon so I can

strap on my hunting knife and go hunting. I
always hunt better by the full moon.

(MIRANDA enters and calls to them.)

MIRANDA: Help me. It's just at the bottom
of
the stairs. Come on!

(THEY go to help her carry in a new red
loveseat sofa—the one from Loew's Paradise
movie theater. JOHN 3 and LILA reenter,
carrying the loveseat with great effort.
MIRANDA directs.)

Up against the wall.

(THEY put it down with grunts.)

It's beautiful.

LILA: I think there's something wrong with
me.

JOHN 3: Me too.

MIRANDA: What?! Oh, come on. It's just a
little loveseat. You act like it's—I dunno, real
heavy or something. Like a car. I didn't ask
you to help me move a car, did I? What
babies! I love you both.

LILA: You love us both the same?

MIRANDA: I love one a little bit more.

JOHN 3: I gotta go.

(HE exits quickly. THEY stare at each other in silence.)

MIRANDA: Well? What do you think?

(LILA goes to the bouquet of flowers and begins methodically tearing the flowers apart.)

JOHN 1: LILA tears up her heart—

JOHN 2: —and Miranda begins to grow.

JOHN 3: For some of us—it's the only way.

MIRANDA: Oh...

(MIRANDA begins to pick up the flower petals LILA has thrown on the floor.)

We gotta throw all those loose things in the garbage from now on. Once the baby comes—we gotta make sure she doesn't choke. That happens too much lately.

LILA: That's it. The fleet's out.

MIRANDA: What do you mean?

LILA: I mean "no," not in my house. How could you?! Why would you bring a baby into my house? A baby that belongs to some guy you picked up—that you just picked up in order to get away from me? To run from the one person who really loves you? When I hold you and you let yourself slip under my skin, there's only us there. Just us. Only us two. Where do you think this baby's going to live?

MIRANDA: Right here. A baby will be good for us. She'll make things good for us—make us responsible. Someone to live for. That's what she is.

LILA: And what the fuck am I? You can't solve your life like this. No one can. People think babies change things—but that's just on the outside, inside things still burn. And if you're burning like that, you're gonna scorch that kid. Children carry their scars on the inside. That's why they're so beautiful and that's why so many people got this need to hurt them. They say it's protection, they say it's concern—but really it's all for them. Don't have a baby. You'll just give it your sickness. That's not love.

MIRANDA: You're just jealous—and you don't gotta be. This baby is ours. She won't have our sickness, she'll grow into something beautiful with both of us here to water her.

LILA: It's not a fucking garden, Miranda. What you got inside you, shits and eats and cries—and why should I care about that. When I cry, do you come to me? But you'll have to go to that thing inside you. There'll be no room for me—there's so little room to begin with... You don't understand that, I bet. You don't know death like I do. It doesn't hang on you like mist in a rainforest. That's me. I'm misty for you all the time now. My desire is drowning me. One of us has to go.

MIRANDA: You're lying. You don't have the balls to throw me out.

LILA: I don't need balls. I have the marks on my brain from your spiked heels. Shoes humans can't walk in—Shoes for goddesses—stupid ones who don't even know how to walk.

MIRANDA: What do you expect me to do?

LILA: Kill it.

MIRANDA: I thought if anyone you would be the one—you would understand. Wrong again...

LILA: Get rid of it and stay with me. Only my arms, Miranda. Remember when you said that?

MIRANDA: No, Lila. I don't.

(LILA throws a lit candlestick at MIRANDA, who dodges it and then stamps it out with her feet while singing.)

"La cucaracha, la cucaracha! Ya no puede caminar!"

LILA: You are a roach. A Puerto Rican roach filled with white crusty roach babies. Somebody needs to step on you and make your milky insides run. Make those insides flow like lava down the outer lips of a volcano. That baby is your eruption. You're gonna cut off your roads, if you keep it. It's gonna turn your insides to rock. There'll be no way back.

MIRANDA: I'm not Puerto Rican anymore. You turned me into your volcano, about to explode into turquoise blue. Maybe they make maternity pants that color. I love that color. It reminds me of you.

(LILA runs out screaming.)

There you go again. What's the use of that? Screams don't change anything. They're like boat-rides in the dark. Who do you pretend to be that night? Somebody in love—but there's a ghost sitting next to you...some ghosts never leave you alone. Especially with a stiff sea

135

breeze tangling your hair and forcing your eyes to close. Making you look deep on the inside—begging for love. But all you see when you open your eyes is the space where love used to be and that space is filled with dirt. (Pause.)

MIRANDA: (Continued.) Is that what I am? If I gathered up all my body dirt—like toe jam, cooter crud, eye snot, nail dirt, navel lint—would I have the sum total of my life in things I could wash away with soap?

(Pause.)

I know exactly when it started... I wanted to be a fairy princess. "No," Mami said. "You got a pirate's face. I bought the eye patch. You're gonna be a pirate." "Why can't Dolores be a pirate?" "She's too pretty to be a pirate, baby. You know your sister's the prettiest girl on the block. Everybody says so. You say so." "Yeah, I say so. But we could both—" Then she slapped me. "Dolores is the princess and you're the pirate so stop whining about it. Or I'll smack you again." "Don't smack me, Mami." All I wanted was to be the fairy princess. But Mami said I had a homely face, which I thought was like a face you were comfortable with—like in your home. But then I found out what it really meant. I got the kind of ugliness that is so deep you can't see it. It lives in my shadows.

Only something from the inside out could take away that kind of darkness.

(LILA comes back in with a stuffed white whale and hands it to MIRANDA.)

LILA: This is a present from Marilyn. She wishes you luck, Miranda. She wants you to take this and start a new life with it—

MIRANDA: (Tossing the whale aside.) I'm not going anywhere.

LILA: Yes, you are. You're getting out of my apartment and giving me back my life. You see, I don't have to be my father anymore. And you just keep making me act like him.

MIRANDA: Where do you expect me to go?

LILA: Home.

(LILA exits to the bedroom. MIRANDA speaks to her unborn child.)

MIRANDA: I remembered how to hope today... I hoped that you might be my home. Your father looked just like me, baby. I got shortcuts with him I don't got with nobody else. And you'll make me into an angel—just like in my book...

(She feels her uterus beginning to convulse. The instrumental part of "Detour Ahead" begins to play softly in the background.)

Oh, little girl, don't do like that! Why are you doing like that?!

(The pain of the convulsions brings her to her knees. A light illuminates the white whale as MIRANDA reaches for it. SHE rocks in pain as the lights cross to JOHN 1, 2 & 3 sitting on a bench at East River Park. We hear "Detour Ahead" continue to play.)

Chapter Twenty-six

(At East River Park, the pier, and the Museum. JOHNs 1, 2, & 3 sit on a park bench. MARILYN sits at the pier, reading a book.)

MARILYN: This is a cute part.

(Reading from a thick book.)

Chapter one hundred and twenty-two: "Um, um, um. Stop that thunder! Plenty too much thunder up here! What's the use of thunder? Um, um, um. We don't want thunder; we want rum; give us a glass of rum. Um, um, um!" Sailors say the craziest things.

JOHN 1: I like the fresh air.

JOHN 3: I like the mindless activity that lets you spend a lot of time thinking.

JOHN 2: I like the shore leave. Sweet, sweet PUSSY!

(THEY burst out laughing.)

MARILYN: People who drink too much rum always say crazy things. Those island beverages are the hardest to control—especially when you mix them. But what else is there to do on an island, anyway?

(We hear the sound of footsteps and MIRANDA beginning to speak softly. Her speech is murmured under the dialogue of the JOHNs and MARILYN.)

MIRANDA: There's this preacher slash cook guy named Fleece—what a name huh? So clear—the sheperd of the creatures of the sea. Anyway, he gives this sermon to the sharks—reminding them how much they're like angels even though they're killers. He says that the only difference between them is that the angel has a boss, and it being God and all, they don't get into the same kind of trouble. When you spill so much blood filling your belly, you can't hear any good advice. Your ears get jammed full with another animal's flesh, and you fool yourself into feeling so content, that it's easy to swim away—never looking back. That's how I used to be, little girl.

JOHN 3: Who's that?

JOHN 1: You're not supposed to talk to footsteps in the dark—you're supposed to run.

(THEY laugh again.)

MARILYN: It's sad how everyone wanted that white whale dead just so they could go home and relax. Or maybe stop by my place and have a little drinkie first. Sailors are so easy to please.

(MIRANDA appears cradling the stuffed white whale, now stained with blood, in her arms.)

MIRANDA: Hey young sailorboys! Have you ever picked your teeth with Halibut bones? I do. I do it cause I'm a fish too. Loose, a loose fish. Come here Sailorboy. You can kiss me for a dollar.

JOHN 1: No thanks.

MIRANDA: A quarter then. All I need is a quarter...

JOHN 2: She's wacked. Isn't that your girlfriend, John?

JOHN 1: Not mine. Yours maybe.

JOHN 3: Well, she sure ain't mine.

(HE searches his pockets.)

Sorry... I don't got any more change.

MARILYN: But that's only because they don't understand love yet—all they know is that at dawn, they go back to the ship in order to go somewhere else. Where ever the wind and orders from someone they never met, will take them—To fight a battle or play at fighting one.

JOHN 1: Isn't it time to go back to the ship?

MARILYN: They think that in order to be free they must live out someone else's purpose—they must deny any knowledge and remember that people are only objects with hearts to be destroyed. That's what the manual says anyway. Never look the enemy in the eye. My first husband was in the army. Uniforms still make me sad.

JOHN 2: There'll be other sailors coming this way soon. Ask one of them. We gotta go.

MIRANDA & MARILYN: (MIRANDA puts on a MARILYN MONROE voice.) I'm not really interested in money. I just want to be wonderful.

(This gets the MEN's attention. LILA enters and sits on the pier.)

MIRANDA: I gotta be somebody else, because I have to travel over water soon— and I have to be careful—with the baby and all. She doesn't like the sea. She doesn't understand it. There's scary places on the other side of the river. But she'll be safe in my arms.

JOHN 2: Shit! I think she's gonna start singing fucking sea chanties any minute now. Hey lady, how about one?

MIRANDA: (Singing in a mock ancient seamen's voice.) Oh! Jolly is the gale, and the joker is the whale, A Flourishin' his tail,—/ Such a funny, Sporty, gamy, jesty, jokey, hokey-pokey lad is the ocean, oh!

JOHN 3: Guess you like books, huh?

MIRANDA: Some books have words worth remembering.

(MARILYN gives LILA the book, who reads from it.)

LILA: I remember the taste of each tear I kissed from her cheek. The taste of her sadness, one with my own. Our lives dripping from the sweat of our love. My fingers searched and entered every hole shaped like my fingers—a perfect fit. That's how I knew it was love. And how I knew love was over. The waters of sadness can't float love for long. Too much the same—too much like me...

(MARILYN turns the page for her. SHE continues to read.)

These young sailors didn't know what to say to this woman who appeared out of each of their nightmares. They could never understand that she was my dream. Who would be the first to say that he had slept with a stranger that may have robbed him of his soul? At least they were sad about it. That was unusual. Each one had a thought—

JOHN 1: I'll give it up for lent.

JOHN 2: It's the thing I fear the most.

JOHN 3: It is always dangerous to love.

JOHNs 1, 2, 3 & LILA: If you need it, it can destroy you.

(MARILYN moves back to her museum area. MIRANDA moves to address MARILYN.)

MIRANDA: Got a quarter?

MARILYN: Sure, honey.

(SHE reaches under MIRANDA's skirt and pulls out a quarter.)

Here's one. That's all you have left. Some things go so quickly.

MIRANDA: I got a phone call to make. I gotta get across the river.

MARILYN: Yeah... I made two phone calls from a park just like this one. Called over and over, and still no one... but, anyway, I bet you're different.

MIRANDA: My baby—

MARILYN: Yes, they do that... two of mine... well, sometimes it's better that way.

MIRANDA: I used to think I knew what was better. Now I don't.

MARILYN: Finally... You're ready for the trip of your life.

(MARILYN takes the book out of LILA's hands and reads from Moby-Dick's epilogue.)

"The drama's done. Why then here does any one step forth?—Because some do survive the wreck."

MIRANDA: That white whale never shoulda let them kill her. Should never have stuck around—getting angrier and angrier—only to get the harpoon in the back. Why'd she have to fight something that could never understand her? She shoulda just started over—shoulda just gone home. It's time.

(MIRANDA takes the book from MARILYN, closes it and holds it tightly to her chest. A light illuminates a pay phone. Blackout.)

<u>End of Play</u>

LIZ ONE
(Her Secret Diaries in the Land of 1,000 Dances)

by

John Jesurun

For Lolin

About the Playwright

JOHN JESURUN is a playwright,director,designer living in New York. His presentations integrate elements of language, film, architectural space and media. His exploded narratives cover a wide range of themes and explore the relation of form to content.They challenge the experience of verbal, visual and intangible perceptions. His work is distinguished by his integrated creation of the text,direction, set and media design. Born 1951 in Battle Creek, Michigan. B.F.A. Philadelphia College of Art/1972. M.F.A. in Sculpture from Yale University/ 1974. 1976-79/Television Content Analyst for CBS.1979-82/Assistant to producer/ Dick Cavett Show producing shows on John and Mackenzie Phillips, John Hammond Sr., Odetta and Tito Puente.

In 1982 he began began his theatrical career at the Pyramid Club on the Lower East Side with his groundbreaking serial play CHANG IN A VOID MOON, now in its 60th episode. (Bessie Award). Since 1984 he has written,directed and designed over 25 pieces including: the media trilogy of DEEP SLEEP (1986 Obie Award, Best Play), WHITE WATER and BLACK MARIA , NUMBER MINUS ONE, DOG'S EYE VIEW, RED HOUSE, SHATTERHAND MASSACREE, PHILOKTETES, EVERYTHING THAT RISES MUST CONVERGE, SLIGHT RETURN, IRON LUNG, BARDO, SEPTET and SNOW. His company has toured extensively in Europe and the United States. His work has been produced and presented by numerous venues including La Mama, the Kitchen, the Walker Arts Center, On the Boards, Brooklyn Academy of Music, the Wexner Center,Kampnagel

Theater, Prater Theater,National Theater of Mexico, Mickery Theater, Theater am Turm, Granada Festival, Eurokaz Zagreb, Bogota International Festival,Vienna Festival,Kyoto Performing Arts Center and Spoleto USA. His short films have been shown at festivals and alternative spaces in Europe and the US. He is the recipient of numerous grants including the: Rockefeller Foundation Playwrights Fellowship, Guggenheim Foundation Fellowship, National Endowment for the Arts Playwrights Fellowship, and the MacArthur Fellowship. His work is published by Performing Arts Journal, BackStage Books, Theater Communications Group, and Sun and Moon Press. In 2009 NoPassport Press published his media trilogy DEEP SLEEP, WHITE WATER, and BLACK MARIA with a preface by Fiona Templeton.

For all performance rights to John Jesurun's work contact the author c/o shatterhand2@earthlink.net website: johnjesurun.googlepages.com

LIZ ONE (Her Secret Diaries in the Land of 1,000 Dances) was originally performed at the Chocolate Factory in New York October 14th-31, 2009. It was produced by the Chocolate Factory with additional production support by Monarch Theater, NY.

Text, Direction, Stage and Video Design by John Jesurun. Lighting by Jeff Nash, Assistant Director: Kevin Hourigan, Technical Director: Logan George, Production Manager: Jennifer Ortega, Additional Video Design by Logan George, Music: Pamelia Kurstin, Costume Design: Molly Deale, Chair Design: José Ho, Sound Consultant: Curtis Webster, Intern: Pauline Tong Tong. Photography: Paula Court.

Cast: Liz One: Black-Eyed Susan
Twin Glimmer: Benjamin Forster.

Quoted Texts Include: "Memo from Turner" by Jagger/Richards, "On Providence" by Seneca "The Cloud of Unknowing" of unknown 14th Century English authorship. "The Spanish English Girl" by Miguel de Cervantes, "La Dragontea" by Lope de Vega Carpio

The playwright would like to especially thank Ellen Stewart, La Mama, MacDowell Colony, Monarch Theater, The Chocolate Factory, Brian Rogers, Sheila Lewandowski, Jennifer Ortega, Curtis Webster, Madeline Best, BeforeYour Eyes, Irene Young, Sanghi Choi, Frank Hentschker, Hebe Joy, Paula Court, Daniel Nelson, Caridad Svich, Jane Stein and NoPassport Press.

Websites: johnjesurun.googlepages.com
Chocolate Factory: www.chocolatefactorytheater.org

LIZ ONE

The stage is a long narrow strip of space that is wider than deep. The entire back wall of the space serves as a large screen which alternately becomes two side by side screens. These screens will project live video and pre-recorded images. In the center of the back wall hangs a large round convex mirror. Underneath this is a large white minimal throne like chair. Identical round convex mirrors on each end of the space slant outwards. Next to each of the side mirrors is a mounted camera. The actors will speak into these cameras at different times. There is also an aerial camera trained on the center mirror and what it reflects.

Cast of Characters:

LIZ– Queen Elizabeth I of England
TWIN GLIMMER– Her courtier

All photos from the premiere of <u>Liz One</u> are courtesy of John Jesurun and photographer Paula Court.

1. QUAESISTI A ME

TWIN GLIMMER: (Reciting, from "The Cloud of Unknowing.) Quaesisti a me. Luscili, quid ita, si providentia mundus ageretur, multa bonis uiris mala acciderent. Lette not therefore, bot travayle therin tyl thou fele lyst. For at the first tyme when thou dost it, thou fyndest bot a derknes, and as it were a cloude of unknowyng, thou wost never what, savyng that thou felist in thi wille a naked entent unto God.

And therfor schap thee to bide in this derknes as longe as thou maist, evermore criing after Him that thou lovest, for yif ever shalt thou fele Him or see Him, as it may be here, it behoveth alweis be in this derknes. And yif thou wilte besily travayle as I bid thee, I triste in His mercy that thou schalt come therto.

(Then from "Memo from Turner," altered.)

"Did not I see you down in San Antone on a
hot and dusty night?
We were eating eggs in Sammy's when the
black man there drew
his knife.
Aw, you drowned that Jew in Rampton as he
washed his woolen
fez,
You know, that Spanish-speaking gentleman,
the one we all

called Lopez.
Come now, gentleman, I know there's some
mistake. "

Te convinco non inhumanitatis solum sed
etiam amentiae. I convict you not only of
cruelty but of madness.

"How forgetful I'm becoming, now you fixed
your bus'ness
straight."

END OF SCENE

2. Paper Mountain

LIZ: What is this mountain of paper?

TWIN GLIMMER: Intercepted Letters.

LIZ: Ours or theirs?

TWIN GLIMMER: Theirs.

LIZ: From?

TWIN GLIMMER: Everywhere.

LIZ: There must be three hundred.

TWIN GLIMMER: Your spies have been
busy.

LIZ: Forging. How many of these interceptions are forged?

TWIN GLIMMER: At least fifty.

LIZ: We have intercepted fifty of our own forged letters? How am I to maintain a grip on political reality if fully and at least one sixth of that reality is false? Give me that!

(LIZ grabs a letter.)

TWIN GLIMMER: It's from Mary to the Philip minion.

LIZ: Real or unreal?

TWIN GLIMMER: Real. Read.

LIZ: "I intend to cede and grant by will my right to the succession of this crown of England to the King your master." Is there a legal will stating such?

TWIN GLIMMER: Philip has ransacked archives in Rome and all over France to find some version of it but to no avail.

LIZ: (Reading letter) "I, Mary, leave to Philip all the rights and interests I may have in the government in the kingdom of Scotland, since my son, James, remains obstinately outside

the Catholic church." Send these ones to
James with the others.

TWIN GLIMMER: Philip daily flings a
glittering web of smuggled entrancement and
interference. Gilded and gelded Jesuits
transmigrate on schedule with the cormorants.

LIZ: James is as Protestant as he is bent. For
God's sake, they are both bent in different
directions. Bent and Protestant we shall be.
Even if the whole island swings that way we
will not suffer this Jesuitical onslaught of
flailing rosaries and candy-ass bishops. What
can we give that sultan in Istanbul to keep
him driving Philip's quadrophenia?

TWIN GLIMMER: We're already selling
them powder and arms. There are one
hundred Turkish prisoners that Drake
captured from the Spanish raids in the Indies.
The Spanish had made them into galley slaves.

LIZ: Have them repatriated to Istanbul
immediately. As a gift from me. Leak it to one
of their spies here in court. We must convince
the Turks that they have nothing to gain by
making a truce with Spain. Spread the rumor
that Sultan has promised me that he will
attack Spain if Spain attacks England. And I
want those slaves dressed well when they are
returned. What's this?

TWIN GLIMMER: Another one of the missives from our English ambassador in Paris falsely telling us that he has inside information that Philip will never move against us. And that therefore we should reduce our spending on defense.

LIZ: Poison his croissants! And what is all this Lucretia stuff our little Maria Nuñez keeps talking about?

TWIN GLIMMER: Lucretia de Léon, a fifteen year old Iberian clairvoyant.

LIZ: Must they continue with their nonsensical attempts to find the favor of a god who is himself a somnambulist? What has she dreamed?

TWIN GLIMMER: She dreams against Philip. His own daughter Isabella appears and says: "Look Your Majesty, Spain is lost, Your Majesty is aware of the fame my grandfather Emperor Charles V left behind. The name of the Catholic monarch Ferdinand also lives even though he has been dead many years and the names and glories of the holy kings of France are known everywhere. As for you, Philip, it is only said that you have impoverished your kingdom."

LIZ: We must marry her to James.

TWIN GLIMMER: She has also dreamed that there will be a large naval battle in which Drake defeats the Spanish navy.

LIZ: When?

TWIN GLIMMER: In eight months time.

LIZ: Then she must marry Drake.

TWIN GLIMMER: Nuñez advises against it – she says that Lucretia is a maternally driven lunatic who one day will be burned.

LIZ: She must be saved.

TWIN GLIMMER: She will be burned. May I describe the next dream?

LIZ: Alright, but it better be good.

TWIN GLIMMER: It is circulated by print and poem on the Spanish continent that on December 14, 1587, she dreamed of you seated with a disemboweled lamb in your lap, thrusting your hands into the eviscerated cavity and bathing them in blood. You are accompanied by a woman dressed as a widow who refuses to drink the blood of the lamb. At this refusal you angrily unsheathe a sword and decapitate the woman.

LIZ: We know who the headless woman is. But who is the lamb?

TWIN GLIMMER: They say the lamb is Edmund Campion.

LIZ: Seditious chatterbox! Bite your tongue before I bite it off for you. Must I continue this dialogue with the devil? I flew through horrific and intricate constellations of pain to twist his tongue away from the eyes of our axe. But he loved God more than life. A tainted lamb not worthy of sacrifice. Though I did love him.

TWIN GLIMMER: Enough to transform him into a living quadrangle like…

LIZ: …human garbage? He was a wasp in the wine!

TWIN GLIMMER: Try this one. (Reads.) "Wife of many and of many the daughter in law, oh infamous Queen. No Queen but a she-wolf, lustful and bestial."

LIZ: More bad Catholic exile poetry? Saint Edmund Campion would dethrone us all. What were his last words? "In condemning us, you condemn all your own ancestors, all our ancient bishops and kings, all that was once the glory of England —The Island of

Saints, and the most devoted child of the See of Peter."

TWIN GLIMMER: That is real poetry.

LIZ: What else has Lucretia de Léon to say?

TWIN GLIMMER: To Philip's daughter she prophesies: "Poor Isabella, your hair will become the shoes of your father's enemies."

LIZ: Who is that hideous gaggle over there? Their hair looks to be the shoes of their enemies' fathers.

TWIN GLIMMER: The Americans, they are a haggard bunch now having lost everything, returned defeated from the Roanoke colony.

LIZ: Send them back.

TWIN GLIMMER: They have been back but the colony has disappeared.

LIZ: Then they must start another one!

TWIN GLIMMER: Also, some children and cats were killed in our recent attack on France and we just feel awful about it.

LIZ: Tragic. Write them a letter and sign it for me, will you? The usual.

3. Location

LIZ: The space you are seeing is vulnerable to the memory and the will. And so the locations of near and far, here and there, then and there, here and now are not relevant.

TWIN GLIMMER: In my mind I am slowly trying to push her influence into the background. So what you will be seeing will in fact be the background of the picture in disregard to the foreground. I have taken the Queen's advice and exercised a polite restraint—a staying away from. And I have naively burned the diary. As for those who thought I knew better, I have memorized most of it—which I will be telling you. But I will forget it as I speak it so don't ask me to repeat it because I will not be able to. I will have safely receded into a cloud of unknowing. A narrator without opinion. But I may occasionally slip and fall victim to my human urge for recognition.

LIZ: I actually lived in the background of the world, not in the glittering foreground. I sat behind a series of veils, real and imagined and watched the strings pull him in every direction.

TWIN GLIMMER: I was one of those veils. I got a few shots in but for me it was a long slow beheading. So I will now retire into the background. As through a cloud. That's my inheritance, my comeuppance. As I was her comeuppance.

END OF SCENE

4. Water

LIZ: (Gazing into a glass of water.) The god of water—violent, phantasmagoric! Cleansing. And now you know everything is clear, Minister of the Interior and Minister of the Exterior—which means that you know nothing—or less than what you did before— when you thought you knew nothing. But how is it that your intelligence continues to become less while your knowledge is constantly increasing in size?! (She throws her glass at GLIMMER.) How can that be?!

TWIN GLIMMER: So now we will begin to form a strategy in cement.

(In this scene, all LIZ's capitalized words are forcefully spoken simultaneously by GLIMMER.)

LIZ: Which means YOU as my diplomats will always side with those without conviction. Regardless of what I think. You will always side with those non–entities who are just like you—those who would do the same for YOU. In the name of diplomacy you will

NEVER take a side and therefore always be a dummy and morally IRRELEVANT.

TWIN GLIMMER: In the service of a greater good, that being....

LIZ: ME! You will be WRONG in your way of thinking—in the way you reach a decision—which is in fact not a DECISION AT ALL but an...

TWIN GLIMMER: ...accommodation, a form of trade, business.

LIZ: Your words must be like pink rosebuds dipped in harmony, dripping with ironclad insincerity. It is during these very flowery moments that you must whisper to yourself softly the words— "Petit pays, je t'aime beaucoups. Petit-bourgeois, je t'aime beaucoups." Your benevolent selfless, self serving actions will be the gorilla glue that keeps England from coming apart! And we are thankful to you for sparing us the guns and knives and bad words and shouts and anger outwardly displayed and feelings kept INSIDE where they should be and where they come from and where they should stay forever! Where they should stay forever... and you will replace them with the NOTHING we get in return for our dishonesty and good will and compassion!

(Standing behind her, GLIMMER holds dagger up to stab LIZ.)

Why is it that my ministers bring me NOTHING for such a great investment of rose colored treachery? Drop the chalupa! Drop it!

(GLIMMER drops the dagger.)

Moron! How dare you imagine such a thing! Chihuahua-brain! Are you French?! Get him out of here! One more thing—I am who I am. You are nobody till somebody kills you. Go make him into somebody.

TWIN GLIMMER: Yes, Your Highness.

LIZ: JUST STATE THE FACTS, you spinning, shit crazed dung beetle! Don't you know I hate these nonsensical, circular, assassination attempts that end nowhere—or worse—where they began! What do you say Rosebud?

TWIN GLIMMER: I think there is still a class war going on. In here and everywhere.

LIZ: Some idea the servants and the two-bit aristocracy got wind of a few months ago and never let go of. They hold onto it like a dog that won't let go. Must I continuously have to deal with a jack-assed, lock-jawed court? And what kind of asses jawbone advice are you giving me?!

TWIN GLIMMER: They love you.

LIZ: They restrain at certain moments but don't be fooled! As you are yourself restraining right now! How dare you restrain and kowtow in my presence! You pretend to relent as if you think restraining would please me. And then they demand the same entitlements that they think their "friends" are getting. And they won't give in. So I throw them a piece of moldy Stilton. And they come running. Even if they have to maim each other to get to the table—but all in apparently polite conversation. They exact their price— they cut a cheesy deal and it is silently and efficiently transacted amongst themselves. And then they loosen their lockjaw for a bit. But like all peons they have strong jaws but their teeth are NOT SHARP!

TWIN GLIMMER: Not exactly a Norman invasion if you will.

LIZ: NOT! They take what they think is theirs as if it is their right, their freedom. But it's not theirs, it's MINE—and THEY are MINE. As if they are my fancy-pants cousins in the big houses—who DO take their entitlement because they ARE entitled. Not because they are free but because they are FREE to take it. And I am free to let them take it.

TWIN GLIMMER: What's wrong with that?

LIZ: EVERYTHING, you moron! They want to be a big dog too. I am the only big dog here—get it?! It's a petty game of growl and sneer.

TWIN GLIMMER: They come in here and present a personality and position that is attained but not born into. And I have to accept that BULLSHIT?! And their mouths have the nerve to say to ME—"Oh, thank you very much."

LIZ: But their eyes say to me—"You were born with yours—now I will take mine out of my own free will... And resentment of the Queen's birthright. "

TWIN GLIMMER: They have the NERVE to believe that power grabbed is accomplishment attained. That whatever way, they will take it. From ME if necessary! And they resent HAVING to take it but they hope they can arouse some resentment in me. The way they feel it daily as low class peons. That's what they want! To give a petty little pinch. As if that is how power works. That is the extent and purpose of the CLASS WAR. For the moment. To make a SUPERIOR feel a similar, simultaneous resentment. To share petty feelings equally. As if that would make everyone equal. And I know they will be back later to claim some more resentment. It is a shock they think they can inflict politely. They are hounds rushing to their own slaughter!

LIZ: I will never relent, never resent. Do I have to kill everyone to stamp this impertinence out?! And where is MY SOUL in all of this? Inside this piece of CHEESE I fear. And where are all these weird ideas coming from!?

TWIN GLIMMER: The colony of Roanoke.

LIZ: Think so? But what I admire about the Americans is their complete and flat footed lack of pure empathy for anyone including themselves. It's almost pagan.

TWIN GLIMMER: I lived there for a year and don't consider myself an American anymore at all.

LIZ: Then you will live there for fifty more until you consider yourself one! Someone find him a rowboat and get him out of here. I am offended! How long has that colony been lost? More John Barleycorn on the rocks!

TWIN: Chalupa is the imperial Spanish word for dagger.

5. Story

TWIN GLIMMER: There was the story for a long time that she had for years hidden in the private areas of the palace, a young male servant, a changeling with a smile colder than ice. Then the story circulated that there were actually two, and that one was a ghost. And then another story that the changeling was in fact a girl dressed as a male.

LIZ: We are not dealing in magic realism or mystical ghost stories here. These boys were known in local folklore as the Glimmer Twins. I reiterate that it was a myth of sorts that circulates in these backward types of Northern countries.

TWIN GLIMMER: They were thought to be her own children fathered either by her private doctor Lopez or possibly even…the rumors of her virginity were never believed. She slowly built a wall of lies around these twins as a means of protecting them. And then, when they were properly sealed away in the background, she continued to live in the foreground. That being said, let's get on with it. She then asked me, the twin who wasn't a ghost—to help her with her diary as she was reaching the age where she was failing to distinguish the background from the foreground. I had to help her set the record straight. To repaint certain areas of what was already being sketched in as forgery by those around her. In regards to her own life, the appearance of things became more important than the actuality—especially since she wasn't going to be an actuality much longer. So the reality would live in the diary and the appearance would live in apparent actuality.

LIZ: Day after day, rewriting and then un-writing and then rewriting it. We got carried away with the power of our process. This constantly adjusted, accommodated memory eventually became the reality between us.

TWIN GLIMMER: Even I came to believe it and become one of its false operatives. I am now a successfully fictitious invention inside her story. This I did myself to save my own self. It's a relief not to be real anymore. It's very safe. Safer than death. I'll go over a few main points from what is commonly thought to be the background of her life. But in reality it is the foreground to you. Everything you were taught to believe about her actually took place in the background of her life and was in fact a secondary kind of reality to her.

END OF SCENE

6. Diary

LIZ: We will go back as far as necessary. The diary won't be entirely true but it won't be entirely fictional either. Upon my death you will send a copy to...

TWIN GLIMMER: Scottish James.

LIZ: James already has one. He's been advising me on it.

TWIN GLIMMER: Why him?

LIZ: Guess.

TWIN GLIMMER: You are planning to pass the crown to him.

LIZ: Who knows where it will land but it may have to be that way.

TWIN GLIMMER: Because I am a bastard.

LIZ: I am a bastard.

TWIN GLIMMER: From your whore mother's womb did you fly like a nest of tiny vipers! How is it that you have survived so long?

LIZ: How is it that you have survived so long? Everyone and their mother has been trying to kill me. From Spain to France to Scotland to Poland even, I believe. Wherever that is. They even say the Emperor of Cipangu wants to kill me—or marry me. I sent a ship there with your brother three years ago!

TWIN GLIMMER: I hope it is lost. How can so many people hate you?

LIZ: And what do you all have to gain by my death?

TWIN GLIMMER: I would only gain sorrow.

LIZ: I think it's pathological. That's what Dr. Lopez says.

TWIN GLIMMER: That apostate witch doctor?! He may be trying to kill you as well.

LIZ: Dr. Lopez? I doubt it. He's my faithful doctor. He knows what no one else knows. If he wanted to kill me he could have done it long ago.

TWIN GLIMMER: Drop the Virgin Queen stuff. There are those who say you are lovers.

LIZ: How dare you bring up such thing! Tiny sparrow, how have you got so cruel in these days? Jealousy.

TWIN GLIMMER: I think so.

LIZ: Dr. Lopez? No, my dear. He will not kill me. If I die it will be at your hands before his. How long has that little Jewish girl, Maria Nuñez been here?

TWIN GLIMMER: Too long, she wants to go home. You see how she has aged since she's been in England too long.

LIZ: She must marry you.

TWIN GLIMMER: She doesn't want to.

LIZ: Do you want to marry a Jew?

TWIN GLIMMER: It could come in handy but I don't think it will benefit your grand-children in the long run. Although they say they are wonderful lovers. As you well know through doctor Lopez.

LIZ: Everyone wants to marry her. She's beautiful and dark and does sing like a lark.

TWIN GLIMMER: She wants to go back to Spain

LIZ: They'll kill her and her family. I can't let her go.

TWIN GLIMMER: She's not well liked by the...

LIZ: Who? The white cow-ladies in waiting that faun around her hoping to bring her down.

TWIN GLIMMER: She can't stay forever.

LIZ: Where can she go?

TWIN GLIMMER: To Antwerp.

LIZ: A step closer to that fool of a Spanish King. I told you I wanted him killed. Why is he still alive?

TWIN GLIMMER: Why are you still alive? We are trying.

LIZ: They are trying. Has that academic hack translated the latest Iberian diatribe against me?

TWIN GLIMMER: It is called "La Dragontea", trashing you and Sir Francis Drake. The Invincible Armada. They say Philip is planning another one.

LIZ: Bring it on motherfuckers. Who wrote it?

TWIN GLIMMER: Some sycophantic scribbling scribner to the Spanish King. Lope de Vega Carpio.

LIZ: Ridiculous name.

TWIN GLIMMER: They say he has written fifteen-hundred plays.

LIZ: Is he two-hundred years old?

TWIN GLIMMER: Hardly. He's forty.

LIZ: Have the Lord Chamberlain's Men perform it once it's translated. I would love to have the Jews perhaps read it to me in Spanish…which I understand very well but I want to see how good this writer sounds in his own language before your translators mash it up. Is it a play?

TWIN GLIMMER: It is an epic poem.

LIZ: Then you read it.

TWIN GLIMMER: Why do you continually make me read what I cannot understand?

LIZ: I would like to hear it now.

TWIN GLIMMER: I would not.

LIZ: The English Queen desires to hear "La Dragontea" read in Spanish. Read!

TWIN GLIMMER: You know how it pains my tongue to read so badly this twisted language.

LIZ: Read, bitch!

TWIN GLIMMER: (In halting, badly pronounced Spanish.)
"Canto las armas y el varon famoso
Que al atrevido ingles detuvo el paso
Aquel Nuevo argonauta prodigioso
Que espanto las estrellas del Ocaso
Canto el esfuerzo y brazo belicoso
De un espanol en tan dificil caso
Que en la fuia mayor de su discurso
Detuvo como remora su curso."
("La Dragontea", Lope de Vega Carpio)

LIZ: Detuvo como remora su curso!!!!
Faggotry! Popery! Epic poems and plays? Do you think I don't know what's going on?! Faggotry and propaganda for the crown and cross! Your pronunciation is getting better. Practice with Maria Nuñez! And what about the other pamphlet?

TWIN GLIMMER: It is a novelette, "The English Spanish Girl" in which you appear...

LIZ: Whatever, let's get back to the edict. I want you to familiarize yourself with the text of the edict in Latin as that is all we will be speaking in when the minister arrives. He speaks Polish. I do not. We both speak Latin and we will speak Latin. He can see that I have the blood of kings on my teeth in any language.

TWIN GLIMMER: How odd only to have learned Latin and not at least French or English.

LIZ: Donkey! Very few people in this world speak English and as we are in the minority let us conform discreetly and patiently till the day comes. Quickly, bring the text, dépêche-la mode!

END OF SCENE

7. African Invasion

LIZ: Speaking of Drake, where is that midnight rambler? Tell him to get the hell out of there and haul his ass back here. The Mediterranean is a desert swamp beyond my control and so I will not have it. Cannot have it. Drake can only do so much until we are up a step then maybe.

TWIN GLIMMER: He has no ass to haul.

LIZ: What do you mean?

TWIN GLIMMER: He's dead.

LIZ: Cannot be true.

TWIN GLIMMER: They are all dead

LIZ: How many?

TWIN GLIMMER: Two-thousand.

LIZ: How can they all be dead?

TWIN GLIMMER: The Spanish killed them all.

LIZ: Don't say that.

TWIN GLIMMER: We could say the Africans killed them all. We have no information on the Spanish being involved. The Africans killed them all.

LIZ: With what?

TWIN GLIMMER: Shall we say disease? Not one has returned in three years.

LIZ: Then say they are all in Ireland.

TWIN GLIMMER: Where they surely will be killed your ex-favorite's bungling. The Spanish ambassador seems to know.

LIZ: Have him poison himself! Why did I listen to those Levites? Are they trying to fuck us up?

TWIN GLIMMER: What would they get out of it?

LIZ: There must be something wrong, call in Lopez.

TWIN GLIMMER: He has nothing to do with this, he's been dead for months.

LIZ: Drake told me to send more and more and I did. And now they are all dead! I would have rather attacked Cádiz again.

TWIN GLIMMER: It was sacked so well in Drake's last sacking that there was nothing left in the sack. But this African spot would have given us a point to attack from again and again

LIZ: And again and again they are all dead. In France, in Holland in Ireland. Hanging with English heads up and down the highways and byways. Who has done this?

TWIN GLIMMER: He is called L'Étoile Dakar.

LIZ: That be French! What are the French doing down there?

TWIN GLIMMER: They tried to take the towns ten years ago.

LIZ: And you didn't tell me?

TWIN GLIMMER: They failed.

LIZ: And now we fail. Why didn't I know about this?

TWIN GLIMMER: Essex told you.

LIZ: When I was drunk so he could get me to sign that order so he could get a cut. I'll give him a cut. Dakar? What are we doing so far down on the map?! Even I know that. We were supposed to take over a small kingdom in North Africa—relatively simple or so you said, paleface! Who's idea was this!? Kill them, destroy the map and never mention a word under pain of mutilated death.

TWIN GLIMMER: Am I dreaming? How is this happening? Why is it happening? Why did I make it happen? Who am I? Who are you?

LIZ: How did they get so far down on the map, you knucklehead?

TWIN GLIMMER: They were blown off course by the same winds that blew off the Armada.

LIZ: So God has willed it. He has overruled me.

TWIN GLIMMER: God in the service of the fancy-pants sad sack in Rome.

LIZ: Blown off course? We do not get blown off course.

TWIN GLIMMER: We have and we are.

LIZ: You mean the whole announcement last year about the Algerian towns we took was fabricated? What did indeed happen? Out with it.

TWIN GLIMMER: They were blown off course and massacréed by L'Étoile Dakar. So we hear.

LIZ: And the Sir Douglas Quintet?

TWIN GLIMMER: Wiped out and the rest were made slaves. They will never be recovered or brought back. Enslaved in some pagan jungle to interbreed with the locals. I don't know who is more unlucky.

LIZ: Pandemonium. One word of Africa again and you will be sold as a slave.

TWIN GLIMMER: We were to be positioning ourselves directly across from Cádiz and thereby check them from movement and increase our southern stratagem.

LIZ: By what? By making deals? I don't make deals.

TWIN GLIMMER: We had set up the Jews to do it. They sold us out we think.

LIZ: Do you have to blame everything on them? That's what got the Spanish in trouble.

TWIN GLIMMER: Trouble? They have the biggest empire in the world and the best poets and painters and playwrights.

LIZ: Cervantes is overrated.

TWIN GLIMMER: And gold.

LIZ: They have gold.

TWIN GLIMMER: They are GOLDEN. They have a planet of gold and what do we have?

LIZ: We have me.

TWIN GLIMMER: They were blown off course.

LIZ: …and now my tranquility has been destroyed. Cancel the poetry reading tonight. Send the French minister and his Egyptian catamite home. 'Tis then when the hurdy-gurdy man comes singing songs of love.

TWIN GLIMMER: We were to meet up with their Sultan and buy his town.

LIZ: Buy it?

TWIN GLIMMER: With the help of the Jews.

LIZ: Jews buying a town for England?

TWIN GLIMMER: It was a small town.

LIZ: It couldn't have been that small if we were to garrison two thousand men there.

TWIN GLIMMER: They were to invade and conquer the town and make slaves of its inhabitants and take over the surrounding area with the help of the enemies of that said kingdom.

LIZ: Continue.

TWIN GLIMMER: And then they were blown off course in the middle of the…in the middle of the storm.

LIZ: Who attacks in the middle of a storm?

TWIN GLIMMER: It was a great idea to attack under cover of the storm.

LIZ: No it wasn't.

TWIN GLIMMER: But some were blown ashore and the rest blown to Senegal where the Étoile absorbed them. So we hear.

LIZ: Absorbed.

TWIN GLIMMER: Three years later. They are beyond the reach of heaven.

LIZ: It's their own fault for being so greedy.

TWIN GLIMMER: They were doing for you. We dance to your drum.

LIZ: There is nothing down there but jungle and bungle. Slaves and gold and slaves and gold. Is that our future?

TWIN GLIMMER: Why not?

LIZ: Gold is poison made for the Spanish soul.

TWIN GLIMMER: Why do you deny that you sent us there?

LIZ: Where is that pre-nuptial agreement? I never did such a thing. I said investigate the African option.

TWIN GLIMMER: With an army of fifteen-hundred?

LIZ: I thought you said it was two-thousand?

TWIN GLIMMER: Roughly.

LIZ: How many English souls roughly are dead in Africa now because of…

TWIN GLIMMER: …your…

LIZ: …stupidity. Cousin Mary isn't involved in this thesis is she?

TWIN GLIMMER: Both Marys are dead.

LIZ: Well, I mean her ghost so to speak, her minions, her
hopefuls, well wishers and ambulance chasers.

TWIN GLIMMER: The ones you didn't kill, Scottish James did. Most of the remainders were sent on another African expedition as you requested.

LIZ: Good. What play did you say they are putting on tonight?

TWIN GLIMMER: Johnson and Nash. "Isle of Dogs."

LIZ: Recite.

TWIN GLIMMER:
"Weren't you at the Coke convention back in
fifteen-sixty-five?
You're the mis-bred, grey executive I've seen heavily
advertised.
You're the great, gray man whose daughter licks policemen's
buttons clean.
You're the man who squats behind the man who works the
soft machine.
Come now, gentleman, your love is all I crave.
You'll still be in the circus when I'm laughing, laughing in my
grave.
When the old men do the fighting and the young men all
look on.
And the young girls eat their mother's meat from tubes of
plasticon.
Be wary of these, my gentle friends of all the skins you
breed.
They have a tasty habit—they eat the hands that bleed.
So remember who you say you are and keep your noses
clean.
Boys will be boys and play with toys so be strong with your
beast.
Oh, Lizzie dear, doncha think it's queer? So, stop me if you
please.
The twin's are dead, my lady said, "You gentlemen, why you
all, you ALL work for me."

(From "Memo from Turner", altered.)

END OF SCENE

8. A Twin Glimmer Returns from Japan

LIZ: Well, it took you long enough to get back! Where have you been!

TWIN GLIMMER: You know very well where I was.

LIZ: Cipangu?

TWIN GLIMMER: Yes, but they imprisoned me and beheaded my crew.

LIZ: What did the Emperor say?

TWIN GLIMMER: He is not visible to the public and he's controlled by the military I think.

LIZ: You think! What about the statues? Did you bring back the idols?

TWIN GLIMMER: They were destroyed in the typhoon. I only have this one small Buddha.

LIZ: Buddha? Is that their god? Did you bring any scriptures?

TWIN GLIMMER: Didn't the Jew give you the ones he smuggled in?

LIZ: Bernstein, the dentist? Yes, but he can't even read them. I got that Jesuit out of prison and he is translating under threat of circumcision. But how do we know he's correctly translating these scriptures?

TWIN GLIMMER: We have to cross check it with that Dutch trader I've sequestered.

LIZ: He is only to translate in your presence. Have you read any of it?

TWIN GLIMMER: It's vaguely familiar.

LIZ: Are you lying to me?! Have the Jew check it over. Is it at all like Greek?

TWIN GLIMMER: It's all scribbles!

LIZ: You are so thin! What have you been eating?

(TWIN GLIMMER takes a few grains of rice out of his pocket and drops them in her lap.)

LIZ: What is it?

TWIN GLIMMER: This is what they eat over there.

LIZ: In prison?

TWIN GLIMMER: Everyone eats it.

LIZ: Then they are all in prison.

TWIN GLIMMER: That is the tenet of the religion.

LIZ: Is it some form of papism?

TWIN GLIMMER: Not at all, they are all happy to be degraded.

LIZ: Then not like the Catholics who are not happy UNLESS they are degrading someone.

TWIN GLIMMER: They hate the Pope. And have been slaughtering Jesuits.

LIZ: Good. How did you get out?

TWIN GLIMMER: The Dutch.

LIZ: Have the Jews been there already too?

TWIN GLIMMER: There are some hidden among the Portuguese.

LIZ: Have the Cipangans read the Jewish bible?

TWIN GLIMMER: One man is translating it and he is the only one who really can know all this. I couldn't bring him with me. The Emperor owns him. Our money is no good there. They have so much silver that it is worth nothing to them.

LIZ: Slavery?

TWIN GLIMMER: They don't need slavery, they have this religion I told you. I had been studying in their church with their monks who are also very thin. The entire country is thin. They have no cows.

LIZ: Can you teach me anything? In secret of course.

TWIN GLIMMER: I can only repeat. I hardly know what I'm saying. But it is so powerful that it doesn't matter. You shouldn't do this. They'll kill you.

LIZ: They'll kill you first. I am the Queen, it is my pleasure. We will call it music lessons. I am not a pagan but between the bishops and the prince of Rome I cannot bear the strife and doubt, there must be another way. Let's begin. I haven't done very well in the years of your absence.

TWIN GLIMMER: I've done much better than you because I've learned to forget.

LIZ: Because you are probably stoned out of your mind. And so the one thing you did remember was how to forget.

TWIN GLIMMER: The music lesson?

LIZ: And I never listen to music. It triggers the worst form of sentiment. Not good for this vocation. And so now you've become some kind of weird amoral Buddha worshiper?

TWIN GLIMMER: It's not so bad. The incense can be sickening, the silence can be deafening. But I can still go to mass without offending the statues in the cathedral. I live in clear silence.

LIZ: Nothing is clear to me. What happened to you over there?

TWIN GLIMMER: Nothing and I'm glad about it. It's called deep smiling.

LIZ: What's that?

TWIN GLIMMER: Just smile deeply and meaninglessly.

LIZ: And keep going on.

TWIN GLIMMER: You always did that so well. I envied you.

LIZ: Yes, but now I can't stop. If I stop I die. There is nowhere else to go in my mind.

TWIN GLIMMER: Breathe in deep.

LIZ: I can't, there's nowhere for the air to go.

TWIN GLIMMER: Of course there is. It goes to your brain and clears it out.

LIZ: Like sotweed.

TWIN GLIMMER: Not really, but similarly. Breathe the air in to your brain.

LIZ: What brain? I will have no brain left after I kill my cousin.

TWIN GLIMMER: Didn't hear that. The thinking. Love it or leave it.

LIZ: I don't love it so I will leave it.

TWIN GLIMMER: I'm afraid they won't let you. I won't let you.

LIZ: But you left it.

TWIN GLIMMER: I left it but I never left it because I didn't love it.

LIZ: You loved thinking.

TWIN GLIMMER: It completed me, made me into something I thought I couldn't be. And so I loved it and still love it even though I have been disassociated by mutual agreement since Cipangu. My personal spiritual situation didn't allow me to continue. At least not in that way so I continue in this way.

LIZ: What way?

TWIN GLIMMER: Doing this with the incense and occasional documents and other slightly...

LIZ: ...tainted...

TWIN GLIMMER: ...corrupt things.

LIZ: Like...

TWIN GLIMMER: ...it's all legal there. Or barely or looked over and every one does it.

Or I have will have to leave the country and go abroad for my business sometimes.

LIZ: Importing statues.

TWIN GLIMMER: Marginal, and some sort of child prostitutes. In Cipangu, no one gets upset about it—it's fairly normal practice. I was living in a paradise where everything is legal.

LIZ: And everything is possible.

TWIN GLIMMER: Slaughtering Jesuits was legal, even.

LIZ: Even?

TWIN GLIMMER: Even so, you don't have to go along with it.

LIZ: What are you?

TWIN GLIMMER: A Buddhist, I told you.

LIZ: Pagan?

TWIN GLIMMER: Kind of.

LIZ: Peace of mind?

TWIN GLIMMER: I've made peace with the life style—you have to accept the others to make harmony just like we learned from Jesus. And now I'm a helper—enlightened really.

LIZ: Purgatory?

TWIN GLIMMER: Not really, Nirvana. It's another world and I'm happy here mediating. And doing what I have to—to keep meditating and eating properly.

LIZ: Properly stoned

TWIN GLIMMER: Yes, it is like being stoned. I always thought you were weird.

LIZ: I am weird.

TWIN GLIMMER: But harmony is what we are all after— forgiveness. Just leave me alone, I'm trying to help you.

LIZ: Help me what?

TWIN GLIMMER: I told you—trying to help you get over killing that woman.

LIZ: I haven't killed her yet.

TWIN GLIMMER: That's what I mean. You've got to get over it and get it done, do it. If you can do it in your mind—visualize it— then you can do it. That's what I do now, practice mediation, deep smiling. Indivisualization. Now lets try. Sing.

LIZ: Oh Jesus, I just can't get into this.

TWIN GLIMMER: You must.

LIZ: I don't even know what I'm saying.

TWIN GLIMMER: Just repeat with me, it doesn't matter what we're saying.

LIZ: What if we are saying some evil curse? I'm just supposed to repeat it?

TWIN GLIMMER: Yes.

LIZ: Repeat without knowing? Without believing?

TWIN GLIMMER: Then it works perfectly. Try. I know what I'm doing. On Tuesdays I work at a monastery for grieving children and teenagers of the Catholic beheaded.

LIZ: Sounds awful.

TWIN GLIMMER: You can't help them. But they don't know that.

LIZ: What are you?

TWIN GLIMMER: They must be helped.

LIZ: It appears very civilized.

TWIN GLIMMER: Sing.

(BOTH sing "oooo.")

TWIN GLIMMER: …but just because it appears civilized it doesn't mean that it is. It is barbaric, orderly, sensible, polite. I'm very high. It disguises perfectly the barbarity. Just because you take two baths a day it doesn't mean you're clean.

LIZ: What do you mean—the next life?

TWIN GLIMMER: The other one.

LIZ: And another one after that?

TWIN GLIMMER: And many, oh many.

LIZ: But what does that mean though?

TWIN GLIMMER: Human garbage. I mean they are alive but they are human but it doesn't even matter if they are alive—or kicking. Barely human. I mean they are alive but it doesn't mean they're living. Sing.

LIZ: I don't know, maybe if I looked at that statue it would help.

TWIN GLIMMER: It won't help. I would keep it hidden if I were you.

END OF SCENE

9. Invasion pt. 2

LIZ: What is he, some kind of a king or warlord?

TWIN GLIMMER: They say Étoile is a feeling, not a person.

LIZ: Impossible, a nation cannot be ruled by a feeling. That is incorrect.

TWIN GLIMMER: …although he is rumoured to be a woman.

LIZ: What is going on down there? What have they done to my navy?

TWIN GLIMMER: There are reports that Étoile sold some of our ships to the Spanish navy and they are now being navigated by swarth-bearded gypsies from Granada.

LIZ: Horrors. A woman has done this to me? My scourge in this life seems to be women more than men. Men fall so easily underfoot.

TWIN GLIMMER: Retaliate?

LIZ: Are you kidding me? You dimwitted monkey gone to heaven. Dost thou think I can send a wave of mutilation across the sea to some god-forsaken place. For what? To turn them all into pixies?! Let us stay in our own reality and mentality at least for this century and not wade out again into unknown waters with armies and navies of ignorant buccaneers and mercenaries.

TWIN GLIMMER: That bitch! Does she know that the King she has offended is a woman too?

LIZ: She could give a shit apparently.

TWIN GLIMMER: Anyone of our kind is equally as useless to her, man or woman.

LIZ: She's smarter than I am then. We are all as white as they are black. Cover it up. Curtail anyone that knows about this. This could bring me down. Have a mass said. Where is that scroll with those crazy Cipangu prayers on it? Give it to me.

TWIN GLIMMER: I burnt it. It was liable to be found by one of your spayed and spinstered ladies-in-waiting...

LIZ: A spinster they call me.

TWIN GLIMMER: ...and called witchcraft.

LIZ: Skip it then. I had it translated into Latin and memorized it. I was just testing you.

TWIN GLIMMER: Did I pass or fail?

LIZ: Both. We've burned a few heretics in our time for less. This would have been beyond the beyond if it had been found. What about the prayer beads and the statue?

TWIN GLIMMER: The statue has been painted over as a monkey. The beads are sown into your dress with pearls. You will have to pray with them by stroking your dress.

LIZ: That will be your job, you funky lemonhead. I won't have to kill you after all.

10. The Burial of Count Orgaz

(LIZ and TWIN GLIMMER stand in front of large projection covering the entire wall behind them. It is "The Burial of Count Orgaz" by El Greco.)

LIZ: What is this thing?!

TWIN GLIMMER: It is a gift from Drake. He's brought it back from his latest Spanish raid.

LIZ: On its own ship? Reveal it! What is it?! Explain the
monstrous papist iconography.

TWIN GLIMMER: It's glorious!

LIZ: I am the only glorious thing in this state.

TWIN GLIMMER: No one else will do.

LIZ: They paint so well. But all of this superstitious symbolism. Explain it. I will have nightmares. But what is happening here? Is this a cruel joke?!

TWIN GLIMMER: It is called "The Burial of Count Orgaz".

LIZ: He brings me a picture of a burial?! Who is Count Orgaz? I have never heard of him. Call for Lopez and see if he or any of his Jew friends know this man. Is it hopefully somehow an Iberian nobleman we have killed? Is it a revenge painting? Continue...

TWIN GLIMMER: Saints Augustine and Stephen, in golden and red vestments, bend reverently over the body of the count, who is clad in magnificent armor that reflects the yellows and reds of the other figures. The young boy at the left is the painter's son, Jorge Manuel. On a handkerchief in his pocket is inscribed the artist's signature and the date 1578, the year of the boy's birth. The men who attend the funeral are unmistakably prominent members of Toledan society. The painting has a chromatic harmony that is incredibly rich, expressive and radiant. On the black mourning garments of the nobles are projected the gold-embroidered vestments, thus creating an intense ceremonial character. In the heavenly space there is a predominance of transparent harmonies of iridescence and ivoried greys, which harmonize with the gilded ochres, while...

LIZ: OK, OK! I get the picture, now beat it!

TWIN GLIMMER: I suppose he thinks he's going to heaven? Where shall we put it?

LIZ: The archbishop won't like it.

TWIN GLIMMER: Because there are no naked women… or men.

LIZ: The English cannot paint the naked body—they never get to see it unclothed in its entirety. A pity. This is fifty times better than any English painter. Who painted it? Bring him to the court.

TWIN GLIMMER: Domeniko Theotokopoulos.

LIZ: A Greek, trapped in Spain painting for the kings of the world! Get it out of here. Must I have to look at this thing to make me realize our enemy's power? Tell Drake I am most displeased and to personally come and get this trash out of my household. No, I do not like it.

TWIN GLIMMER: You just loved it

LIZ: I have just unloved it. Burn it.

TWIN GLIMMER: We cannot burn a religious painting

LIZ: It is a heretical instrument of Catholic ideology. We will burn "The Burial of Count

Orgaz. Cremate it and send it to the hell it represents.

TWIN GLIMMER: But our artists can study it and improve their skills.

LIZ: Learn to paint in the manner of this obvious and surly insult to the very being of our island? The gold, the arrogant faces, why should we study them? Why would we want to paint like that? I find it over realistic. And frightening. Ungodlike.

TWIN GLIMMER: God never meant images to look so real. It is an insult to his creation. An affront. As if what he has made is not good enough.

LIZ: And no more portraits!

TWIN GLIMMER: You just don't want the portraits to reveal your real face. You don't want to sit still for long enough to notice that time has surprised you. You bear the look of it on your face. The permanent smack of fear, the shock of the old. The raised eyebrows and relentless sag of living skin. Liz, the here-and-now has become the then-and-there.

LIZ: Get out of my sight, you ugly hunchbacked catamite.

TWIN GLIMMER: I can only say the truth.

LIZ: Liar.

TWIN GLIMMER: Truth.

LIZ: Liar!

TWIN GLIMMER: How many times have we had to rewrite the truth as a lie? Here in these very chambers? You know it as well as I do.

LIZ: We rewrite it every day, rewind the time and wind it out in a different color for the benefit of the English island planet...

TWIN GLIMMER: ...and the hardworking uneducated and malnourished mental dwarfs who keep it floating.

LIZ: Why are we floating? For why, wherefore do we float? For a reason? For God? Or our new religion? For Luther? For Mary for Harry? Four million souls floating on the bloody velvet eyelid of Europa. What is this for? What do we represent? Who are we? We are not what these others are but wherefore, what are we then? We refuse to relent and be what they are. Why? Look! A tiny infant bee has tittered its last breath on the painting. Born too late in the season.

TWIN GLIMMER: Perhaps we were born too late in the season of the world. We are overtaken in a single glance by the firstborn race depicted in that painting. Swarthy and dark as they are.

LIZ: We are overtaken, subdued, just look at it! It's laughing at us and it's not even real but it is so real that we can hear the laughter. Who is that child in the front laughing at us?

TWIN GLIMMER: They say it is the young prince of Spain.

LIZ: You just said it was the child of the painter. Why does everyone keep lying to me?

TWIN GLIMMER: I didn't want to bring up the idea of the male heir to their throne.

LIZ: That again?!

TWIN GLIMMER: How can we compete against them but with greedy pirates like Drake and slithering ladies in waiting and jerks up and down the muddy highways and byways of our creation and habitation. What is the use of an English man learning Latin anyway? Where will it ever get us? Who of us will ever get to Rome? If it really exists.

LIZ: Must we continue to be the blancmange of Europe? Cuddling up here on our rocky raft. I have never even met cousin Mary who is trying to kill me. Our whole lives we are so uncivilized that we cannot even meet for fear. The fear. The fear of our minions killing each other or us or both. So as not to kill ourselves or each other we have kept away from each other. We are so uncivilized that whole decades are but plots unfolding and exploding and corroding and corrupting us as we watch them enacted for entertainment in plays that only dare to weakly whisper the truth. Our imaginations are weak as poetry.

TWIN GLIMMER: You've been prudent, in forty years you have only beheaded five people.

LIZ: …Is that including doctor Lopez?…They wanted him dead, what could I do?! On certain days of the year I cannot be King— that is the deal. He wasn't trying to poison me. In the tortures they thought he'd reveal the whereabouts of you. He never knew. He finally had to say something, anything. They had to kill anyone, someone. They were never comfortable with a Jew in the house.

TWIN GLIMMER: Them Anglo-Saxon ghostface killers do weave a bloody web on your behalf.

LIZ: …and then blame it on the terrific anger of the she-Pope I am become. Drawn and quartered, my dear doctor Lopez! He escapes the Spanish torturers only to be chopped and fried by the English ones. Poor sad Jew, doomed as Jesus the day he was born. Not god nor poetry could save him. I have never met nor will never meet my cousin James of Scotland who they say is also trying to kill me. He can have this throne if we can kill all the people that stand in his path. A united island finally—is that all we are living for?—is that meaningful? Should the island be united? I will never meet him for fear that we will in the seconds before and after find good reasons to obliterate each other. So we politely rule by letters which are read by I don't know how many people in between under pain of death. So we write them in code which they decipher to their own whims as they did with the Lopez letters. Our most trusted friends are not trustable. I do not trust you and you must never trust me. So I must live in a state of distrust and mistrust. I would one day kiss your face and the next day rip it off. Didn't I tell you to burn that painting! One of the figures has the face of Lopez, remove it!

TWIN GLIMMER: Where shall I burn it?

LIZ: You will burn it in my serene presence and the all too mortal presence of the entire court. Instead of burning heretics let it be said that Liz burns paintings of heretics. Heretics burnt by proxy, cheaper and less bloody.

TWIN GLIMMER: But it will be a frightful sight.

LIZ: Out in the courtyard, let us set up as for a masque. I shall ignite the fire myself.

TWIN GLIMMER: Do you think it is advisable that the Queen be seen burning a painting?

LIZ: It is a lesson the court must learn and I will be the teacher.

TWIN GLIMMER: The bishops may object to the figures of clergy in the painting being burned.

LIZ: For that very reason we will do it. They'll think it's a message from Lopez.

TWIN GLIMMER: And then shall we have music?

LIZ: Don't they do that in Spain when they burn Jews and heretics?

TWIN GLIMMER: So Dr. Lopez once told us.

LIZ: Then we will burn a Spanish painting to English music. Invite all the known and suspected spies so they may report it back to that nitwit Emperor Felipe. You have sent Dr.

Lopez's remains to the Sultan in Jerusalem for burial as I requested?

TWIN GLIMMER: Yes. Would you like to choose the music?

LIZ: No, I think Mr. Devereux, my doomed favorite will choose one of his favorite musical masterpieces.

(They watch as the painting slowly burns to Nirvana's "Smells Like Teen Spirit" sung by Scala.)

END OF SCENE

11. Invasion pt. 3

LIZ: Is they Turks?

TWIN GLIMMER: Something like that, but not really.

LIZ: Mohammedans?

TWIN GLIMMER: Not sure but they are very black, the blackest of all.

LIZ: Woe betide them, ghostface. I thought we had sent a delegation down there, dustface.

TWIN GLIMMER: We did, but to the country next door.

LIZ: Can't they help us?

TWIN GLIMMER: They are cousins.

LIZ: So what?!

TWIN GLIMMER: Their code of honor is more primitive than ours and so does not permit anything that might be construed as betrayal.

LIZ: Leave them to their own devices but I do not want them sailing up here on one of our own ships to cut us to shreds in the middle of the night for their illegal pagan sacrifices. I know they suffer immeasurably like dogs and artists but let them stay out of our orbit. If the world is flat let them stay in their corner. Keep an eye out or I will put your eye out. My Africa-phobia is raging tonight. I shall not sleep.

END OF SCENE

12. Providence

LIZ: Shall we read alternate lines?

TWIN GLIMMER: Seneca?

LIZ: On Providence.

TWIN GLIMMER:

"Let every season, every place, teach you how easy it is to
renounce Nature and fling her gift back in her face."

LIZ:
"In the very presence of the altars and the solemn rites of
sacrifice, while you pray for life, learn well concerning death."

TWIN GLIMMER:
"The fatted bodies of bulls fall from a paltry wound, and
creatures of mighty strength are felled by one stroke of a man's hand; a thin blade severs the joints of the neck and when the connection between head and neck is so cut the whole great mass collapses."

LIZ:
"The soul is not deeply buried and need not even be rooted out with steel. There is no need to probe for the vitals with a penetrating wound, for death lies near the surface."

TWIN GLIMMER:
"I have appointed no specific spot for the lethal blow, where ever you choose, you are vulnerable."

LIZ:

"Even that which we call dying, the moment when the breath forsakes the body, is so brief that its fleetness is imperceptible."

TWIN GLIMMER:
"Whether the throat is strangled by a knot, or water stops the breathing, or the hard ground crushes in the skull of one falling headlong to its surface, or flame inhaled cuts off the course of respiration, be it what it may, the end is swift."

LIZ:
"Do you not blush for shame. You dread so long what comes so quickly!"

("On Providence", Seneca)

This I quoted to Dr. Lopez but he continued to live in philosophical torment til the very end.

TWIN GLIMMER: Can we continue with the diary?

LIZ: Look at the sky. From underneath this universe of twins glimmering we will work our way backward.

TWIN GLIMMER: We see it again in our memory but we know it is not presently happening and so we are afraid at our inability to decipher what is in front of us until reassured by the narrating voice of reason. Which is our own.

LIZ: Don't repeat this idea. It has a distant mental influence.

TWIN GLIMMER: It has surfaced in Rome.

LIZ: The church in Rome is nothing but a club of lost philosophers in perpetual revolt.

TWIN GLIMMER: They have become each other's torment even long before they arrive as turds in hell.

LIZ: I'm not worried if there is life after death but if there is death after death. Again and again, that's what worries me. Why did you bring me those Cipangan scribblings?

TWIN GLIMMER: God speaks through me.

LIZ: And I am left to speak through God. That is frightening. That is the difference between us.

LIZ: Let's stop for now. I'll be coming into the foreground as needed by the others. I don't need them but I need them as much to summon me for that is my reason for being and if they don't summon me I will not continue to exist.

TWIN GLIMMER: Poor Doctor Lopez, his face turned to bacon. Letters to James? The diary?

LIZ: So am I compelled?

TWIN GLIMMER: If you don't, someone else will.

LIZ: But you told me to keep that in.

TWIN GLIMMER: No, no, take it out.

LIZ: What will we put in its place?

TWIN GLIMMER: I'll think of something.

LIZ: You took out the whole African adventure.

TWIN GLIMMER: We'll put it back in.

LIZ: It's a charming detail that no one knows about. But put in that last letter to Mary

TWIN GLIMMER: You asked me to take it out again yesterday.

LIZ: No, it must go back in. I have to save my reputation.

TWIN GLIMMER: It's a forgery.

LIZ: It is true in my mind and so it will be true on paper.

TWIN GLIMMER: I did burn it. It took me three days in that little fireplace. But I have consigned it to my memory. If it was all lies I would have not burned it. But because it was the truth we had to burn it. I could have burned certain pages but the truth and the lies were so will mixed that it actually became a perfect description of a reality. In that sense it was truthful.

LIZ: Sometimes it's better to burn the truth or the truth will end up burning you. It would have been traced back to my authorship which is… a partial lie. Of course you are not really hearing this. Only the twin self of my mind is hearing this and trying to remember against all odds. You are an invented audience of one. I am alone in the white room of my mind.

TWIN GLIMMER: You mean I'm not even real?

LIZ: Inside this room you are. Outside it you are not. I'm so sorry to tell you.

TWIN GLIMMER: So I must never leave.

LIZ: It would be like a beheading. A final separation of glimmering thought and speech.

TWIN GLIMMER: I do know that I wasn't the only glimmer in the crown. One night as a small child I awakened and found my brother trembling violently and asking if he could speak to me. He walked to the window and gazed into the darkness and explained that he had beenstudying the concept of infinity with our tutor. I never saw him again except as a spirit and no one ever mentioned him again. They said he'd become one of the four thousand holes in Blackburn, Lancashire. He's still suffering, I know it. I thought he had run away.

LIZ: Or died. Never mention that again,

TWIN GLIMMER: (Shouting.) I do know that I wasn't the only glimmer in the crown. One night as a small child I awakened and found my brother trembling violently and asking if he could speak to me. He walked to the window and gazed into the darkness and explained that he had been studying the concept of infinity with our tutor. I never saw him again except as a spirit and no one ever mentioned him again. They said he'd become one of the four thousand holes in Blackburn, Lancashire. He's still suffering, I know it. I thought he had run away!

LIZ: Or died. Never mention that again. You must have been dreaming. You have no brother. Sleep on your left side. That side of the mind has less of a memory for these things Now we are going to move on to the question of Maria Nuñez…

END OF SCENE

13. Confidante

TWIN GLIMMER: As you can see, I am not her minister and confidante Cecil. I am closer. Cecil is only the ink. Very grand. The writer writes in ink but never touches it. I have been touched. Day after day, I am thoughtfully and thoughtlessly put down and picked up and picked up and put down again and again to make the words come out. I hold the withering hand and lovingly guide the words along the page. Sometimes I lay on the table and watch what I have written burn on the hearth. The only other witnesses being the squinting crickets who warm themselves by its light. But that's only my point of view. I wonder what they think they are seeing. I wonder if they see me at all. So the writing turns from one thing into another into another thing and then finally into another thing in a place.

END OF SCENE

14. The Spanish English Girl

TWIN GLIMMER: When the theaters came to the palace I and my brother—even after he became a ghost, would be released to perform inside the plays presented. But we always had to return by sunrise. I cut now immediately to the 1599 story by Cervantes called "The Spanish English Girl"—in which Elizabeth herself is a character. She had it smuggled into court along with many other hideous pamphlets against her printed all over Europe at the time. Although, this one was quite lovely. It reads: "When they arrived at the palace, and entered the vast hall in which her majesty was seated, Isabella's escort halted at the lower end, and she herself advanced alone in all her inconceivable beauty, producing an effect like that of a brilliant meteor shooting through the sky on a calm clear night, or of a sunbeam darting at the first dawn of day through a mountain gorge. A comet she seemed, portending a fiery doom to the hearts of many in that presence hall."
("The Spanish-English Girl", Cervantes)

END OF SCENE

15. High Reality

TWIN GLIMMER: The diary now shifts into high reality and then to the low reality of chapters expurgated. Yes, it's true I did carry on for years with Maria Nuñez without Liz's knowledge or approval. When the time was coming, I mean the time near her passing when she stood for days in silence as it has been recorded-it wasn't all silence. I stayed on for a day or so. My twin's ghostface allowed him to safely stay behind as well. The three of us made the final corrections. Scottish James would remove me. There was a natural inner brutality, a silent and controlled nature he shared with Liz… It was left in some people when they were changed from animal to human in the womb. Somehow left behind in them in a tiny corner, a little piece of heartlessness. The bitter wind of her globe-stricken stare peering from an empty sphere forced me to withdraw as into a cloud.

LIZ: Twin Glimmer, is you there?

TWIN GLIMMER: It is not recorded in the diary that I did go on to marry the beautiful Maria Nuñez several months after my own death. Liz had prearranged the painstakingly meticulous forgery of my own beheading by James. After my beheading we left England forever. In deference to the Queen, I will let her have the last words…which I dutifully transcribed from behind a veil in her chambers. And then we will withdraw into the background. From a younger age my nose could sense like an animal when her lovers came and went. Even I remained in the background of these exciting events. It was a pity to see her lover Essex ascend into the cloud. Impedio dolore animi ne de huius miseria plura dicam. "I am prevented by my grief of mind from saying more about this man's unhappiness."

END OF SCENE

15. Essex

LIZ: You and I have decided that we will think through this cloud of unknowing. How we will get from here to there. We will not step over each other but through each other as through a cloud. It is not about avoiding pain—it is about accepting pain. So we will not avoid. We would sit and read the manuscript entitled "The Cloud of Unknowing" through in Latin—over and over. And so how to do it. You and I would read it together and so we will again.

TWIN GLIMMER: "Our intense need to understand will always be a powerful stumbling block to our attempts to reach God in simple love….and must always be overcome. For if you do not overcome this need to understand, it will undermine your quest. It will replace the darkness which you have pierced to reach God
with clear images of something which, however good, however beautiful, however Godlike, is not God."

("The Cloud of Unknowing")

LIZ: And so, you, however Godlike, are not God. And so, we, however Godlike, are not God. And so, our intense need to understand must be overcome finally and once again. Once we are gone from each other we must overcome that intense need to understand again. That I can…and I would, turn you into a place of nothingness. In doing so, I turn myself into a place of nothingness. But it won't be the same place. How do you turn a person into a place? Into space? The shard of space where he met his end. Against a modest pile of paint. A person into a place, a being into a thing, a thing into a space, a thing into a thought into a space into a place. A thought into a space, a person into a thought, bold and bloody, dark and bright, something into nothing into something again into nothing again.

TWIN GLIMMER: A thought into a space, a person into a thought, something into nothing into something again into nothing again. Don't you remember me anymore?!

LIZ: There is a polite restraint, a staying away from, a keeping distance from others misfortunes. Just don't say anything, don'tget upset or outraged at the injustice of it. Don't feel sorry. Or feel sorry, but not too sorry. Indicate that it must somehow be their own fault and so do not to get involved with someone who has brought this on themselves.

Although they may not deserve it. As they enter a place of nothingness.

END OF PLAY

STAGE NOTES: LIZ ONE

(Her Secret Diaries in the Land of 1000 Dances)

<u>Interview with Tom Murrin</u>

For almost 30 years, writer/director John Jesurun has been surprising and delighting audiences with his unique eye, ear and mind for a sophisticated, mysterious and repeatedly brilliant kind of theater. All his shows are different, and he has often been years ahead, utilizing the media technology other directors now routinely incorporate into their pieces. This past spring he staged a show called <u>Firefall</u> at Dance Theater Workshop, with a dozen young actors with laptops and a huge backdrop screen that had a constant video feed from the Internet, which the onstage actors were able to interact with, even to the point of purchasing items from eBay while the show was going on. With <u>Liz One (Her Secret Diaries in the Land of 1000 Dances)</u>, John focuses on Queen Elizabeth I of England, who is played by Black-Eyed Susan, an original member of Charles Ludlam's Ridiculous Theatrical Company. Ben Forster co-stars. I spoke with John, an old friend.

Hi John. How did a show about Queen Elizabeth come to you?

I've wanted to do it for a long time. I've been writing bits and pieces over the years. It's Black-Eyed Susan as Queen Elizabeth the 1st and her secret diaries (an unwritten history that I've made up) which no one has heard before. Ben Forster plays a variety of people, but mostly he is her son that nobody knows about, a son that she's hidden away in the palace.

Yes, the Virgin Queen is not exactly known for having a son.

Well, she and he decide to re-write her history. She's writing her diary from the end of her life, and going backwards. It goes all over her life, going over some of the familiar issues that we know about, and some other things as well. For example, that she never had any children and was a virgin to the end of her life. That never happened, according to the play. That's one of the main ideas that explains why Ben is there.

So Ben is her co-biographer of sorts?

He is re-writing her life with her, and he sometime argues with her too, like about why he is not going to inherit the throne after her. There is a back and forth relationship between

Ben and Susan. Parts of it we wouldn't have known, and some things could have happened. Like she becomes really interested in Buddhism. There's a scene when someone comes back from Japan and tries to teach her how to meditate, and she gets interested in this. It's funny and very serious too.

So this is a Queen Elizabeth we haven't seen before.

There's religion and her fight with the pope, and her fight with Spain. They have become Protestants in England by then. There's a lot of interesting things which might have happened because she was very educated. I have her smuggling in books and pamphlets so she can see what is being said about her in other countries at the time. The other countries were Catholic and they wrote horrible things abut her. She was called "She-Wolf." It's a very behind the scene, internal look, what you see behind the face of power. You hear conversations most people would never hear, her private image, hiding her son away, having people killed.

How about video?

I'm trying to keep it fairly simple, keeping the focus on Susan, and Ben too. The video will be used in a portraiture way, to get close-ups on their faces. Not a huge Internet thing, but a focus on the actors, really; a look at two actors within the story, in an intimate way. And also, it gives Susan a chance to be in the spotlight. She's great in this part.

DÍAS Y FLORES

A play by Oliver Mayer

About the Playwright

OLIVER MAYER is the author of over 20 plays, including most recently THE WIGGLE ROOM and WALLOWA. Other plays include: DIAS Y FLORES, LAWS OF SYMPATHY, CONJUNTO, YOUNG VALIANT and BLADE TO THE HEAT. He recently debuted FILO AL FUEGO (the Spanish version of BLADE TO THE HEAT) in Miami. His literary archive is available through the Stanford University Libraries. He won an Alfred P. Sloan Initiative Science and Technology award for DARK MATTERS, an original play about particle physics. "The Hurt Business: a Critical Portfolio of the Early Works of Oliver Mayer, Plus," is published by Hyperbole Books; "Oliver Mayer: Collected Plays" is published by NoPassport Press. He wrote the libretto for the opera AMERICA TROPICAL, composed by David Conte, published by E.C. Schirmer and Sons. An associate professor at the USC School of Theatre, Oliver is Resident Faculty Master at Parkside International Residential College. He is the winner of a USC Zumberge Individual Award, and a USC Mellon Mentoring Award for Excellence in Faculty Mentoring of Undergraduates. His life's goal is to forge new ground as an American playwright, not simply for myself but for new generations of new American writers searching to find their reflection onstage.

For all performance rights to Mr. Mayer's work contact David Baird ay Kinetic Management at dbaird@kinetic.ws

A Note from playwright Oliver Mayer:

Plays are bundles. We playwrights bundle thoughts and feelings—words, music, actions, dreams—and present the bundle to each night's audience (a bundle of its own).

This bundle is old, new, borrowed and blue: But mostly new. I bundled observations on the changing ethnic nature of New York City with the blood consciousness of a man in love, not knowing where that love might lead. When the play came to me, I was reading The Arabian Nights – a book that legend says you should never finish on pain of death. So this bundle is by design open-ended, not quite finished.

The garden is real—you can visit it the next time you're on 13th Street between Avenues A and B, on Manhattan's Lower East Side. The paqueteria is on one level akin to Fed Ex and DHL; on another it is a storehouse of dreams.

Thanks to Silvio Rodriguez for the songs in the play. One day we dream of presenting the play in Cuba in honor of him and his monument of work.

Love and solidarity to Luis Alfaro, and to Armando Molina: Each in our way, we have been finding voices for ourselves and our city for the better part of twenty years, and it's a beautiful thing to come together with this play. Last but never least, this is for mi mas roja flama.

Días y Flores

During the world premiere performance, directed by Luis Alfaro at Company of Angels (CoA), Los Angeles, CA, on January 16, 2009, the cast of characters appeared as follows:

CAST OF CHARACTERS

Sherezad	Marlene Forte
Farruco	Melvin Rodriguez
Pantys	Justin Huen
Silvio	Miguel Angel Caballero

During a subsequent production for the Avante International Hispanic Theatre Festival at the Prometeo Theatre in Miami, FL, on July 24, 2009, produced by Mario Ernesto Sanchez and Joann Yarrow, the cast of characters appeared as follows:

CAST OF CHARACTERS

Sherezad	Marlene Forte
Farruco	Oliver Mayer
Pantys	Xavi Moreno
Silvio	Miguel Angel Caballero

PLACE: 13th Street between Avenues A & B, The Lower East Side, NYC (Loisaida)

TIME: Very recently.

ACT ONE

"They stood between their hands, bending
and leaning from side to side in their beauty
and loveliness as if they were moon."
-- The Arabian Nights

Rimsky-Korsakov's "Scheherazade" in
darkness.

Scene one

(The Lower East Side. Morning. Sunlight.

FARRUCO DIAZ enters limping. He jingles when he walks—a ring of keys on his belt. SHEREZAD joins him. BOTH have coffees to go.)

SHEREZAD: (Finishing a story.) "Se va, se va, se fue." (Trying to decipher it.) Going, going, gone?!! Is that a curse? How is a break-up like a homerun?

FARRUCO: If it's a walk-off. If it wins the game.

SHEREZAD: A walk-off? I'm the one who walked!!

FARRUCO: —off.

SHEREZAD: Do I win?

FARRUCO: Do you?

SHEREZAD: Does winning feel like dying?

FARRUCO: Sometimes.

SHEREZAD: Nobody just walks off. You leave a little piece of your soul with every swing.

(HE drinks.)

Ugh! Not sweet enough! So yeah. I broke up. Again. (Then, singing...) "ALONE AGAIN, NATURALLY..."

FARRUCO: Good riddance to the dude and his baseball metaphors. I bet he was gay. (Off HER reaction.) You just haven't found the right guy.

SHEREZAD: And you never found the right girl! Why'd you never get married to that sweet girl in Passaic—?

FARRUCO: Don't say her name. It colors the day, and it's not a fun color, okay?

SHEREZAD: What's in a name anyway? And who are we to talk? What were our parents thinking? Sherezad? Farruco?!! They coulda named us after movie stars. I coulda been Marilyn or Doris. You coulda been Steve or Warren. Instead we sound like a couple of refugees from a falafel shop!

FARRUCO: Do you never get tired of talking?

SHEREZAD: I got rabia. In my blood, in my heart! And what's in my heart must come out! I'm Cuban, I gotta talk, I gotta sing! I get this filin, my heart goes tilín tilín, and I open my mouth and words, songs, everything just pours out of me!

FARRUCO: (Touches her forehead.) You got a lot of stories in there.

SHEREZAD: You like that, I got a million more.

FARRUCO: Sis, I love the wheels you roll on.

(SHE watches FARRUCO limp.)

SHEREZAD: How's your wheels?

FARRUCO: They hurt.

SHEREZAD: Knee?

FARRUCO: There too.

SHEREZAD: Even after the surgery?

FARRUCO: Still hurts.

SHEREZAD: Where?

FARRUCO: In the bone.

SHEREZAD: Did you try hydrotherapy?

FARRUCO: Can't swim.

SHEREZAD: Chinese medicine?

FARRUCO: Hate needles and I don't like tea.

SHEREZAD: Then I guess we'll just have to cut 'em off.

(Looks around the office.)

Are you kidding me? Those are the same calendar girls that were on the wall—what?—twenty year ago?

FARRUCO: Thirty. How can you take 'em down after you've established a relationship? I've been going steady with these mamitas for a long time!

SHEREZAD: Buy a PENTHOUSE! Live a little.

FARRUCO: This is my life.

SHEREZAD: That's sad!

FARRUCO: Hey. This business bought us our freedom.

SHEREZAD: You wanna be free? Sell it. Sell it all!

FARRUCO: No way!

SHEREZAD: Sell the house at least.

FARRUCO: Jersey's home!

SHEREZAD: Jersey's the pits!

FARRUCO: Traffic is. But the house? She, it's just like it used to be. The piano's there. (Remembering.) You used to tinkle them 88s like the Latina Spitfire Gershwin!

SHEREZAD: Used to. And it wasn't Gershwin. If anybody, it was Schubert.

FARRUCO: Then the Cuban Schubert.

SHEREZAD: The Cuban Schubert was Lecuona.

FARRUCO: Then the Lecuona of Union City! Look, I can take a sick day, we can take the tunnel home, and you can play for me— hell you can play all day if you want.

SHEREZAD: Hell no!

FARRUCO: I'm not that dark gay guy! I'm your brother, and I say sing. Sing!

SHEREZAD: Let's make this a no-music day, okay?

FARRUCO: Whatever you say. Today belongs to you, She. And the City is gleaming.

SHEREZAD: City don't gleam.

FARRUCO: It's a relative gleam. Come on, I think I just heard Pantys come in.

(FARRUCO opens the door. SHEREZAD follows. They enter the PAQUETERÍA main room. Shelves of homemade packages: plastic, cardboard, Tupperware, even suitcases. PANTYS sits working a laptop at the front counter by the cash register, bopping along to BANDA on the radio.)

PANTYS: Qué onda, Jefe!

(PANTYS sees SHEREZAD.)

Wow! You must be—

FARRUCO: Turn that shit off!

PANTYS: It's just banda.

FARRUCO: Put some salsa!!

PANTYS: Sure Boss, but the customers—

FARRUCO: This is the Loisaida!

(FARRUCO draws a line with his foot.)

This is a no-banda zone!!

PANTYS: Mande.

SHEREZAD: Mande? Command me? Don't say that to a Cuban, cause he will! Fuck "mande!"

(PANTYS smiles to her, bows almost imperceptibly.)

PANTYS: Para servirle.

SHEREZAD: Serve me? You ain't from around here.

FARRUCO: This is Pantys.

SHEREZAD: Pantys?

PANTYS: Boss talks about you all the time.

SHEREZAD: Oh yeah? He can't shut up either.

(FARRUCO turns on SALSA. He dances one-legged in the old style.)

FARRUCO: Azúcar!

SHEREZAD: That's wrong in so many ways!

FARRUCO: This is for la raza!!

SHEREZAD: La raza?

FARRUCO: La raza cubana!! Come on, Sis!!

SHEREZAD: I think I'll sit this one out.

FARRUCO: Your loss! Coño! I'm a hot papichulo!

(SHEREZAD turns the SALSA off.)

PANTYS: Gracias.

SHEREZAD: Okay, Mister Hottie. Already limping. You wanna go completely lame?

FARRUCO: Just representin', She. Our peeps!

SHEREZAD: "Peeps?" Is this how you talk these days?

FARRUCO: Just staying hip. Walking the talk.

PANTYS: Most of our customers these days don't speak much English anyway.

FARRUCO: They barely speak Spanish either.

PANTYS: They speak Mexican Spanish.

FARRUCO: Like I said.

(FARRUCO extemporizes sing-song "Mexican Spanish" with attitude.)

SHEREZAD: Hey! Mexicans speak beautiful Spanish!

FARRUCO: In Cancun! But on Avenue C it sounds pretty stooopid! Now you wanna be hip... then you gotta represent, you gotta do it New York style,—

(FARRUCO extemporizes "Cuban Spanish"—superfast and urban.)

FARRUCO: (Continued.) When in Rome, baby. When in Rome!

SHEREZAD: What's that smell? Definitely not Rome. Is that... mole?

FARRUCO: (Sniggers.) How'd you guess?

(PANTYS moves from one package to the next.)

PANTYS: Mole poblano, mole de guajalote, mole verde,—

SHEREZAD: That's a lotta mole! Didn't know so many New Yorkers are cooking Mexican these days!

PANTYS: They're not cooking. Their mamás are.

FARRUCO: These packages aren't going out. They're coming in.

SHEREZAD: But there's Mexican restaurants everywhere!

PANTYS: No es lo mismo.

SHEREZAD: (Examines packages.) Tamales, pan dulce, tortillas—

FARRUCO: Makes you kinda miss a good old-fashioned Porta Rican mofongo—

SHEREZAD: (Holds up a package.) What is this?

PANTYS: Birria.

SHEREZAD: Goat?

PANTYS: Cooked in its own blood.

SHEREZAD: Too much information.

PANTYS: From Tulcingo, Mexico.

SHEREZAD: How much does it cost to send this?

FARRUCO: Forty-five smackeroos.

SHEREZAD: For forty-five bucks, half the bodegas in town'll get you a goat!

FARRUCO: It's not the birria, Sis. It's just that everybody misses home. And they're willing to pay for the taste. It's what keeps us in business. Fed Ex is too lazy to drive into the Mexican outback for a tupperware of Grandma's birria. But we will.

(FARRUCO works himself up. Continues.)

We'll go where only mad dogs and Englishmen go out in the mid-day sun, to this godforsaken town, this,—

PANTYS: Tulcingo.

FARRUCO: Tulcingo!—Everybody's from Tulcingo these days! The entire male population has landed in the Tri-State area— And even though they're probably all living in the same apartment, they're still willing to shelve out forty-five dollars for a taste of down-home cooking. Hey, wouldn't you?

PANTYS: My mamá don't cook so good.

FARRUCO: Well I would. I would pay just about anything to taste Mom's cooking one more time!

(Out of the blue, He is crying.)

SHEREZAD: Sweetie—!

FARRUCO: Déjame! This place is a dump! And it smells like a South Texas taco stand! It's sweltering in here! Turn on the air for chrissakes!

PANTYS: It's on.

FARRUCO: I'm getting hot flashes! Carajo!

(FARRUCO exits into the back room. After a moment's silence,—)

PANTYS: He's like that all the time. Llorando, sin causa. Maybe he's losing his mind?

SHEREZAD: Aren't we all?

PANTYS: He gets real angry about mejicanos. Almost like he's... a racista.

SHEREZAD: My brother is not a racist!

PANTYS: Some cubanos are.

SHEREZAD: Not us! We're not Miami Cubans! We're good Jersey Cubans! We grew up with Puerto Ricans and Dominicans and a few misguided white people too.

PANTYS: No mejicanos.

SHEREZAD: There weren't any!

PANTYS: There are now.

SHEREZAD: It's really changed that much?

(Off his silence.)

Where you from?

PANTYS: Tulcingo. But I don't like birria. I'll take John's pizza any day.

SHEREZAD: Real New Yorker.

PANTYS: I'm getting there.

SHEREZAD: Cut my brother a break. He has a hurt heart. He's gotta heal his heart.

PANTYS: And yours?

SHEREZAD: My heart is fine.

(Off his reaction.)

I'm fine! It was just a break-up. Not a tragedy. We were going to be buried—I-I mean married.

(Trying to ignore the flub.)

I got off easy.

PANTYS: Maybe Boss will stop crying now that you're back.

SHEREZAD: Who says I'm back? I'm just here now!

(FARRUCO reenters. No more tears. He smokes a cigarette. He turns the front door sign OPEN.)

FARRUCO: You're home. That's all that counts.

SHEREZAD: Hey, put me to work.

FARRUCO: Nah, Pantys and I got a system.

SHEREZAD: Okay. I'll take a walk around Tompkins.

FARRUCO: Watch your back. Alphabet City's too amped for your El Lay radar—or is it gay-dar?

SHEREZAD: Shush.

(SHE exits through the front door.)

FARRUCO: Fucking space cadet, huh?

PANTYS: She's nice.

FARRUCO: She's really messed up. If you knew anything about women you could tell.

PANTYS: You sure you should be smoking?

FARRUCO: I gotta do something with my hands!

(HE crushes a cigarette.)

Carajo! I'm choking on this goddamn mole! When did New York turn into TJ? What the hell happened to my city?

PANTYS: Maybe we oughta take a walk too.

FARRUCO: Keep an eye on her. Just in case.

(FARRUCO exits through the front door. PANTYS turns on BANDA.)

Scene Two

(Dias Y Flores Park, 13th Street between Avenues A and B. SHEREZAD walks by.

Turns back. The gate is locked. SHE lingers.
About to keep moving when—)

(An unseen GUITARIST begins to play "Días
y Flores." SHEREZAD stares in, looking for
the source of the sound. Emotions welling
up, she locks her fingers in the chain-link
fence.

MUSIC stops as FARRUCO appears.)

FARRUCO: You look like Artemis.

SHEREZAD: Artemis our cat?

FARRUCO: When she died.

SHEREZAD: Thanks! She must have been
about a hundred years old!

FARRUCO: At least. She used to sleep on
Mom's old bedspread, purring. One night I
came home to no more purrs. She went under
the house like animals do. I gotta remember
that when it's my time. If you can't find me,
look under the house, okay? She went down
there to let go in the dark. But something
made her not want to go away just yet. And to
get back home, she had to climb our chain-
link fence. I found her the next morning. Her
body rigid, holding on. One paw, like yours,
locked in the link. Halfway between the

darkness and the light. Between home and wherever the hell she had to go.

SHEREZAD: I look like that?

(SHEREZAD lets go of the fence.)

FARRUCO: Not anymore.

SHEREZAD: Is that when you started crying?

FARRUCO: Who says I cry?

SHEREZAD: A man can cry, it's cool.

FARRUCO: Not so cool when you're running a business, trying to compete with DHL and Fed Ex. "Oh yeah, let's send our package through the crying guy!"

(Slight pause.)

Stupid ass stuff makes me cry. My midnight sandwich the other night? It wasn't particularly good or bad, but I bit into it and it was like a fucking flamenco song! I had these waves of pure emotion, like a Lorca poem, like a matador on his last day on earth—and I wept on the bread.

SHEREZAD: But did you eat it?!!!

FARRUCO: You bet your ass I did. I'm just really really alive these days. And it kinda fucking hurts.

(MUSIC returns. The gate (magically) swings open.)

(SHEREZAD about to enter. FARRUCO drifts away.)

SHEREZAD: Where you going?

FARRUCO: This ain't my song. I got enough pain. (Winking.) See ya later.

(SHEREZAD comtemplates her next step. Enters the garden. It is an oasis from the city, full of hanging vines and fruit and exotic flowers and running water—yet walled in by buildings. SHEREZAD finds the source.)

(SILVIO is a scruffier, grungier and younger version of Dream Silvio, more New York, more sexy. But the music he plays and sings is the same. Not needing to speak, he points his guitar towards her and continues the song from the beginning.

At first, she opens her mouth as if to sing. But instead she just breathes, taking it in.)

SILVIO: (Singing and playing:)
"LA RABIA EL ORO SOBRE LA CONCIENCIA

LA RABIA COÑO PACIENCIA PACIENCIA"

SHEREZAD/SILVIO:
"LA RABIA ES MI VOCACIÓN..."

(SILVIO stops playing. They stare at each
other for a long moment.)

SHEREZAD: Tilín tilín.

SILVO: Excuse me?

SHEREZAD: Hey.

SILVIO: Hey.

SHEREZAD: Am I foaming at the mouth?

SILVIO: Do you have the flu?

SHEREZAD: It's the song. It's on my skin.
I feel it rushing in my head.

SILVIO: Not your head.

SHEREZAD: What? My heart?

(SILVIO shrugs. Begins to play a new
song—"Quién Fuera.")

SILVIO: Your kidneys, liver. Shoulders, hips.
Chest, stomach, neck.

SHEREZAD: Just say my body. I'm old enough to be your mother.

SILVIO: This is not a come-on.

SHEREZAD: Comes on mighty fast.

SILVIO: Thought is at the speed of light. Speech is at the speed of sound.

SHEREZAD: And music?

SILVIO: Music is magic. (He sings and plays:)
"ESTOY BUSCANDO UNA PALABRA EN EL UMBRAL DE TU MISTERIO"

SHEREZAD: You're looking for a word at the threshold of my mystery? Fresco!

SILVIO: "QUIÉN FUERA ALI BABA? QUIÉN FUERA EL MÍTICO SIMBAD?

SHEREZAD: Sinbad?

SILVIO:
"QUIÉN FUERA UN PODEROSO SORTILEGIO? QUIÉN FUERA ENCANTADOR?"

SHEREZAD: Who was the Enchanter? There's some kinda weird ju-ju going on here!

SILVIO: Always. Every time we meet.

SHEREZAD: But we've never met before.

SILVIO: Then in a dream.

SHEREZAD: I don't dream.

(Slight pause.)

Wait a sec. Are you fucking with me?

SILVIO: I'm just singing a song here.

SHEREZAD: Sinbad comes from the Arabian Nights.

SILVIO: Ever read it?

SHEREZAD: I've cracked it open a few times.

(THEY shake hands.)

SHEREZAD: (Continued.) Sherezad Diaz.

SILVIO: Silvio Flores.

(SILVIO snaps his fingers.)

Sherezad? Like the ARABIAN NIGHTS!

SHEREZAD: Exactamundo. One thousand and one nights of pure talk.

SILVIO: Lotta action in that talk. Stakes were hight. She had to talk to say alive.

SHEREZAD: No one's trying to kill me— unless it's killing me softly.

(SILVIO plays a lick of "Killing Me Softly"— then shifts back.)

SILVIO: What's in a name?

SHEREZAD: Quite a lot. Try walking down the street in Union City and your mom screaming "Sherezad!" out the window. Talk about a curse!!

SILVIO: It's a gift.

SHEREZAD: That keeps on giving. Like malaria! I don't know if it's my name, but I get this filin which makes me want to just open my mouth and—

(SHE starts to cough.)

SILVIO: Talk?

SHEREZAD: Talk, sing, scream.

SILVIO: You Cuban?

SHEREZAD: Of course I'm Cuban!

SILVIO: Cuban Cuban?

SHEREZAD: I cried when Celia died. I wanted to send Elian back to his dad! Cuban with a brain! Y tú?

SILVIO: I like Celia but I didn't cry. Didn't care about Elian one way or the other.

SHEREZAD: Not your generation. I'm a gusano. I got seniority! You're a marielito. A scrub. A newbie.

SILVIO: Hey. I'm Cubano Cubano.

SHEREZAD: I wouldn't go bragging about that.

SILVIO: Me enamoré de Cuba.

SHEREZAD: I left when I was two. Cried for three months straight. We lost our first apartment because I wouldn't shut up.

SILVIO: You miss home.

SHEREZAD: I didn't want to go. But I had to. Otherwise there's no fairytale.

SILVIO: Fairytale?

SHEREZAD: If we never left. If there was no Castro, no Miami Sound Machine. If we had stayed home, we'd all be boring, blissed out, drinking mojitos and checking out each other's butts on the Malecón.

SILVIO: Sounds like a fairytale to me!

SHEREZAD: No! This is the fairytale.

SILVIO: Alphabet City?

SHEREZAD: Abso-coño-lutely! We had to come. And we had to cry for coming.

SILVIO: Lots of tears in this fairytale.

SHEREZAD: Grim. Quite grim.

SILVIO: But with a certain Arabian sexuality.

SHEREZAD: You think?

(As an answer, HE plays…)

SILVIO:
"ESTOY BUSCANDO UNA ESCAFANDRA…"

SHEREZAD: I'm searching for—a diving suit?

SILVIO:
"AL PIE DEL MAR DE LOS DELIRIOS…"

SHEREZAD: At the ocean edge of delirium?
Hmmn.

SILVIO:
"QUIÉN FUERA JACQUES COUSTEAU?
QUIÉN FUERA NEMO EL CAPITÁN?"

SHEREZAD: Captain Nemo?

SILVIO:
"QUIÉN FUERA EL BATISCAFO DE TU ABISMO?
QUIÉN FUERA EXPLORADOR?"

SHEREZAD: My explorer?

(THEY move closer with each exchange.)

SILVIO:
"CORAZÓN, CORAZÓN OBSCURO..."

SHEREZAD: Heart in darkness...

SILVIO:
"CORAZÓN, CORAZÓN CON MUROS..."

SHEREZAD: Heart with walls...

SILVIO:
"CORAZÓN QUE SE ESCONDE..."

SHEREZAD: Heart that hides...

SILVIO:
"CORAZÓN QUE ESTÁ DONDE CORAZÓN,
CORAZÓN EN FUGA
HERIDO DE DUDAS DE AMOR..."

SHEREZAD: Wounded by doubts of love?

SILVIO and SHEREZAD are about to
touch, then—

SHEREZAD: (Continued.) I gotta pee.

(As she heads for the bushes.)

Scene Three

(The Paquetería. Visibly less crowded with
packages. Pantys reads from a worn
paperback. Farruco enters. He carries a plastic
bag from Tower Records. He makes a big deal
of sniffing the air, looking around at the
relatively empty room.)

FARRUCO: No more Mexes?

PANTYS: Been and gone.

FARRUCO: No more mole, thank Cripes!

PANTYS: Shipment arrives tonight from San
Salvador.

FARRUCO: (Screws up his face.) Pupusas?
Puts the quease in cuisine. It's Wetback

Central around here! If our customers ain't from Old Mé-ji-co, they're from Guate-Salva-Duras!

PANTYS: (Quietly.) They're from here.

(Slight pause.)

How's your sister?

(FARRUCO starts to get worked up again.)

FARRUCO: It's like magic, you know? She comes and I just regress. It's like when you go to a high school reunion, and the school bully puts you in a headlock. I mean, I thought we were past this!

PANTYS: She put you in a headlock?

FARRUCO: No! She makes me feel like young! I left her at the park, and my knee felt pretty good. So I started walking towards the Bowery. Remembering the way it used to be, before the condos and the fashion patrol. I was walking pretty fast, and I caught my reflection in a shop window, and SHAZAM!! I got a deja vu!! I saw myself back in 1960-something! Leather jacket, greasy head of hair, right outta WEST SIDE STORY. Fresh off the Havana banana boat. Living on the Lower East Side before it was Loisaida. Couldn't speak a word of English, but I sure as hell could sing it! With a Bri-ish accent no less!

PANTYS: British?

FARRUCO: Bri-ish! Everybody cool was Bri-ish. Chad and Jeremy, Marianna Faithfull, Herman's Hermits—helluva lot cooler than being Cuban back then! Why be a second-class shitizen when you could be Peter Noone? (HE sings...)
"MISSUS BROWN YOU'VE GOT A LUVLY DAUGHTER,"
—Oh yeah! I bet you that song never made it out to Tulcingo.

PANTYS: You kidding me? Los ingleses son los mas chingones de todos, que la chingada!

FARRUCO: What do you know about it?

PANTYS: (Sings.)
"WHAT WOULD YOU DO IF I SANG OUT OF TUNE?
WOULD YOU STAND UP AND WALK OUT ON ME?"
(Continuing.) El Club de los corazones solitarios del Sargento Pimiento!!

PANTYS: Pimiento!!

FARRUCO: Oh!! Sergeant Pepper's Lonely Hearts Club Band!!

PANTYS: Seguro! Los Beatles! Remember that album cover? With all the faces of the legendary people? I used to dream that one day I would be one of them.

FARRUCO: What? A lonely heart?

(PANTYS goes silent. FARRUCO pulls out a cd from his bag.)

FARRUCO: (Continued.) Anyways, I went and bought this.

FARRUCO plays "El Watusi" by Ray Barreto.

PANTYS: This isn't Bri-ish.

FARRUCO: No shit, Sherlock. It's LA-IN!! Nuyorquino style!

PANTYS: Latin?

FARRUCO: LA-IN!!! From back - in - the - day!!!

(FARRUCO boogaloos, even on a bad wheel. Performing for PANTYS, he hip-hops and break-dances until,—)

FARRUCO: (Continued.) OWWW!!! CARAJO!!!

PANTYS: Boss,—

FARRUCO: Get away!!

(PANTYS shuts the music off. Farruco stands, pretzel-shaped.)

FARRUCO: (Continued.) Oh man!! How did that kid in the Bowery turn into this—this—monster!?? Fucking Quasimodo!!

PANTYS: Ni modo. Bossman, I used to have back pain too, but then I read this book HEALING BACK PAIN by el doctor John Sarno, and unless you just lifted 300 pounds or fell out of a second story building—it's not your back. Money? For me it was money.

FARRUCO: You don't got any money.

PANTYS: That's why I had pain. No money. No love.

FARRUCO: You still don't got those things.

PANTYS: I can make money.

FARRUCO: And love?

PANTYS reveals a paperback.

PANTYS: Stories. I read good ones.

FARRUCO: Ay monito, you got it worse than me.

FARRUCO breathes. Finally straightens himself.

PANTYS: Ask yourself what hurts.

FARRUCO: Come-mierda! Don't talk to me about pain. You don't got the slightest idea what pain really is. Pain is my life! To be forced to leave the place of your birth, never to return! To get older every day, and to know that the island has already forgotten you. To live here, but dream there. Forever.

(Silence, until FARRUCO decides to break the mood by laughing at himself. He hums the tune to "El Watusi" as he returns to work.)

PANTYS: You're a sensitive guy.

(Slight pause.)

Musical.

FARRUCO: My first language.

PANTYS: And a very good dancer.

FARRUCO: Shoulda seen me on two good legs.

(Slight pause.)

You're pretty sensitive yourself.

PANTYS: It's my cross to bear.

FARRUCO: I said sensitive, not Christlike!

(Silence. PANTYS returns to his book. FARRUCO sneaks a look outside.)

PANTYS: You want me to go look for her?

FARRUCO: She'll find her way home.

(PANTYS holds the book but does not read. FARRUCO lingers. Nearly speaks to PANTYS, but does not.)

Scene Four

(The Garden. SILVIO plays. SHEREZAD, behind bushes, pees.)

SHEREZAD: RABIA. Oh what a filin. Like this kid in junior high, wore a long coat even in the summer, acne, the whole shebang. He never spoke. Lunchtimes he'd take his sandwich into the bushes and eat it like an animal. He was a freak, except.... Except he could play. Rachmaninoff. Liszt. When he thought no one was listening, he'd play the piano till he was drenched in sweat. Nobody knew but me. Because I was hiding in the bushes, listening! Lost in the romance, the

filin! And here I am back in the bushes. Like
an animal. Listening to the romantic stuff.
Lost in the music. I'm in the middle of an
ocean of stories and I can't fucking swim! Fate
is a bitch. With this RABIA stuck in my
throat. And I can't stop talking. Something
wants to come out of me but it's stuck in the
back of my throat and it won't let go!

(SHE hacks from behind the bushes.
SILVIO stops playing.)

SHEREZAD: (Continued.) I think maybe
we're moving a little too fast. I mean you're
beautiful, marvelous, fantastic. But I'm
coming off a major crack-up. I'm in shock,
I'm concussed, I'm NUMB! My heart is...
FUZZY, and my head never was too clear to
begin with. Plus I'm not really here. So we're
definitely moving way too fast, aren't we?

(SHE emerges.)

Or are we moving anywhere at all? I talk and
talk and all you do is play Cuban songs in the
sun like any young man should. I came in here
of my own accord. I brought my pain in here.
And I'd never in my right mind think of you...
the way I'm thinking of you. It's the song! The
song is in my blood! And I'm a Jersey Girl! I
thought Billy Joel was in my blood, I mean,
SING US A SONG YOU'RE THE PIANO
MAN, right? I'm the piano man! But I'm

feeling shit I haven't felt since, I dunno, a long time!

SILVIO: (Sings.)
  "ESTOY BUSCANDO MELODÍA..."

SHEREZAD: I'm looking for a melody!

SILVIO: (Sings.)
  "PARA TENER CÓMO LLAMARTE..."

SHEREZAD: I don't know what to call me either!

SILVIO: (Sings.)
"QUIÉN FUERA RUISEÑOR?
 QUIÉN FUERA LENNON Y MCCARTNEY?"

SHEREZAD: Lennon and McCartney?!!

SILVIO: (Sings.)
"SINDO GARAY, VIOLETA, CHICO BUARQUE?
  QUIÉN FUERA TU TROVADOR?"

SHEREZAD: Mi trovador?

SILVIO: Your troubadour.

SHEREZAD: What if I don't got one?

SILVIO: Imposible, como un cubano sin sabor.

(THEY drift toward a kiss.)

SHEREZAD: Are you my troubadour?

(SILVIO pulls back.)

SILVIO: Not me.

SHEREZAD: I don't see anybody else around here.

(SILVIO sets his guitar down.)

SILVIO: Songs aren't mine.

SHEREZAD: Whose are they?

SILVIO: Silvio Rodriguez. My art father.

SHEREZAD: Never heard of him.

SILVIO: That's because of the embargo.

SHEREZAD: We embargo music?

SILVIO: Especially music. We're breaking the law. Trafficking in contraband música.

SHEREZAD: Oooh a rebel.

SILVIO: I usually lie all the time. But I can't lie to you. Not about these songs.

SHEREZAD: Why?

SILVIO: You're wounded by doubts of love.

SHEREZAD: Me? What about you?

SILVIO: Okay. Us. Somos cubanos.

SHEREZAD: By blood. So what?

SILVIO: What the blood feels, and believes, and says, is always true.

SHEREZAD: This'll never work. Impossible, crazy,—

(THEY kiss.)

SHEREZAD: (Continued.) Beautiful.

THEY Make out. Her eyes open, his closed.

SILVIO: I want my cookie.

SHEREZAD: I want my cookie too.

SILVIO: I got your cookie, right here.

SHEREZAD: Um. Can you uh open your eyes please?

SILVIO: Shut yours.

SHEREZAD: Just open them.

SILVIO: Why should I?

SHEREZAD: Because you should.

SILVIO: I don't need to see, I see inside!

SHEREZAD: Well I'm out here!

SILVIO: (His chest.) No, you're in here.

(SHEREZAD pulls away.)

SHEREZAD: Oh man! You're a smooth operator! What was I thinking? Cubans think you're God's gift with a perfect dick!

SILVIO: That's me. Soy Cuba!

SHEREZAD: I'm Cuba too!

SILVIO: You? Ha!

SHEREZAD: That's why you can't lie to me.

SILVIO: You don't even understand my songs!

SHEREZAD: They're not yours! You are NOT Cuba! You're a kid with a sexy song and too much time on your hands. Get a job!

SILVIO: This is my job! I'm the groundskeeper! Sorry if that's not what you're looking for! It's not like I play for the Yankees!

SHEREZAD: Well you just struck out.

SILVIO: (Mock baseball announcer.) Se va, se va, se fue!

(SHEREZAD goes scarily silent.)

SHEREZAD: What did you just say to me?

SILVIO: Take a Spanish class.

SHEREZAD: I know the words. (Growing paranoid.) Who told you to say that to me? Oh my God, is this some kind of set-up?

SILVIO: You got a problem, Lady!

SHEREZAD: I do—it's you!!!

SILVIO: Quiet!

SHEREZAD: Did you just tell me to be quiet? No, you didn't just tell me to be quiet!!

SILVIO: I did!

SHEREZAD: I'm quiet. I'm just thinking real loud.

SILVIO: I come here to sing some songs and meet some chicks, no big thang. And you come with your Cuban drama and mess it up! Why you gotta curse me?

SHEREZAD: You want a curse?

SILVIO: I'm looking at one.

SHEREZAD begins to arch her back, like a cat.

SILVIO: (Continued.) You're that crying baby making life hell for everybody within earshot. Okay, so you got rabia. What are you gonna do about it? (Waits to a response.) Nothing!

(SILVIO slings his guitar over one shoulder. Starts out of the park.)

SHEREZAD: LA RABIA ES MI VOCACIÓN!!!

(The skies darken overhead. SHEREZAD opens her mouth, starts to hack. Catlike, she turns around and releases the human equivalent of a fur-ball. As she does, SILVIO suddenly stops awkwardly at the chain-link. He tries to walk, but finds he is stuck. He turns in fear.

SHEREZAD takes a big gulp of air, feels her chest and lungs to test their openness. SHE notices the fur-ball. With her foot she kicks it aside.)

SILVIO: Mierda.

SHEREZAD: Go!

SILVIO: I'm going!

(HE's stuck.)

SHEREZAD: Quit fucking around.

SILVIO: It's like my leg is made of—

SHEREZAD: Stone?

SILVIO: You cursed me!!!

SHEREZAD: I didn't do nothing! I didn't even speak. If anything, I shut up.

(SILVIO genuflects wildy.)

SILVIO: Bruja!!

SHEREZAD: You really can't move, huh? (Giggles.) Wow! What are we gonna do?

SILVIO: We?

(SHE leans against the chain-link. So does he. As the sky darkens,—)

Scene Five

(The paquetería. PANTYS with a dolly loaded with boxes.)

PANYS: (Sings.)
 "ALL YOU NEED IS LOVE...
 ALL YOU NEED IS LOVE...
 ALL YOU NEED IS LOVE, LOVE...
 LOVE IS ALL YOU NEED."

(PANTYS opens the door. FARRUCO eats from an open care package.)

FARRUCO: Provecho!

PANTYS: Boss! What are you doing?

FARRUCO: Is this birria? Bloody good. But I need some pan cubano to sop up this mess!

(FARRUCO rummages through boxes till he finds homemade tortillas.)

PANTYS: Jefecito. You don't wanna do that.

FARRUCO: And I always thought they were Mexican frisbees! Look fast!

(Tosses one at PANTYS.)

PANTYS: That belongs to somebody!!

FARRUCO: Cool out!

PANTYS: This is not cool!

FARRUCO: I wanna see what all the fuss is about!

PANTYS: I'll take you to a restaurant!

FARRUCO: NO ES LO MISMO!! Can't you understand? I want to taste Tulcingo! I wanna see what forty five bucks worth of home tastes like!

(FARRUCO bites into the tortilla.)

UGH! How can you eat this? You dumbass Mexes can't even make a decent piece of bread, aprieta el culo!

PANTYS: QUIT PUTTING DOWN MEXICANS!!

FARRUCO: Don't take it personal. What do you care anyway? Your home is here. And these? They're just a bunch of fucking boxes! It's just BUSINESS!!!

(FARRUCO knocks boxes off shelves.)

PANTYS: Not that one!! (Saves it.) Es mío.

FARRUCO: Yours? From... home?

(Long pause.)

Will you... open it?

(PANTYS nods in silence. Opens it. Both stare at its contents.)

FARRUCO: (Continued.) Panties? Is that why they call you...? Coño!

PANTYS: My mother sends them to me.

FARRUCO: Maravilla.

PANTYS: I wear them.

FARRUCO: I guessed that.

PANTYS: I have a reason.

FARRUCO: I'm sure you do.

PANTYS: Soy... hermafrodita.

FARRUCO: Exsqueeze me?

PANTYS: Que tengo dos sexos a la vez.

FACCURO: Whoa. You mean you're gay? Bisexual? Que tú juegas a los dos bandos?

PANTYS: I'm like some earthworms and mollusks and a lot of plants.

FARRUCO: Androgynous?

PANTYS: Hermaphrodite.

FARRUCO: Wow.

PANTYS: I've never just told anyone. Not unless—

FARRUCO: Unless?

PANTYS: Unless he had to know.

FARRUCO: I certainly didn't have to.

(PANTYS weeps silently.)

FARRUCO: (Continued.) Monito! It's okay! Double the pleasure, double the fun!

(Not knowing what else to do, FARRUCO embraces PANTYS. They say this way, breathing in sync.)

PANTYS: If you were an animal, what animal would you be?

FARRUCO: A wolf. A lone wolf. Y tú?

PANTYS: A chocolate covered scorpion.

FARRUCO almost lets go, but doesn't.

FARRUCO: I think it's great. I do. I'm interested. Not like that, but. It's a kind of a miracle. Something out of a fairytale.

PANTYS: It's a curse.

FARRUCO: Also in fairytales. I'm trying to think this thing through. I gotta admit, I might have a problem with the equipment— the male stuff. It's all a great big mystery! Clits are hieroglyphic. But cocks!??

PANTYS: Please. No más. It's a mistake.

FARRUCO: No mistake. I'm not gay. But this is Kismet. And you just can't mess with Fate.

(THEY kiss.
Thunder and lightning.
"Sheherazade" by Rimsky-Korsakov.)

End of Act One

ACT TWO

"Music scotch-tapes the whole world together
—doesn't it?"
—HM Koutoukas, With Creatures Make My
Way, 1965

Scene One

(The garden. Dark clouds over the sun.
Shadows of overhanging trees. Sudden gusts
of angry wind.

SILVIO, lamer than ever, hugs himself for
warmth. SHEREZAD plays with the fur-ball.
Bats it around like a cat.)

SILVIO: Is that was I think it is?

SHEREZD: What does it look like?

SILVIO: It looks like a fur-ball.

SHEREZAD: Really?

SILVIO: But I've never seen one that size.
And I've only seen them come out of cats.

SHEREZAD: Where did it come from?

SILVIO: It came outta you.

SHEREZAD: No it didn't.

SILVIO: Yes it did.

SHEREZAD: Don't be stupid.

SILVIO: I admit I had my back turned. But about the time this thing happened to my leg, you hacked out a loogie—

SHEREZAD: I did not!

SILVIO: It was really gross. And you're playing with it right now.

SHEREZAD: I can't help it if I'm congested!

(SHE opens her mouth to speak. Instead hacks. Barely stops herself from throwing up something else.)

SILVIO: Congested. Right.

SHEREZAD: (When she can speak.) Something's stuck in there.

SILVIO: Drink some water.

SHEREZAD: I'm getting this filin.

SILVIO: Oh shit, you're into santería!

SHEREZAD: No! I'm hearing Beethoven.

SILVIO: What?

SHEREZAD: They asked Einstein what death meant. He said, "No more Beethoven." (After a slight pause...) Or was it Mozart?

SILVIO: (Creeped out.) Why are you talking about death?

SHEREZAD: Not death. Something worse.

SILVIO: Rabia?

(SHEREZAD nods.)

SILVIO: (Continued.) What do you know about it?

SHEREZAD: I know it in the ache of my bones.

SILVIO: (Sneering.) What? Crying for Cuba?

SHEREZAD: Not Cuba. The music.

(Feeling it as new.)

SHEREZAD: (Continued.) Palms sweating. Stomach turning. Fingers palsied. (Flexing her fingers.) But you still got to play, She. You walk towards the beast like a virgin to a black dragon, blood sacrifice. You search for escape. Signs say EXIT in red, but there will be no exiting this nightmare. You want to break every finger of your hand, one at a time. You pray for fire, earthquake, flood, even if it takes you too, along with the piano, to the bottom of the sea.

SILVIO: What's wrong with you?!!

SHEREZAD: You're having a breakdown. Right there on the keys. You can't play another note. Beethoven's Pathetique has you by the ass. And you'll never make music without fear again.

(SHE hiccups.)

SILVIO: You broke down in the middle of a piano recital.

SHEREZAD nods.

SILVIO: (Continued.) Tears, wailing—the whole shebang?

(SHE nods again.)

SILVIO: (Continued.) Wow. Maybe you oughta try the guitar.

SHEREZAD: Pathetique would sound pretty dumbass on a guitar.

SILVIO: (Shrugging.) Try it.

(SHE picks up the guitar. Strums.)

SHEREZAD: Sounds like a dead cat.

SILVIO: Cradle it, like a woman.

SHEREZAD: Why should I have to fuck it to play it.

SILVIO: Make love to it. Tiene un famban barretoso.

SHEREZAD: Did you just tell me this guitar has a fat juicy ass?!!

SILVIO: Feel.

SHEREZAD: (Feeling.) Wow.

(SILVIO takes the guitar back.)

SHEREZAD: (Continued.) Don't be jealous! And don't underestimate me. Last time you did that I turned you to stone. (Off his horrified reaction.) That was a joke!

SILVIO: See me laughing? My leg is killing me! Look, no offense—please!—but I think this furball loogie thing has something to do with your fear of music thing which may have something to do with my leg. The last thing I remember was telling you to shut up. So maybe we oughta reverse that. Talk, sing, play! Listen, my super's kid plays piano. Maybe you can play for me,—

SHEREZAD: Didn't you hear anything I just said?

SILVIO: I heard that you love to play. So play.

SHEREZAD: Piano is my man. He doesn't have a fat ass. He has a perfect body, black and beautiful. But I can't play him anymore.

SILVIO: Why?

SHEREZAD: I just can't! I reveal too much! Playing is like you seeing me in my underwear!

SILVIO: Now I'm really confused. Are you telling me you're not wearing any underwear?

SHEREZAD: It's what I wear closest to my skin!

SILVIO: That's sexy.

SHEREZAD: No it isn't.

SILVIO: It can be. If you'll let it.

SHEREZAD: Sexy? (Giggling.) Really?

(SILVIO eggs her on.)

SHEREZAD: (Continued.) After school I'd play my piano. My brother would sit outside on the street, just under the window listening to me. Then this guy—

SILVIO: A guy? Cubano?

SHEREZAD: White guy. Wore his hair long.

SILVIO: Yuck.

SHEREZAD: He looked nice! Lived across the street. I'd see him through the window. This one day I was playing and I looked down and there he was, sitting with my brother! My heart went tilín tilín! I played the Pathetique like I'd never played it before. Farruco thought I was playing for him. But I was playing for the guy across the street. Oh, what a filin.

SILVIO: Did you fuck him?

SHEREZAD: No! "Did I fuck him?" I was a kid!

SILVIO: If I was your brother, I'da beat the shit outta him.

SHEREZAD: Why?!!

SILVIO: It's a guy thing, okay?

SHEREZAD: Whatever. (Smiling to herself.) It was sexy.

(SILVIO stretches his lame leg. It's starting to get better.)

SILVIO: Play me this Pathetique.

SHEREZAD: No fucking way.

SILVIO: Just do it. Gimme a break. This whole day has been pretty damn unusual.

SHEREZAD: Well I'm not the usual chick you pick up in the park!

SILVIO: That's for damn sure. (Flexing his leg.) Feels like my leg is coming out of a deep sleep.

SHEREZAD: You see? It wasn't me! You're gonna be fine! We're both gonna be fine—!

(CELL PHONE rings. The ring tone is a Beethoven theme.)

SHEREZAD: (Continued.) Oh shit. Only a couple of people have this number. (Checking his phone.) Comemierda!!

(SHE steps away to take the call. SILVIO stumbles.)

SILVIO: Hey. Uh.

SHEREZAD: This'll only take a second.
(Into the phone.) Why the HELL are you
calling me?!!

(SHE steps out of the park. Every time she
raises her voice Silvio reacts as if her words
are pins and he's the pin cushion. Without the
chain-link for support, he fights a losing battle
to stay upright.)

SILVIO: Um.

SHEREZAD: (Into the phone.) How do you
know I'm in New York? No you are not
coming out here! Te vas al carajo!! (To
Silvio.) This is gonna take a minute.

(SHE walks further away, continuing to
scream into the phone. SILVIO rubs his
frozen leg.)

SILVIO: Sonofabitch. I am getting way too
old for this. Going from bed to floor to couch
depending on the girl, mooching meals and
clothes and presents and cash on the back of
música that isn't even mine, from females
who are one helluva lot less than free—and
for whom? Them, or me? It just ain't worth
the energy. I'm fucking done! Is this my life?
(Looking around.) This fucking place that
time forgot. Goddamn garden. Shitty park.

(SILVIO pushes his guitar away.)

SILVIO: (Continued.) Bullshit songs. Half-ass poetry. Bodega dreams of a Floating Island that was never even there. And here? (Bitterly.) This concrete tomb is my home.

(HE talk-sings Nuyorican poet style.)

"The Lower East Side
 At times I drift away in dreams of a better
yesterday - - But man, like we
are never really free - - with all my tomorrow
 in yesteryear sorrow. The Lower East Side is
 taking my life away --
I fight to leave
 I fight to stay...
The Lower East Side
 is taking my life away.
Not one damn block belongs to me...
 Not one damn block belongs to me."

(HE looks up. SHEREZAD—no phone—stands listening.)

SHEREZAD: Me neither.

SILVIO: Boyfriend.

(SHE shrugs.)

SHEREZAD: What that your poem?

SILVIO: Miguel Piñero.

SHEREZAD: Another art father.

SILVIO: Yep.

SHEREZAD: Can you walk?

SILVIO: I don't know.

(SHEREZAD picks up the guitar.)

SHEREZAD: The Island is there. And even if it isn't, it's in the music.

(Starts to walk away with it.)

SILVIO: Hey!

(SILVIO rises.)

SHEREZAD: Just checking.

(SILVIO limps to her, takes the guitar, leans on it like a cane.)

SILVIO: Play me the Beethoven. And quit fucking around. It really hurts.

(SHE looks him up and down.)

SHEREZAD: It does, doesn't it.

(THEY exit the garden.)

SHEREZAD: (Continued.) Wait a sec.

(SHEREZAD returns. Stands and stares at the fur-ball. SHE deposits the fur-ball in the bushes and, not knowing what else to do, genuflects.

SHE exits the garden and joins SILVIO.)

Scene Two

(The paquetería. FARRUCO and PANTYS embrace. PANTYS rests his head on FARRUCO's check, while FARRUCO talks.)

FARRUCO: I thought I knew you. And me? It's no secret, you read me like a book. There's not a lot to hide between us. Or is there?

(Slight pause.)

FARRUCO: (Continued.) So? Cuéntame. How different are you? How wondrous? How strange?

(PANTYS straightens. FARRUCO rests his head on PANTYS's chest.)

PANTYS: Aquí soy yo. This is me. I left Tulcingo. I wanted the fairytale. The faraway place with the beautiful people and the exotic love lives of novelas. I wanted to be a part of this story. Aquí.

FARRUCO: This? (Looking around.) Really? My condolences.

PANTYS: It's all a big story. Yours, mine. We don't write it. It writes us. (Smiling.) In Tulcingo, Manhattan was Breakfast at Tiffany's. The Knicks. The Twin Towers. Now I'm here and it's what it is. Dreams become reality. I don't mind. (After a slight pause...) Do you?

(FARRUCO opens his mouth, absolutely unsure what will come out. SHEREZAD enters the store with a still-limping SILVIO. SHE has a coffee, HE has a beer in a paper sack. FARRUCO releases PANTYS. THEY pretend to work apart.)

SHEREZAD: Miss me?

(FARRUCO sees SILVIO, who still limps.)

FARRUCO: Who's this guy?

SHEREZAD: We met in the park.

(FARRUCO and SILVIO size each other up. *There may be a resemblance.)

SHEREZAD: (Continued.) Do me a favor, close up please? We gotta go home, like right now.

FARRUCO: How come?

SHEREZAD: I gotta play the piano.

FARRUCO: (Suddenly brightening.) Really?

(FARRUCO turns the sign CLOSED.)

FARRUCO: (Continued.) He's coming?

SHEREZAD: I gotta play for him.

FARRUCO: For him?

(FARRUCO turns the sign OPEN.)

SILVIO: What's the problem?

FARRUCO: Can't go. (Then, off her reaction...) Traffic.

SHEREZAD: Are you fucking kidding me?

FARRUCO: I'm neither fucking nor kidding.

SILVIO: Joder!

FARRUCO: No cursing! There's a lady present.

SILVIO: The lady curses like a lumberjack!

FARRUCO: The lady is my sister. She can say whatever the fuck she feels like!

SHEREZAD: Farruco. I told him I'd play for him. It's medicinal. I did something to his leg.

FARRUCO: Your leg? Estás cojo?

SILVIO: Como tú.

FARRUCO: No shit.

(THEY compare limps.)

SILVIO: Your sis put a curse on me.

SHEREZAD: Did not!

SILVIO: Maybe she put a spell on you too.

SHEREZAD: Shut up!

FARRUCO: Did you?

SHEREZAD: (Shocked.) I did not make you lame! How could I wish lameness on you?

FARRUCO: Not wish. Curse.

SHEREZAD: How could I do that to you? That would be like cursing myself!

(SHE hiccups.)

SHEREZAD: (Continued.) Ohmigod!

(SHE gags.)

PANTYS: (Coming to SHEREZAD's aid.) Permíteme. But this is not physical.

(PANTYS breathes with HER.)

PANTYS: (Continued.) You see? All you have to do is breathe. (Indicating SILVIO.) As for the young man, unless he fell out of a two-story building, it's not his leg. (To FARRUCO.) Yours either, Jefe.

FARRUCO: Y tú qué sabes? You think I'm making this up?

PANTYS: Boss,—

FARRUCO: Don't fucking speak another word.

(FARRUCO limps away.)

PANTYS: Como usted mande.

(PANTYS returns to his work.)

SILVIO: Ow.

(SILVIO slumps to the floor. SHEREZAD weeps.)

FARRUCO: What, She?

SHEREZAD: I crippled you!

FARRUCO: I don't blame you, Sis. You took something with you when you left. I thought you'd eventually bring it back. But whatever it is, or was, it's gone.

SHEREZAD: I had to get away.

FARRUCO: And I had to stay.

(Each stands apart, staring at the other. Finally, FARRUCO breaks it.)

FARRUCO: (Continued. To SILVIO.) Hey Kid. You hungry?

SILVIO: I'm always hungry.

(FARRUCO tosses him a care package.)

FARRUCO: Have some pupusas.

SHEREZAD: What are you doing?!!

FARRUCO: Eat what you want. It's a Going-Out-of-Business party. I'm done.

(FARRUCO exits limping into the back room. There is silence except for eating and weeping. Then MUSIC from the back room. FARRUCO reenters.)

FARRUCO: (Continued.) You wanna hear pathetic? Beethoven Pathetique. Second Movement, Opus 13—lucky 13.

SHEREZAD: Turn it off!

FARRUCO: This is my heart! Our very own concert pianist on Bergeline! Our baby Cuban Beethoven! Sitting by the window on the street, listening to you play for us!

SILVIO: (Sniggering.) Wasn't for you, man.

FARRUCO: How the fuck you know?

SILVIO: She played, but not for you.

FARRUCO: I was there, you little fucker!

SHEREZAD: I can't stand this!

(SHEREZAD marches into the back room. MUSIC cuts off. SHEREZAD returns with the CD in two pieces.)

SHEREZAD: (Continued.) Yeah, I played the Pathetique. And look at us! We're all pathetic as hell! Probably that poor ponytailed white guy is somewhere crying too—and he's probably bald! We're all cursed!

(SHE exits. FARRUCO follows her, limping. After a moment…)

SILVIO: How can you stand this place? (Gesturing.) This homesickness.

PANTYS: Nothing quite like mother's cooking.

SILVIO: Yeah, but it's everybody else's mom. Everybody else's home.

(SHEREZAD bursts back in. FARRUCO bursts in behind her.)

FARRUCO: She! Stay!

SHEREZAD: I'm going back to Hollywood. Someone pretty fucking smart said you can't go home again. I'll call ya from the airport.

FARRUCO: El Lay is evil!

SHEREZAD: And New York is good? North Jersey is the Garden of Earthly Delights? It's not the place—it's us. Wherever we go, we turn it all into mierda! Look at me! One fuck-up after another, to this very moment! No kids! No love in my life! And look at you!

Never married, no one to come home to, and that poor sweet woman in Passaic—

FARRUCO: Don't say her name!

SHEREZAD: That poor lady who loves you—

FARRUCO: It's outta bounds!

SHEREZAD: I gotta go.

FARRUCO: If you go, you go with rabia. And rabia is all you leave us.

SHEREZAD: So? LA RABIA ES MI VOCACIÓN!!

SILVIO: (Wincing in pain.) Eso es! That's the curse!

SHEREZAD: Please. Rabia is all you sing about in your magic garden.

SILVIO: Magic? That shitty park is all I got left of home!

SHEREZAD: Cuba?

SILVIO: Fuck Cuba. I never been there. I'm from here!

SHEREZAD: Then what's your problem?

SILVIO: MY NAME!!!!

SHEREZAD: Flores? What's wrong with Flores?

SILVIO: SILVIO, coño!!! Name a kid Beethoven, then ask him to write a symphony. Name him Michael Jordan, then ask him to fly. Name a kid Silvio Rodriguez, the greatest trovador on the planet and then give the kid a guitar? Joder! Suddenly all this Cuban romantic mierda starts coming outta me, and I can't shut it down por nada!!

SHEREZAD: Then sing your own songs.

SILVIO: You think I haven't tried? These songs are in my blood! I got no business sense! No employment prospects! All I can do is play guitar in the park!

SHEREZAD: And pick up chicks.

SILVIO: Why not? It's my fucking park!

SHEREZAD: Your park? You're the groundskeeper!

SILVIO: MY PARENTS FUCKING BUILDED IT!! (After a slight pause.) Built it.

FARRUCO: They built it? Coño. I helped them. Twenty years ago.

SILVIO: Thirty.

FARRUCO: (Remembering clearly.) Heroin addicts burned the building to the ground, all the way down to the basement. Us locals got together. Brought soil, mulch. Seeded, brought in trees for shade. Played música on the hi-fi—Ray Barreto. Hung a Cuban flag out the window. Weekends we'd sit outside and drink rum and eat a whole pernil! Man, we had some great block parties. That was New York, baby! Man, your parents were Nuyorquinos!

SILVIO: They were freaks. Like you. Parents are supposed to leave their kids estates! 501Ks! Mine left me a half-dead garden and a buncha scratchy Silvio LPs.

SHEREZAD: 501 jeans—401Ks. Quit crying. Move on with your life!

SILVIO: Move on with yours!

FARRUCO: Your parents? Did they... die?

SILVIO: Everybody gotta die sometime.

FARRUCO: How?

SILVIO: Every LATIN cliche known to man! Overdose, knifed, shot, AIDS because they were too macho to get checked, tons of fatty food and alcohol, and basic unadulterated LONELINESS. Sound familiar? (In FARRUCO's face.) How you gonna die?

SHEREZAD: Leave my brother alone.

(Slight pause.)

SHEREZAD: (Continued.) I need a cigarette.

FARRUCO: Me too.

(SHEREZAD and FARRUCO exit together out the front door.)

Scene Three

(SHEREZAD at the chain-link. SHE does not enter the garden. FARRUCO is several steps behind HER, but finally HE joins HER. FARRUCO lights two cigarettes a la the old movie Now Voyager—Paul Henreid and Bette Davis Cuban style.)

FARRUCO: Wanna go home?

SHEREZAD: Jersey?

FARRUCO: Cuba.

SHEREZAD: Oh.

FARRUCO: We can do it.

SHEREZAD: I almost went. Had my passport and everything. Went to a party, Hollywood Latinos, Cubans from Vegas. A man I never met before came up to me. "You going to Cuba? You're a stooge for Fidel! You're giving American dollars to a dictatorship with concentration camps for gays!" He was shouting, crying, calling me everything but a communist. And I was standing there with a glass of white wine in my hand.

(Slight cough as SHE remembers, her hand out miming a wine glass.)

SHEREZAD: (Continued.) Well, after the wine landed on his face, I got outta there. But I was discombobulated. And I never went.

FARRUCO: I bet Fidel's been dead for years.

SHEREZAD: Fuck Fidel. We're Americans, Farruco. I'm sick of remembering and I'm tired of crying. I'm done with the past.

FARRUCO: (Touching the chain-link.) I took you here once.

SHEREZAD: You did?

FARRUCO: Long time ago. Some kind of pachanga. All the papichulos were checking you out. You didn't know how cute you were! That day my City was like a big open flower after rain on a sunny day.

SHEREZAD: I don't remember.

FARRUCO: You don't? You're the only person left who would. And you don't remember? You really don't remember?

SHEREZAD: (Struggling to remember.) I think I remember those bushes.

FARRUCO: You do?

SHEREZAD: I think.

FARRUCO: (Almost crying.) You sat by those bushes!

SHEREZAD: See? I remember!

(SHE touches FARRUCO's face.)

SHEREZAD: (Continued.) I remember you. My ideal guy.

FARRUCO: Y tú? The jewel of Havana. La perla más rara,—

SHEREZAD: Please.

FARRUCO: El más delgado pétalo de hielo. I can see you, sitting knock-kneed under that tree. My baby sister in the sun.

SHEREZAD: Why can't I find a guy like you?

FARRUCO: Why can't I find a girl like you?

SHEREZAD: Spoilt for life. (Slight pause.) I remember that sweet girl in—

FARRUCO: Don't say her—

SHEREZAD: Mona. (Slight pause.) She's entitled to the dignity of her own name. See, there's no magic in a name.

(Suddenly she starts to cough, to hack. The worst yet.)

FARRUCO: Sis!

SHEREZAD: Something—stuck— choking—

(SHE grabs the chain-link with both hands.)

FARRUCO: You are not the cat.

SHEREZAD: I think I am.

FARRUCO: Eventually we're all the cat. But not yet.

(SHEREZAD looks into the future.)

SHEREZAD: I'll be alone. I'll talk and talk and no one will be there.

FARRUCO: I'll be there.

SHEREZAD: Where's my Prince Charming? My Arabian Knight?

FARRUCO: Estoy aquí! Maybe this is what Arabian Knights look like these days!

SHEREZAD: But you're not MY Arabian Knight.

FARRUCO: Don't be so choosy.

SHEREZAD: Will you really be there? Corazón?

FARRUCO: I don't know, Corazón. I'd die for you. But I can't live for you.

(HE looks into the future.)

FARRUCO: (Continued.) A Thousand and One Nights is not a death sentence. Add it up! What is it? Three years? Get over yourself. You're cursed. Okay. You know what I say?

Te bendigo. I bless you. Now take the
bendición and go forth unto the world! Go
with someone you love, or go it alone! But
you GOTTA LET GO!!!

(HE gently pries her hands off the chain-link.
They go together.)

Scene Four

(The paquetería. FARRUCO and
SHEREZAD enter the front door. SILVIO
and PANTYS are waiting for them.)

FARRUCO: What? (To PANTYS.) What are
you waiting for? Oh yeah.

(FARRUCO pulls out a money clip.)

PANTYS: Put it away!

(FARRUCO pockets the money.)

FARRUCO: I can't do anything right by you
anymore, monito.

PANTYS: Don't do anything.

FARRUCO: We're not even friends anymore?
Guess not. I know you too well. (Looking
around.) What a mess.

PANTYS: We opened one more package.

(PANTYS and SILVIO reveal a TOY PIANO.)

FARRUCO: Leave her alone, guys. Let her be. There's no magic, no curse. It's all just stuff we have to get over, on our own.

(FARRUCO starts to put it away.)

SHEREZAD: I'll play.

FARRUCO: What? (No reponse.) For me?

SHEREZAD: Not for you.

SILVIO: To un-curse me?

SHEREZAD: Not your curse. (Slight pause.) I'll play for me. And for Pantys.

FARRUCO: Why Pantys?

SHEREZAD: Because he loves my brother.

(SHE examines the keyboard.)

PANTYS: It's a good one. Japanese!

SHEREZAD: It's just music. We feel what we feel. It's nobody's fault, is it? You can't stop how you feel, right?

(SHE studies the keys. Finally plays the
melody to Beethoven's Pathetique. Stops
short.)

FARRUCO: Don't stop!

SILVIO: Just play.

SHEREZAD: I can't!

SILVIO: Then sing!

(As the music retards to a complete stop,—)

SHEREZAD: (Sings.)
"OH MELANCOLÍA
NOVIA SILENCIOSA
ÍNTIMA PAREJA DE AYER"

FARRUCO: Intimate couple from yesterday.

SHEREZAD: (Sings.)
"OH MELANCOLÍA
AMANTE DICHOSA
SIEMPRE ME ARREBATA TU PLACER"

SILVIO: Always disturbing my peace.

SHEREZAD: (Sings.)
"OH MELANCOLÍA
SEÑORA DEL TIEMPO
BESO QUE RETORNA COMO EL MAR"

PANTYS: Kiss that returns to the sea.

SHEREZAD: (Sings.)
"OH MELANCOLÍA
 ROSA DEL ALIENTO
DIME QUIÉN ME PUEDE AMAR...!"

(EVERYONE emits a sigh.)

PANTYS: Eres chingona! Chingonaza!!

SHEREZAD: Am I foaming at the mouth?

SILVIO: I think I am.

(SILVIO moves his leg.)

SILVIO: (Continued.) Am I un-cursed?

SHEREZAD: I don't know, are you?

FARRUCO: We can repack everything! Por qué no? We can finally put the pain behind us!

(PANTYS quietly packs his things.)

FARRUCO: (Continued.) Monito. Where you going?

PANTYS: Been a long day, Boss.

FARRUCO: Are you all right?

PANTYS: I'm not any one thing.

FARRUCO: You coming back tomorrow?
Pantys?

(PANTYS exits. FARRUCO stands, struck
numb and dumb. SHEREZAD notices
PANTYS's paperback.)

SHEREZAD: Coño! You know what he's
reading? The Arabian Nights! The curse! It
never ends!

FARRUCO: (Takes the book.) Do you think
maybe he needs this?

(FARRUCO runs out the door.)

SILVIO: (Watching him.) No limp.

(Silence. HE waits. Finally shrugs and starts
to limp away. At the door,—)

SHEREZAD: Okay. I cursed you.

SILVIO: Of course you did.

SHEREZAD: I didn't think it would really
work.

SILVIO: Don't fuck with Cuban women. But
I'm drawn to the flame.

SHEREZAD: Then go.

SILVIO: To Cuba? Maybe. Come with me.

SHEREZAD: That's tempting Fate, kid.

SILVIO: Fuck Fate.

(SILVIO takes her hands, kisses them.)

SHEREZAD: What's that for?

SILVIO: I un-curse you too.

SHEREZAD: You cursed me?

SILVIO: Many, many times.

(One last hand kiss.)

SILVIO: (Continue.) That's with eyes open.

(SHE kisses HIS hands.)

SHEREZAD: That's with eyes closed.

SILVIO: Wow.

(THEY kiss lips.)

Scene Five

(The garden at dusk. PANTYS sits alone.
FARRUCO listens at the chain-link.)

PANTYS: (Singing.)
"LA RABIA SIMPLE DEL HOMBRE SILVESTRE"

FARRUCO: (Quietly). The rabia of the wild
man.

PANTYS: (Sings.)
"LA RABIA IMPERIO ASESINO DE NIÑOS"

FARRUCO: Of empire and child murder.

PANTYS: (Sings.)
"LA RABIA SE ME HA PODRIDO EL CARIÑO"

FARRUCO: That has rotted away my caring.

PANTYS: (Sings.)
"LA RABIA MADRE POR DIOS TENGO FRÍO"

FARRUCO: By God I'm cold.

PANTYS: (Sings.)
"LA RABIA ES MÍO ESO MÍO SÓLO MÍO,..."

(FARRUCO enters the garden.)

FARRUCO: It's not only yours. (Pause.)
Look uh. Take a few days off. (Slight pause.)
How much time do you need? That much?
Okay. I guess I understand. Where will you
go?

PANTYS: Tulcingo. (Then off FARRUCO's reaction.) Why are you laughing?

FARRUCO: After New York City? The hub of the universe? What're you gonna do?

PANTYS: Go home.

FARRUCO: Oh.

PANTYS: I'm not going to remember. And I'm not going to cry.

FARRUCO: What's left?

PANTYS: I'm just going to keep reading.

FARRUCO: The story?

(FARRUCO gives PANTYS the book.)

PANTYS: I read it twice. Your name? It's not in there. Sheherezade is on every page. But Farruco—no hay ningún Farruco!

FARRUCO: Not my curse.

PANTYS: Then what is?

FARRUCO: Dad named me Farruco after King Farouk. A playboy, a gambler, lots of beautiful women. Why didn't any of that rub off on me?

PANTYS: Hazme un favor.

FARRUCO: Mándame.

PANTYS: Come. As my guest. First Mexico City. Then Tulcingo.

FARRUCO: Oh I don't know if I can take all that banda your people listen to. (Slight pause.) That was a joke.

PANTYS: My people? We listen to many things.

(PANTYS exits, leaving the book behind. FARRUCO stands in the middle of the garden.

SILVIO returns to the garden and plays "Días y Flores."

SHEREZAD enters, walking past FARRUCO. Close as they are, they remain alone. SHEREZAD goes to the bushes. Returns with the fur-ball in her hand. SHE makes a wish.)

SHEREZAD: DIME QUIÉN ME PUEDE AMAR

(SHE blows into her first. The fur-ball evaporates into air. SHE suddenly can breathe.)

SHEREZAD: (Continued.) Whew!

(FARRUCO straightens his back.)

FARRUCO: Whew!

(SHEREZAD sees him. FARRUCO unhooks the keys from his belt and puts them in HER hand. HE exits after PANTYS. SILVIO watches him go.)

SILVIO: Se va, se va—

(SHE shushes him.)

SHEREZAD: Se va.

(A gleaming Cuban flag unfurls. Flowers all around.)

END OF PLAY

AFTERW0RD
_STAGES

Part of a life in the theater is that you never quite disconnect from it, no matter how far away you may venture from your chosen stage – or, to be more accurate, the stage which chooses you.

During our recent vacation to Spain -- my wife Marlene and I seeking to leave behind the seemingly 24/7 barrage of plays and more plays by friends, students and colleagues -- I found my sleep filled and my mind racing with fever dreams about productions that needed to be cast (fortunately real existing plays of mine; unfortunately for nonexistent dreamland productions). Waking at 3am in various Spanish hotel rooms, I found myself mulling opportunities for student playwrights back home (chalk it up to jetlag). This life of ours is not easily taken off like a uniform, nor is it segmented into bite-size 9 to 5 chunks of existence.

The world itself seems to be in on this phenomenon. In Sevilla's old town at 1am on New Year's Day with our friends David and Liza Zayas, we got lost getting back to our hotel and walked smack dab into Tony Kushner, also returning from New Year's revelries. I hadn't seen Tony in years, but I have known him since 1989 and the initial workshops of ANGELS IN AMERICA at the Mark Taper Forum. I was just back from my MFA at Columbia, and Tony was one of several young writers of promise. Watching him navigate the life lesson of putting his work onstage showed me how plays can matter, not just historically but in the here and now, not only for us but for generations to come – and how it all came from the mind and heart of the playwright. I was terribly jealous of him and the almost unprecedented amount of effort and faith that went into the creation of the ANGELS phenomenon. Here we were over twenty years later, and it all came flooding back: his slightly airy gentlemanliness, my competitive urges. Like a high school reunion, we only reinforce now who were were then. It's a good thing; competing with Kushner helped me write my early plays. In my work, I always like to challenge the best. How else can one learn the hard truths of one's own limitations and vulnerabilities? How else does one find out one's hidden reserves of toughness, and love for the struggle to at least try to be great in this life?

The competition lies – of course – with one's self. It isn't real – and it is more real than anything else. I know that it's not about Tony, or history, except in relation to me and my dreams as a playwright. And it's based on want more than need. "Why keep doing this?"

the writer ought to ask, often. "Do I need this in my life?" ought to be a recurring question, a kind of thermostat to the playwright's career, dialed up and down depending on one's ability to work, and sleep, and dream.

It all crystallized for me driving by twilight, entering the town of Cordoba in our rented diesel Mercedes station-wagon. Our GPS system, up to that point a god-send, picked that moment to go hay-wire, leading us to several cobble-stoned dead-ends. As it was our first time in Cordoba, we were faced with a challenge. Where to stay and how to get there became my quest. The street signs pointed towards a series of commuter hotels in the flatlands on the outskirts of the old city, now lit up above us in the middle of a large Renaissance shell of stone and marble. Our fatigue made us vulnerable to the charms of these low-energy lotus eaters. But this odyssey called old stores of competitive urges to rise inside me, so I drove into the great snail shell of the old town in its growing darkness. Three times we identified the street and hotel we wished to arrive at; three times we were pushed away, as if Cordoba itself were denying our way. Cars decided to park at the very mouth of our necessary right turn, mindless of traffic rules. One way streets became narrow walkways that could only be managed by driving on the ancient sidewalks, even through Church monasteries lit by

Christmastime candlelight. Defeated, I found
the sign for another hotel and pulled the
Mercedes onto the sidewalk in an awkward
attempt at a parking spot. But Marlene,
equally frustrated, was not beaten. She asked
me one more time to follow our original plan.
"What plan?" I blurted, "We have no plan!"

But I knew we did.

It may have been a plan made in the dark into
the unseen, but it was the kind of plan I knew
better and respected more than a GPS satellite
or a Google Map. Breathing hard, sweating
like a runner, I pulled the car off the sidewalk
and onto the caracole as we tried one more
time, utilizing all our accrued knowledge of
this and other trips into the unknown.
Somehow, this time the secret code of the city
revealed just enough of itself to let us in, to a
hotel providentially named Alfaros –
birthplace of the family name that our friend
and colleague Luis Alfaro today gives life and
plays to.

Parking the car (another adventure!), I realized
we had found a way, somehow, and I knew
the feeling so well that I said to Marlene out
of the blue, "This is a lot like writing a play."

I mean that the finding of the way is the play
– the way it feels and how it tests everyone
involved – writers, actors, audience – so that

321

they see in a snapshot, and feel in a heartbeat, who they are at that chosen moment.

The finding of the play is the style, the tone, the pace, of the play itself. And the getting there is the story – partly GPS'd to be sure – but essentially made new and human by the beautiful and horrendous mistakes made along the way.

The stakes include the occasional fender-bender and/or tiff with your wife. And if at any point it just doesn't feel worth it anymore, then the commuter hotels await with their pre-fixed ease. And the autovia is always there to take you to another easier city, or for that matter to the airport back home to the known, if that is what you prefer.

The Hotel Alfaros turned out to have a pleasant Moorish theme, and to be very near some of the best tapas we ate in Spain. Next day, we walked map in hand around the old city, but soon set it aside and let our feet take us to the ancient Jewish Quarter where Maimonides once lived and formulated his thirteen principles of faith.

Behind the wheel later that afternoon, I saw the old city in the rearview mirror. Cordoba, my old friend, who last night had kicked my ass! Just like the plays (my own and by others) whose characters and words and actions made

me see and feel myself in the shell of my body
– mistakes and glories at every blind turn.

"This is my stage," I said, this time to myself.
You don't find it – it finds you.

Oliver Mayer
January 8, 2011

"marea"

a play by alejandro morales

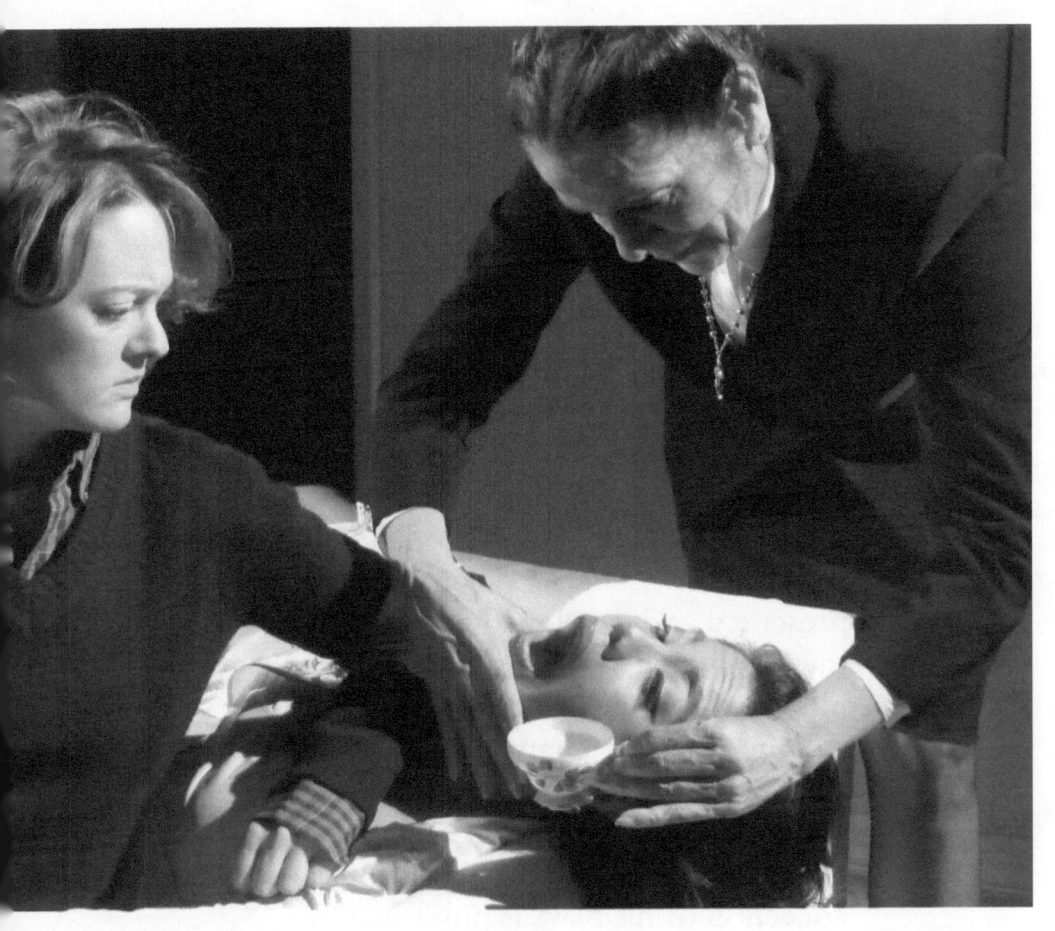

About the Playwright

ALEJANDRO MORALES's plays have been developed and presented at Mabou Mines, South Coast Repertory, HERE, The New York International Fringe Festival, INTAR, and The Public Theater where he was a 2008 Emerging Writer. He is co-founder and Associate Artistic Director of Packawallop Productions, which presents visually-charged original productions that spotlight cultural and sexual identity. Packawallop has also presented and developed four of his plays-- the silent concerto, expat/inferno, castle of blood, william bell, and marea. He is an alumnus of New Dramatists and has been awarded the Whitfield Cook Award for sebastián and The Fringe Overall Achievement Award for expat/inferno. A collection of his plays is published by NoPassport Press, wherein an earlier version of marea was published.

For performance rights to Ms. Morales' work, please contact Packawallop Productions in New York City at alex@packawallop.org

production history

"marea" premiered in 2009 as a packawallop production at HERE arts center directed by scott ebersold. it was cast as follows:

claudia: polly lee

maria: maria christina oliveras

regla: judith delgado

caridad: maggie Bofill

(all photos by alejandro morales)

1.

a new york apartment. it looks spare, clean and stylish. it is a universe of images... in fact, the more images that can flicker on its surfaces throughout the play, the better. there are three doors: one to a bathroom, one to a bedroom, and a third, which leads to we know not where. the bathroom and the bedroom are suggested easily and elegantly. there is a kitchen offstage.

maria appears. she addresses the audience.

maria: the day was like any other except i had forgotten my inhaler.

i was in a hallway at school. college. and the attack came. i couldn't breathe. the hallway was closing in on me and everything was getting dark.

i hear a voice.

italian.

she is behind a door. i reach out to touch the handle. classroom. the door is blue. the door handle is silver and sharp. my hand is sweating.

i can't breathe.

i turn the door handle. i make it turn.

my hand slips and it feels like i'm falling
through the door. falling right through. i am
falling into a dark room.

and then i see her.

her face. her eyes. her nose. her mouth. her
lips. her skin. like porcelain. like paper. and
her hair. phrases and phrases of wild hair i'd
try to read but i failed.

i can almost understand her. i think i can. the
words are like a language i know. i see there
are subtitles. i don't read them. it doesn't
matter what they say. it doesn't matter. it's
her face. her face that's important.

her face looking out. at me. right at me.
straight at me. she burned me. burned me so
thoroughly i felt i'd glow as white as she was.

that was the first time i saw monica vitti in
l'avventura.

end of scene.

2.

maria alone. she holds a camera.

she points it at various things, arranging them as she sees fit. but she never takes a picture.

claudia walks in. she has a jacket and her bag and keys. she has come home from work.

maria points the camera at claudia.

a moment...

maria: stay right there.

claudia: where did you get that?

maria: i bought it.

claudia: huh.

maria: i'm a photographer

claudia: don't take my picture.

maria: why not?

claudia drops her things on the floor and collapses in a chair or the couch.

maria: you're such a slob.

claudia: that's nice.

maria picks up claudia's things and quickly
puts them away. maria returns with a bottle
of wine and two glasses.

maria: drink?

claudia: what flavor?

maria: chianti. it's supposed to be voluptuous.

claudia makes a face. maria does not see.
maria sets to opening the bottle and pouring
the wine.

maria: so?

claudia: don't ask. worst day ever.

maria: what happened? did you talk to—?

claudia: i've begun the conversation.

maria: and what did he say?

claudia: they're still reviewing my outline.
these things don't happen overnight.

maria: i'm excited.

claudia: don't get too excited.

maria: i'm jealous. all the research you get to
do.

claudia: i just got home from work. no research talk right now, please?

maria hands claudia a glass of wine.

claudia: no, that's alright. i don't want any.

maria: i bought the wine for you. for us.

claudia: i hate chianti.

maria: you love chianti.

claudia: do i?

maria: yes you do.

it's our anniversary today...

happy anniversary.

a moment.

claudia: cara...

maria: you forgot.

claudia: you know i'm not good with dates.

maria: i know. you forgot my birthday last month. anyway, it's okay.

maria pulls out a wrapped package.

i got this for you.

claudia: oh god, i feel like an asshole. i didn't
get you anything.

maria: i got myself a camera. why don't we
say it's from you?

claudia: but it's not from me. i didn't even
know you wanted a camera. i thought you
were through with taking pictures.

maria: i saw this one today and i wanted it.
so, thanks! it was very sweet of you.

claudia: it's not like your old one.

maria: that's ok. i like this one. it's small. it
suits my purposes.

she points the camera at claudia.

claudia: don't.

maria: ok. fine. now open your present.

claudia opens her present the way a kid
would. not self-consciously or anything like
that. she just rips the wrapping apart and
tosses it all over the floor. maria picks up the
paper as it gets dropped.

claudia's present is revealed to be a vintage dress. early 60s. it's in excellent condition.

claudia: (stunned.) this is unreal.

maria: i thought of you.

claudia: where would i wear this? i can't wear this. me? i'm a fashion moron, cara...

maria: wear it to class.

claudia: i will not wear this to class.

i don't even know what to say...

maria: try it on.

claudia: now?

maria: no, next month. of course now! (pointing to the bedroom.) get in there and put it on. i want to see what it looks like on you.

claudia: can't i sit here for a minute?

maria points to the bedroom. claudia surrenders and rises from the chair. she goes to the bedroom. maria grabs her by the hand and pulls her to her and kisses her.

claudia: what was that for?

maria: you didn't kiss me when you walked in.

claudia: you didn't kiss me either.

a moment.

claudia: i'll take you to dinner.

maria: you will, will you?

claudia: anywhere you want to go.

maria: the place with the lamps.

claudia: how did i know?

maria: i don't know. how did you?

claudia: don't tease.

maria: i picked the wrong place to have an
asthma attack that day.

claudia: i'll say. stumbling into my class like
that. you were a mess.

maria: but i met you and monica vitti that day.

claudia: she's the one you really love.

maria: is that what you think?

claudia: tell me you love me.

maria: i love you.

claudia: again.

maria: i don't love you.

claudia: (walking to the bedroom.) i deserve that.

maria: (being sincere.) it's not true. i love you.

a moment.

put on your dress.

claudia: ok.

she walks off with the dress. a moment.

maria: were you drinking before you came home? i smelled whiskey on your breath.

pause.

claudia: i had a drink near school. i wanted a scotch while going over some notes.

maria: notes for the monograph?

claudia: yes, for the monograph...that we're not talking about tonight.

maria: sorry... how's the dress look?

claudia: hold your proverbial horses, please.

silence. maria drinks some wine and picks up her camera. she walks around with it, like before. pointing it at things, not really taking photos.

maria hears something. indistinct. whispering? rustling? the sound of waves? perhaps all three.

maria: do you hear that?

claudia: hear what?

maria: that noise.

claudia: i don't hear anything.

the noise comes from the closed door. maria puts down her camera and slowly walks over. puts her ear to the door.

she listens.

silence. maria steps away from the door. claudia steps out. the dress looks stunning on

her. it is a total transformation. she evokes
monica vitti in l'avventura.

a pause.

claudia: well?

maria: state transformandome.

claudia: no, cara, siete voi che mi transforma.
or, you attempt to. does it fit ok.

maria: more than ok.

claudia: i'll settle for ok. on good days, i'm
lucky if my socks match. ... so shall we go?

a moment.

maria: let me take your picture?

claudia: cara...

maria: just so you can see yourself.

claudia: i saw myself in the mirror.

maria: not the way i see you.

claudia: alright.

maria holds up the camera. time is
suspended. claudia stands beautiful and
perfect. maria takes the photo. time resumes.

claudia: let me see?

maria flips the camera around and shows
claudia the photo.

claudia: so thats' the way you see me?

maria: che bella donna siete...

claudia: i don't look like myself.

a moment. maria puts away the camera.

maria: we should go.

end of scene.

3.

maria, alone.

maria: i was cataloguing photos at work when
i saw the island. it was unlike the photos we
normally use in our stock collections. too
much shadow. too much atmosphere. the
film grain made it look like it was dissolving.
or materializing. the island shot up into the
air, a chaotic maze of rock. i traced the edge
of one of the rocks with my finger on my

monitor. i found myself tracing another edge of one of the rocks with my finger on my monitor. i found myself tracing another edge and another edge. nothing made sense.

except the sky and sea in the picture. they were so still, so smooth, they could have been two blades resting next to each other. i touched the edge where they met. i felt it. cut. and then, even though this was a black and white photo, i could swear the water in the picture began turning blue.

i started to take deep breaths. but i couldn't. my fingers tried to clutch at the sea in the picture and they couldn't.

i turned away from my computer. i grabbed my inhaler and i left my desk. i ran out of my cubicle. i ran out of the building. all i could think of was escaping.

end of scene.

4.

maria's apartment. claudia on the floor smoking. maria stands nearby.

claudia: i want to stab him in the ass... he made insinuations. insinuations, cara.

maria: once you get the proposal for the monograph accepted, he'll shut up.

claudia: so what that he got published in film comment. i've written for film comment. years ago. ok. but i've done it. and the department head is practically blowing him.

maria: how much have you had to drink?

claudia: i just had a quick drink after work.

maria: uh-huh.

claudia: i am not drunk.

maria: "i want to stab him in the ass?" sober people say this?

claudia: they're driving me crazy. they deserve to be stabbed in their fat nasty asses.

maria: you just need to get a commitment from a publisher for the antonioni monograph and they'll leave you alone.

claudia: let's get the hell out of here. let's go somewhere. somewhere crazy.

maria: right now?

claudia: just escape.

maria: i like the sound of that.

we'd put on our chic traveling outfits, grab out matching luggage, and walk out of here with giant blank sunglasses on our face.

claudia: airport lounge. i want to go to the airport lounge.

maria: where do you want to go?

claudia: an island.

maria: bermuda?

claudia: cuba.

maria: we're not going to cuba.

claudia: why not?

maria: because we're not.

claudia: say something in spanish.

maria: don't start this with me.

claudia: c'mon. just one little thing.

maria: claudia!

silence.

maria: get up from the floor. you look ridiculous.

claudia: what's gotten into you?

maria is straightening out an already straightened out apartment. she arranges something that to the rest of us does not need arranging, but it's incredibly important to her.

claudia: we're not going to talk about this are we?

maria: i think going on vacation is a great idea. if you want to go to an island, there are several we can go to... st. thomas. st. lucia. you tell me when's good for you and i will arrange it.

claudia: what if i want to arrange it?

maria: you? you can't even arrange to get a publisher to commit to publishing this book you're supposed to be working on.

silence.

maria: i'm sorry.

claudia: i'll see about dinner while you're arranging things.

a moment. the telephone rings. claudia grabs the receiver.

claudia: hello?

silence.

claudia: hello?

silence. claudia hangs up.

maria: who was it?

claudia: i don't know. wrong number. they didn't say anything.

maria: bad connection.

claudia: no. someone was listening on the other end. i heard them breathing.

maria: are you ok?

claudia: i don't know... yes. it's just... nothing.

she walks out.

end of scene.

5.

maria later that evening.

maria: i stare at the wall in front of me. blank. white. i stare at it. waiting. for what? my shadow on the wall. so still. so quiet.

and then something happens.

i am in miami. i am in the house. that house. there is a terrible storm outside. the rain, the thunder threatens to break the windows and flood the room. i worry about the glass. i worry about cutting myself.

i run but in this room there are only windows... and a door. i run to the door and i try to open it.

it doesn't turn. and then i hear... something, no, someone on the other side. and the storm gets louder. thunder. lightning. one of the windows smashes open and i see i have been cut by the glass. i grab on to the doorknob.

i try to open it.

i try to open it!

maria repeats "i try to open it!" while frantically trying to open the door. claudia walks in half-asleep.

claudia: what are you doing?

maria "wakes" with a start.

maria: i... i... must have fallen asleep...

she notices her hand on the doorknob.

it's so strange... this door.

claudia: come to bed. you were dreaming. there's nothing behind that door.

maria: really?

claudia: it's been like that since i moved in. supposedly the apartment door and this one used to be one large unit. it's bricked up now.

maria: there's an apartment next door?

claudia: it's vacant. the old lady next door died and they haven't cleaned it up yet.

are you ok?

maria: (lying.) i'm fine.

claudia: (knowing better.) come to bed and i'll get you a sleeping pill and some water.

a moment.

claudia: what were you dreaming about?

maria turns to claudia. something's off.
claudia senses this. she puts her arms around
maria.

maria: i'm so sorry.

claudia: about what?

maria: (doesn't know what to say, so decides
to say...) keeping you up.

end of scene.

6.

maria alone.

maria: the first part of l'avventura begins on an island.

there's anna and claudia, played by lea marrasi and monica vitti, two good friends on a little expedition with some friends including anna's lover sandro.

something's up with anna. we don't know what. she wants to get away from sandro, but has sex with him anyway. she wants to be left alone yet she jumps into the water for a swim and then claims to see a shark so that sandro can rescue her. and once they get into the island, she disappears.

just like that.

no body. no evidence of escape. nothing. she's gone and leaves claudia behind to look for her.

and i always wondered...

this is hard.

... i, um...

she takes a deep breath and collects herself. silence.

i had an accident while i was on a little expedition of my own with my claudia. well, not really an accident, it was... well, nothing really. but we were in sicily and i was wading into the water up to my calves taking pictures of the ocean, the islands off in the distance, and i guess i wasn't paying attention, because i lost my footing...

... and i...

this is harder.

... i was carried along somewhere, like falling asleep. and i... saw her.

anna.

and i wanted to ask her why? where did she go? and why?

but i came to. claudia pulled me out. i had been sucked under and my camera was ruined. i never bothered getting it replaced.

end of scene.

7.

maria and claudia. claudia has just gotten
home from work. maria holds a manila
folder.

claudia: i want to totally stab him in the ass.

maria: what happened?

claudia: apparently i wasn't evaluated well by
one of my classes last term and word got out.

maria: which class?

claudia: you favorite.

maria: italian post-war cinema?

claudia: they were a tough bunch.

claudia lights a cigarette.

maria: more single malt after work i take it?

claudia: how come you never talk about what
happens to you at work?

maria: i have a boring job.

claudia: let's trade.

maria: i have a better idea.

she hands her the manila folder.

claudia: what's this? i didn't forget something, did i? another anniversary?

maria: you didn't forget anything. have a look in there.

claudia opens the folder. there are black and white print-outs of film stills in there.

claudia: (looking at one still.) look at that. monica vitti.

maria: during the filming of l'avventura.

claudia: (looking at another.) lea massari. she was one prima bambina, wasn't she?

maria: monica's my girl.

claudia: she looks like you here.

maria: who does?

claudia: lea massari. here in this picture on the island. see?

maria: is that the way you see me?

claudia: i'd think you'd find a way to make sure your hair didn't fly around like that in the

wind, by yeah, she really does look like you.
well in this picture at least.

she looks through some of the other stills.

i haven't seen a lot of these before.

maria: i did some research at work and i was
able to get one of my contacts in london to
put me in touch with the people cataloguing
antonioni's personal files after his death. they
sent me some of the stuff they've found and
they'd be willing to cooperate with the rights
to use the stills if you send them your
proposal.

claudia: cara... you've started securing rights
for images i don't know i'm going to use.

maria: but you could use them.

claudia: you don't know what i'm writing
about.

maria: you're writing about antonioni, you
told me. 1960-1962. that's what's in the file.
we just need to get that proposal together and
with these stills, i'm sure it'll sell itself when
you send it to some publishers.

claudia: i'm sure.

why is my writing this book important to you?

maria: it's part of your job. i want you to do
well.

claudia: but... what if i wrote about something
else?

maria: but you're not writing about something
else.

she pulls out another still.

this one is amazing. it's monica vitti just
outside the san domenico palace near the end
of the film.

claudia: cara... i am writing about something
else. i sent in my proposal this afternoon.

a moment.

maria: but you said—

claudia: —i know what i said. i thought...

maria: what? what did you think? tell me.

a moment.

claudia: i thought... if i wrote it... if i
researched...

she pulls out a notebook. there is a flag on one of the pages.

look, i took all these notes and i just couldn't figure out what... i didn't have a thesis. well, at least nothing good enough to get the department head off my back.

maria: the book would write itself. it's a great film. a great film you were teaching when i met you.

claudia: that's not enough for a thesis. not for the kind of thing i need to publish.

but look! i found this quote by antonioni that got me thinking.

she opens the notebook to the flagged page.

claudia: (reading.) "the director gazed at things radically, to the point of their exhaustion. this is dangerous. to look longer than is required disturbs any established order."

maria: i think that's bullshit.

maria collects the film stills. "collects" means organizing the print-outs in some arcane and mysterious fashion that only makes sense to her.

claudia: cara, when i read that quote i don't know what, but i was terrified... and then i thought—

maria: —are you saying i terrify you? you really think that?

silence.

she closes the manila envelope. she calmly gets up and is about to leave the room.

claudia: i wasn't finished.

maria: i really don't care.

claudia: oh, you don't? five minutes ago you cared about my job. you said you wanted me to do well.

that quote led me to a good thesis. a good article and something that... look, i just think you should read it.

maria: what's it about?

claudia: (taking a deep breath.) horror films.

maria: horror films?

claudia: i've discovered these italian horror films that were being made in the early 60s

right around the time of l'avventura... and
they made me think—

maria: —b movies?

claudia: i think this article may open your eyes
to a few things.

maria: oh, really? to what?

silence.

maria: to what?

claudia angrily gathers her things.

claudia: why don't you do a little research at
work and see for yourself?

maria: where are you going?

claudia: out.

> end of scene.

8.

a little later. maria alone. she holds her
camera. she holds it out in front of her face
as if to take a self portrait. she holds her
finger over the shutter release. she does not
press.

a stunning woman around maria's age
appears. she is dressed impeccably. vampish.
dark sunglasses and black gloves. she
advances slowly towards maria.

she holds something behind her back.

when she gets to maria, she puts her visible
hand on maria's shoulder.

maria in fright presses the shutter release.
flash. the woman quickly puts her hand over
maria's mouth.

woman: you have been running. you have
been trying to escape. but i have found you.
did you think i wouldn't? i am the villain and
you are the victim. we belong together, don't
we? don't we?

it becomes clear. it becomes obvious. you
cannot run. you cannot escape. you can close
your eyes but you still see.

she puts her hand to maria's throat and her
other hand clutches at maria's body. the
gesture is violent and sensual.

it becomes clear. it becomes obvious.
inevitable. i will claim you.

maria: your voice... i know your voice.

caridad: of course you do.

maria: who are you?

caridad: you know.

maria: who are you?

caridad: shhh...

she tightens her grip on mria. the phone begins to ring. maria is gasping for air. she clutches at the woman and tears a piece of clothing from her.

the woman is affected by this. the phone continues ringing. the woman disappears.

the phone continues ringing.

end of scene.

9.

claudia walks into the apartment. back from her walk. the phone continues ringing. she sees maria gasping.

claudia: cara...

maria: my bag! get me my bag!

claudia finds maria's bag and hands it to
maria. maria pulls out the inhaler. she takes a
hit.

the phone continues to ring. claudia answers
it.

claudia: hello?

silence.

claudia: hello? who is this? hello?

silence. claudia hangs up.

maria: wrong number?

claudia: again.

are you alright?

maria: i was scared. i couldn't breathe.

claudia: you haven't had an attack in a while.

maria: i got one the other day at work. first
one in a long time.

a moment. maria clutches on to claudia.
silence.

maria: where did you go?

claudia: i walked around. got a coffee.

maria: don't leave me again.

claudia: what's happening, cara?

maria: i don't know. maybe it's turning 30.

claudia: do you need to see someone?

maria: see someone?

claudia: to talk. just sort things out. i can get
you a referral through school.

maria: i'm fine.

claudia: there's things you should talk about...
things you never talk about.

maria: like what?

claudia: your family.

maria: i have no family.

claudia: you have your grandmother.

maria: my grandmother is a crazy woman.
she's the one that needs a therapist. not me. i
just need to figure things out. maybe take up
photography again. that's why i bought that
little camera.

claudia: have you used it?

maria: no.

silence.

maria: i want some music. something.

she puts a cd on. something jazzy. perhaps
giovanni fusco's "eclisse slow" from the
soundtrack to antonioni's l'eclisse.

maria lights a cigarette. she sways practically
standing still, smoking. claudia lights a
cigarette of her own. she stares in an opposite
direction.

claudia: i'm jealous of you sometimes.

maria: of me?

claudia: you have a genetic advantage. your
family dealt with communism. mine dealt
with coupons and casseroles.

maria: where i come from is provincial same
as any other place is provincial.

claudia: since when is miami provincial?

maria: it's filled with conservative, old world
people who can't speak english and lack any

sort of breeding or class. period. full stop.
end of story.

claudia: why don't you ever speak spanish to
me?

maria: because we speak italian. that's what
we do.

claudia: spanish is... home. i can't imagine
what it would be like to have that... that
language. i mean, i'm from iowa and i
couldn't even—

maria: —forget home. where you come from
isn't as important as where you end up. all
successful people are escape artists.
chameleons. the past is only there to forget
and you, cara, should forget that little
midwestern hamlet for good.

claudia: like you've forgotten your
grandmother. or cuba.

a moment.

maria: it's not the same.

she shuts off the stereo. silence.

claudia: why don't you talk about her? or
your parents?

maria: i don't have parents. just my
grandmother. and i don't really have her
either. it's late and we should go to bed.

claudia: i think you need to read my article.

maria: italian horror?

claudia: it's on mario bava's black sunday. it's
a seminal film.

maria: what about it?

claudia: it's about a young woman who
discovers the truth about her family. they're
under the curse of a vampire.

... will you read it?

maria: (muttering.) curses and vampires...

                    end of scene.

10.

time and space shift.

regla, maria's grandmother appears holding a
broken statue of la caridad del cobre. the
scene should be subtitled or, if possible,
dubbed with the actors mouthing the spanish
and the english translation on the soundtrack.

maria: no puedo respirar. (i can't breathe.)

regla: maria, eso te pasa por ser atrevida. (maria, that's what you get for being where you shouldn't.)

maria: abuela, no fue mi culpa. tropese. (grandmother, it wasn't my fault. i tripped.)

regla: esta estatua de la caridad vino de cuba y me la rompiste. (this statue of our lady of charity came from cuba and you broke it.)

maria: perdoname. (forgive me.)

regla: no me pidas perdón a mi. pideselo a la virgen. (don't ask me for forgiveness. ask the virgin.)

maria: me duele el pecho. (my chest hurts.)

regla: pidele perdón a la virgen. (ask the virgin for forgiveness.)

transition. maria runs into the bathroom, closing the door behind her.

regla disappears.

imagery from bava's black sunday (hereafter referred to as la maschera del demonio). images from the scene where the two doctors enter the vajda family crypt and see princess

asa's coffin. claudia is dressed for class and
she lectures as if the audience were her
classroom.

claudia: so if we pay attention to this
sequence, we can see that we are in the hands
of a master with mario bava. he does not see
this as a schlocky little film. he has great
feeling for this story and he wants us to see it
as he does. notice as the doctors enter the
crypt, bava takes his camera... his eye... our
eyes... on a 360 degree seamless panoramic
shot of the crypt. we see the entire set. we
are enveloped inside it.

this is a film about what we see... and what we
don't want to see.

the crypt houses princess asa, a witch who lies
in a coffin with a window on the lid. inside
the coffin we see the mask of satan, which has
been nailed to princess asa's face.

maria is revealed in the bathroom. she is
pressed against the door, breathing hard,
terrified. the woman appears. again, she
holds the razor behind her back.

woman: i was there that day. the day you
stood in the water. with your camera. you
thought you'd "wade in under you calves."

that's who i am, remember?

maria is choking as the air mysteriously drains for her lungs.

maria: let... go...

woman: don't resist. don't resist like you always do. you know you want to reach below the surface. you know this is what you truly desire.

transition. claudia continues her lecture.

claudia: the doctors are attacked by a bat. in the struggle, the window on the lid of the coffin breaks. one of the doctors cannot resist reaching into the coffin, prying off the mask of satan to reveal princess asa's true face.

transition.

maria: (gasping.) your face... your face...

maria manages to snatch the sunglasses off the woman's face.

maria: your face... i know your face.

transition. claudia continues her lecture.

claudia: asa's face is perfect and preserved, except she is missing her eyes. the doctor cuts

himself removing the mask and we see a
close-up of a drop of his blood falling into
asa's empty eye socket.

transition.

woman: of course you do. from   that
day... in the ocean.

maria: no, not that day...

woman: of course that day.

claudia: one drop.

caridad pulls out the razor.

claudia: let me help you.

claudia: two drops.

caridad opens the razor.

claudia: three drops.

maria struggles, but it is no use. the woman
presses her hand against maria's mouth and
runs the razor up maria's leg and cuts. maria
screams, but her scream is muffled by caridad.

woman: breathe...

maria stares at caridad, tense with fear. the woman senses something. she pulls maria close to her, protectively.

woman: tesoro...

transition. claudia continues her lecture.

claudia: there is just enough blood to revive princess asa as this ancient, dark fluid begins to rise inside her skull.

the image of princess asa's face swallows everything. blackout.

end of scene.

11.

maria and claudia. maria has stepped out of the bathroom. she's in her bathrobe. she holds claudia's article in her hand.

claudia: did you read it?

maria: yes.

claudia: and?

maria: i don't feel well. i want to get to bed.

she hands claudia the article. claudia stares at it.

claudia: i really thought you would see something in this article.

maria: i don't want to talk about it now.

a moment...

maria heads towards the bedroom and claudia towards the bathroom in silence. right in front of the bathroom door is a photograph face down on the floor.

claudia: i think you dropped something.

she hands the photograph to maria. maria looks at the photograph. something is wrong.

maria: where did you get this picture?

claudia: it was just here. lying on the floor. isn't it one of the antonioni stills you got me the other day?

maria: those were print outs. this is a developed photograph. and it's not antonioni. i took this photo.

claudia: you haven't taken a photo in years.

maria: this is sicily.

claudia: from our trip? but your camera was ruined. we didn't end up with any pictures.

maria: i almost drowned.

claudia: you did not almost drown. you were knocked over by a wave. the sea was too rough that day …

maria is staring at the photo intensely.

maria: (pointing something out.) what's that?

claudia: it's a fish or a bird or something.

maria: that's not an arm. no one was drowning. not you. not anyone. i was there, remember?

maria: but look—

claudia takes the photo from maria.

claudia: —i'm not in the mood for this.

maria: not in the mood for what?

claudia: go to bed.

maria: you don't order me around like that.

claudia: then stop acting like... like... (she notices something on maria's leg.) is that blood?

maria: what?

claudia: on your leg. you're bleeding!

maria looks. she does indeed have a cut on her leg. she is stunned.

claudia: cara?

maria: oh god...

claudia turns to the bathroom and heads in. as she reaches the door of the bathroom, she sees something terrible. she puts her hand to her mouth.

tableau.

transition into:

end of scene.

12.

regla appears holding the broken statue. again, the scene should be subtitled or if possible, dubbed with the actors mouthing the spanish and and the english translation on the soundtrack.

maria: no puedo respirar. (i cannot breathe.)

regla: trate de arreglar la virgen. (i tried to fix the virgin.)

maria: llama al medico. (call the doctor.)

regla: el pegamento no trabajo. (the glue didn't work.)

maria: llama al medico. (call the doctor.)

regla: es tu culpa, maria. (it's your fault, maria.)

maria: ¿que le paso a mi mamá? ¿dondé esta? (what happened to my mother? where is she?)

regla: es tu culpa, maria. (it's your fault, maria.)

transition. regla disappears.

end of scene.

13.

claudia dumps a bloody towel at maria's feet.

claudia: what's this?

maria: i don't know.

claudia: what is going on? did you do this to yourself?

maria: i don't know.

claudia: this isn't like you.

maria: how do you know?

claudia: you've done this before?

maria: look, i don't know what happened... i was reading your article... i was just reading your article...

claudia: shhhhh... let me see your leg.

maria: (terrified.) no.

claudia: let me see your leg.

a moment. maria parts her robe and exposes her legs. there are multiple cuttings on them. claudia looks away, terrified.

silence.

silence.

silence.

maria: look at me.

claudia: i can't.

maria: you can't?

i see.

so when you want to write about your little vampires with masks nailed to their faces… you can't tear yourself away. it's art. it's… it's… it's the subject of a goddamn! fucking! article! but when it's real, in front of your face…

claudia strikes maria.

silence.

silence.

silence.

transition.

        end of scene.

14.

maria alone.

maria: i see anna on the island. she is running in between the rocks. the crevices. she feels

the jagged surfaces scraping her. her arms.
her legs. she feels the sting of the salt water
on her cuts. did she get lost? was she doing it
on purpose?

above the rocks, she sees the sky. a cloudless
blue sky. she stares at it, trying to figure out
how to describe it. cobalt? turquoise? but it
defies her. it triumphs over her. she can only
say "that is a cloudless blue sky." but it's
more. much more.

claudia appears holding a camera. she points
it at maria.

maria: and then anna sees claudia's blonde
head peering down at her. claudia extends her
hand towards anna and when anna sees the
sky ripple, she realizes the sky is actually the
sea. claudia keeps staring into the water. she
is looking right at anna, but she doesn't see
her.

claudia takes a picture. flash.

claudia takes another picture. flash.

claudia takes one last picture. flash.

claudia is replaced by regla. she holds the
broken statue.

regla: desgraciada. malagradecida. asquerosa. pidele perdon a la virgen. (miserable. ungrateful. filthy. ask the virgin for forgiveness.)

maria: i can't breathe... i can't breathe...

regla: que hiciste, maria? (what have you done, maria?)

maria: it was an accident.

regla: no importa! a la virgen se tiene que respetar. a la virgen se tiene que temer. (it doesn't matter! the virgin should be respected. the virgin should be feared.)

regla sets the statue before maria.

regla: no le tienes miedo a la caridad? (aren't you afraid of la caridad?)

maria: i don't understand.

the woman appears behind maria and puts her hand on her shoulder.

woman: don't be afraid.

regla: esta virgen me recuerda de tu mamá.

a moment. the woman looks at the statue.

maria: (to the woman.) i don't understand.

woman: this statue...

this statue...

... reminds her of your... mother.

regla: le rese a la caridad del cobre...

woman: she prayed...

regla: y le pedi...

woman: and she begged...

regla: por una hija.

woman: she prayed for... for a... a daughter

regla: pero no salia en estado.

woman: she couldn't get pregnant.

regla: y le ofrecí hasta mi propia vida...

woman: she offered her life...

regla: pero día tras día sentia un dolor en mi
vientre.

woman: there was pain... a pain in her womb.
like a fist.

regla: como un puño. y le dije a la virgen que se vaya pa'l carajo.

woman: she told the virgin to go to hell.

regla: ells que fur dichosa. escogida.

woman: what did the virgin know? the virgin had been fortunate. she had been chosen.

regla: ella no comprendía este dolor.

woman: the virgin didn't understand this pain.

regla: vete pa'l carajo, le dije!

woman: she told her to go to hell and then...

regla: salí en estado.

woman: she was pregnant.

regla: tu abuelo estaba orgulloso, pero yo tuve miedo.

woman: she was afraid.

regla: mi furia, mis palabras encabronaron la virgen y pensé que me había maldecido.

woman: her fury, her words angered the virgin and she thought the virgin had cursed her.

regla: pero el parto fue bueno, y mi hija bella.

woman: the birth went well and she... she
found me beautiful.

regla: beautiful.

woman: la felicidad le vino a los treinta años,
por fín.

regla: happiness came to me at thirty. finally.

woman: esos ojitos negros como asabaches.

regla: those little black eyes, like onyxes.

woman: me llamó caridad para que la virgen
no me hiciera daño.

regla: i named her caridad so the virgin
wouldn't hurt her.

caridad: me llamó caridad para que yo fuera
dichosa. escogida.

regla: i named her caridad so she would be
fortunate. chosen.

caridad: and i was. fui escogida.

caridad removes something from her body,
perhaps a piece of jewelry and sets it before
regla.

maria: and then what happened?

silence.

maria: please, abuela, tell me what happened
to her? where has she gone? i need to know.

regla: rompiste a mi virgen. (you've broken
my virgin.)

regla disappears, leaving maria and caridad
alone.

caridad: ya sabes.

maria: you are not her.

caridad: who else would i be?

caridad holds up the photograph of the ocean.

caridad: how far into the ocean did you feel
like walking that day? how much did you
desire to submerge yourself? how intensely
did you long for the silence below the surface?

maria is silent.

caridad: you felt compelled. possessed.

maria: i didn't drown.

caridad: perhaps not then. but your desire
must have been strong enough to cause your
eye to find this arm among the waves of the
caribbean.

maria: that day... the day i walked to the
ocean, i was in italy. that was the
mediterranean.

caridad: no. this is the caribbean. look at the
color of the water.

it's so blue. a distinct shade.

the blue of a vein. you were remembering...

maria: i wasn't remembering anything.

caridad: (singing.)

> ausencia quiere decir olvido,
>   (absence means forgetting)
> decir tinieblas, decir jamás;
>   (means darkness, means never)
> las aves suelen volver al nido
>   (birds desire to return to the nest)
> pero las almas que se han querido
>   (but the souls who have been loved)
> cuando se alejan no vuelven más.
>   (when they go, do not return)

i used to sing that looking out at the water. at the caribbean. turbulent. like a hurricane was happening. a small fishing boat is rocking on the surface. three men named juan sitting there.

maria: that's the story of la caridad.

caridad: they are looking for her. she had disappeared one day on the beach. they scan the surface. the green and blue that turns grey and white in the middle of a storm. they search for anything. a hand, an arm, her dark black hair fanning out among the waves. we hear them talking. we hear them asking: what caused her to do this? what caused her to go out into the sea on a night like this?

maria: that's not the story!

caridad: it's my story. it is also your story.

she extends a hand holding a razor.

caridad: take it.

maria reaches out her hand.

caridad: you are compelled. possessed. i can tell.

maria retreats her hand.

maria: no. i don't think so.

caridad: es imposible escapar.

she folds up the razor. darkness.

end of scene.

15.

in the darkness, we hear regla's voice.

regla: en tu silencio,
      in your silence
         escuchame.
      hear me.
         en tu oscuridad,
      in your darkness
         mirame.
      see me.
         obedéceme
      obey me
         con tu alma,
      with your soul
         con tu mente
      with your mind
         y con tu corazón.
      and with your heart.
         no es a un hombre
      it isn't a man
         que se debe obedecer,
      you must obey

si no a dios el señor.
but god, our lord.
maria...
maria...
maria...
maria...
despierta...
wake up...

claudia: she's waking.

end of scene.

16.

the lights come up on maria tucked into a bed
made on the apartment's couch. next to her
are regla and claudia.

maria: abuela?

regla: maria.

claudia: i called her.

maria: what?

regla: you have been sick.

maria: when did you learn english?

claudia: she's spoke english just fine to me on the phone. (to regla.) she's terrible. she's told me you don't speak any english at all.

regla: i do what i can.

maria: we always spoke spanish. we never spoke english.

claudia: she refuses to speak español around me. we do a little italiano.

regla: are you italian?

claudia: me? god, no. iowa.

regla: i am sure it's very pretty. iowa.

claudia: you don't have to say that.

maria: what are you doing here? que haces aquí?

regla: (to claudia.) my granddaughter always liked the italian. i do not have any idea porqué.

claudia: they're similar, though, aren't they?

regla: that is what they say.

maria: they're completely different.

regla: spanish is so beautiful, so useful, so important if you want good work. that is what i hear. i do not hear any person saying that they must learn the italian. but what do i know? i am a miserable old woman. i am old fashioned and not used to the modern ways. she is the one who knows it all. i suppose she is the expert.

maria: you suppose?

claudia: cara, don't get all crazy. you've had a rough couple of nights. (to regla.) she was clutching her inhaler in her sleep. it must be the smoking.

regla: she smokes?

maria: claudia, i can't believe you would do this.

claudia: you were out cold for two days. what the hell do you expect me to do?

regla: relax yourself, maria, and i will make you manzanilla. that always calmed you.

claudia: manzanilla?

maria: (to claudia.) chamomile. (to regla.) no quiero.

regla: (hissing.) no seas majadera conmigo, hija.

maria: claudia, where's my inhaler?

regla: (to claudia.) she doesn't need the medicine. she needs to calm herself. she is too nervous.

maria: didn't i tell you she's a witch? get me the inhaler. (to regla.) esta es mi casa.

regla: cuidadito, que estas muy equivocada.

claudia hands maria the inhaler and she takes a hit.

maria: my grandfather died because of her. he got sick. instead of a doctor, she brought him a priest.

regla: (to claudia.) please, can you boil some water for the tea?

claudia: i don't think we have any chamomile.

regla pulls out a bag from her purse.

regla: i brought it with me. it is a special blend.

maria: (getting up.) claudia, don't.

regla presses her back down.

regla: quedate! (to claudia.) the water, please.

claudia: sí, señora. (to maria.) you're being
impossible.

claudia leaves the room. regla walks over to
the door and closes it.

maria: quando aprendiste el ingles?

regla: since you left me, i practiced every day.
i was waiting. i was always waiting. day after
day. hour after hour. i was very patient. i
knew it was impossible for you to escape
from me. i was like a mother to you. salute
me the way i deserve, hija. press your lips to
my cheek.

maria: you have not changed a bit.

regla: i am still your grandmother. i don't care
who you think you are, but i still deserve
respect.

maria: i will ask you very politely then. abuela,
please go. i do not want to see you.

regla: but i cannot leave you like this. sick. in
bed. i am taking you home.

maria: this is my home.

regla: your home is with me. in miami.

maria: no!

regla: how care you say no to me?

maria: i don't want to go back to that horrible place. that backwards place. i never belonged there.

regla: of course you did. you are my family.

maria: i wanted nothing more than to escape. to get the hell out and not come back to the... the ridiculousness. it's like... a beast. it's a pair of claws wrapped around your neck, choking you.

regla: and what about here? you are not happy in this house.

maria: i am extremely happy.

regla: you aren't married.

maria: i don't intend to be.

regla: a woman should not be alone. we need to take care of things. things that belong to us. i don't know what i would have done if i did not have you with me after i lost your grandfather and your mother.

maria: i take care of claudia.

regla: that kind of caring is not enough.

maria: why don't you tell me what you mean.

regla: no es mi lugar—

maria: —no. no es tu lugar—

regla: —there are cuts on your legs...

maria: those are scratches.

regla: scratches, eh? don't think i don't see...
don't think i don't know. la americana wants
you out of here. i can tell.

maria: that is not true!

regla: you have tried to run away. you have
tried to escape. but you haven't gone
anywhere at all. i am going to go into the
kitchen and see if your amiguita needs help
with the manzanilla.

maria: you do that.

regla exits. regla enters the kitchen and looks
at claudia, who is arranging the tea cups.

regla: i will make the tea.

claudia: it's no bother.

regla: i will make the tea.

claudia: okay.

she exits the kitchen and goes back into the bedroom. regla begins to make the tea.

claudia: she kicked me out of the kitchen.

maria: what part of "i never want to see her again" didn't you understand?

claudia: you were unconscious. i had to do something. i thought she could take care of you. i'm sorry.

maria: she wants me to go back to miami.

claudia: you're a grown woman. she can't control you. she can't make you do anything you don't want.

but why is it such a bad idea? what is it you're so afraid of?

maria: you actually want me to go with her?

claudia: i didn't say that... i'm just asking—

maria: (realizing regla was right.) oh, god...

she wasn't supposed to come here! she
doesn't exist here! miami doesn't exist here!

claudia: cara...

maria: i'm being sucked back! don't you see
that?

regla appears in the door, holding the tea.

regla: maria, drink this.

maria: claudia, please, help me...

claudia: you're acting like a child, cara.

regla: (to claudia.) please hold her down.

claudia doesn't move.

regla: please hold her down.

claudia holds down maria as regla advances
with the tea. there is a struggle. regla expertly
pries maria's mouth open and pours the tea
down her throat.

maria: it's burning me... i'm being sucked
back.

regla: sleep. you will feel better when you
wake up. and then we can go home.

maria: (crying.) claudia... help...

claudia: (to regla.) what was in that tea?

the tea begins to take effect. maria struggles out of bed. regla tries to grab her.

regla: maria, calmate.

maria musters whatever strength she has left and pushes regla away.

maria: see here. both of you. i will not go. i will not.

she runs into the bathroom, locking the door behind her.

claudia: i don't know what's going on.

regla: give her time.

claudia: i found her two days ago, passed out and calling out for caridad. who is that?

a moment.

regla: it is la caridad del cobre. she is the patron saint of cuba. there is a story that three fishermen, three men named juan were out in the ocean and they thought they saw a drowning girl, but it was the statue of the

virgin floating in the waves. it was a miracle,
the holy mother appearing to them like that.
there is a shrine to her in cobre where people
ask her for miracles.

claudia: does that work?

regla: no. no it doesn't. there are no miracles.
only curses.

darkness.

> end of scene.

16.

maria is slumped against the bathroom door,
drugged from the tea. time is slowly
suspended. imagery from l'avventura flickers
throughout.

maria: (chanting, trying to keep herself awake)
> her face.
> her eyes.
> her skin.
> like porcelain.
> like paper.
> claudia.
> on the island.
i can almost understand her.
> she looks for anna.
> anna has disappeared.
> anna...

freeze frame on lea masari's face in closeup. caridad appears.

caridad: disappeared?

maria: she escaped. she makes a clean and perfect escape.

caridad: is that what you want?

maria: right now? yes. more than anything.

caridad: i can help you.

a moment.

maria: (decisive.) how?

over the following, lea masari's image slowly turns into a closeup of barbara steele in la maschera del demonio.

caridad: in that house. in miami. there was a door that was never meant to be opened. you were told: do not! ni te atrevas! you were terrified, reaching out for the doorknob in the dark. and the knob would grow slicker, slippery with your sweat. you wondered what was behind the door. another set of rooms with people living there? that other set of

rooms, that place, that city, that country that
lay behind the door you called it cuba.

maria: how did you—

caridad: the pictures you drew. the dreams
you had. remember? there was a woman.
very elegant. nice dress. sunglasses. heels.
gloves. she's walking down the street when
she stops for a moment. she opens her purse
looking for something... her lipstick? a tissue?
a piece of candy? she's not really paying
attention to the shadow that falls over her, but
when she looks up... close up on the reflection
of his mouth stretched back to reveal long,
thick incisors and a tiny stream of saliva
sliding out. she runs. she runs as fast as she
can until she gets to the ocean. and she
wonders. does she leap in and drown or does
she stay on the island with the vampire? but
before she decides, before she is able to jump
in, the vampire sinks his teeth into her.

caridad removes her gloves revealing wounds
from slashed wrists.

this is cuba. do you remember?

maria: oh my god...

in a panic, she tries to open the bathroom
door to get away from caridad. caridad
quickly gets between maria and the door.

regla: maria!

caridad: are you insane? she's out there. you can't just run out there like that.

regla: (from the other side of the door.) maria, abre la puerta!

maria: (dizzy.) everything's green and blue...

caridad: she's got hold of you. you have to listen to me.

maria: (dizzier) everything's blue and green and now it's turning grey and white...

caridad: no matter what happens, you have to try opening that door. that unopenable door.

maria: there's nothing behind that door. it's just the apartment next door to this one.

caridad: that's not the door i'm talking about.

maria: i feel sick...

caridad: look at me! listen to me!

the door in miami...

maria: (dizzy.) hand on doorknob. i wanted to make it turn... and one day it happened.

whispering. the door began to speak. they were calling my name. it sounded like my name...

... my name...
... my name...

i tried to open that door, but i never could.

caridad: you need this.

she takes out the razor.

regla: maria, me oyes?

caridad: give me your hand.

maria: no.

caridad: i want to help you.

claudia: cara, please come out. i want to see you.

maria: you want to hurt me!

caridad: tesoro mio, i would never want to hurt you. stop resisting.

mirame...

mirame, marea...

maria: what did you call me?

caridad: marea.

maria: that's not my name.

caridad: don't you think i would know your name? don't you think i would know you?

she reaches out and puts her hand on maria's face. maria looks at caridad.

a moment.

maria reaches out her hand and caridad gently puts the razor in maria's hand.

a moment.

maria slashes at caridad with the razor. she hits caridad's arm. caridad grabs her arm in pain.

caridad: que hiciste, marea?

maria: (dropping the razor) what you wanted to do to me.

she grabs the doorknob of the bathroom door.

caridad: you're making a mistake.

maria: i'm escaping.

caridad: that is impossible, hija.

maria: you don't tell me what's possible.

not you.

maria reaches for a door, she opens it and...

darkness except for the un-openable door, which glows blue.

and then...

end of scene.

1.

projection: the opening credits for a black and white film (reminiscent of black sunday/la maschera del demonio and other italian gothic horror of the period.

el italiano productions presents
an e.b. scott film
the escape

starring

sharon lorraine o'douglass
as "la hija"

juliana hitchcock
as "la abuela"

beatrice luna
as "la madre"

and introducing

mildrina solomon
as "monica"

written by les a. moore

exterior: a dark, gloomy gothic looking manse.
a dark and stormy night. lightning. thunder.
creepy wind rustling through bare branches.
over this image, a title informs us:

"miami"

the projection dissolves as the stage becomes
the setting for the film we are about to watch.
the set is some sort of adaptation of a set
we've seen before. the new york apartment
should magically transform into the miami
house, whether through lighting, projection,
or an "elegant prop" i.e., one object that
manages to symbolically transform the space.
the geography of the house is the same—
three doors. one to the bathroom, one to the
bedroom and one that leads we know not
where.

we hear, among the sounds of the storm, a
faint voice:

voice: (caridad/la madre.)
      es imposible escapar
      los recuerdos del mar.
      es imposible dejar
      los recuerdos del mar.
      es imposible borrar
      los recuerdos del mar.

      imposible escapar
      imposible dejar
      imposible borrar
      los recurdos del mar.

the singing is eerie and ghostly. la hija (a.k.a.
maria) appears. she follows the sound of the
singing. she is in a trance. she follows the
sound to the mysterious door. she tries to
open the door but it does not open. she
keeps trying harder and harder. more and
more frenetically.

from the "kitchen," la abuela (aka regla)
appears. she is dressed in very formal dark
clothes. she has been working in the kitchen.
she wears an apron, which is perfectly white.

la abuela: what are you doing?

la hija stops. she "awakes" with a start.

la hija: abuela!

she notices something is not right.

la hija: what happened? i was sleeping... i
didn't...

la abuela: come over here, child. let me look
at you.

la hija walks over to la abuela. la abuela feels
for a temperature, makes other small random
checks over la hija.

la hija: i'm sorry to wake you.

la abuela: you know i never sleep.

i was in the kitchen. preparing the meat for
our dinner for tomorrow. the knives needed
the sharpening. i like to take my time.
sharpening the knives. very slowly. very
carefully.

you were sleepwalking. this is very unusual
for you, child.

la hija: i was having the most terrible dream.

la abuela: tell me about this dream. perhaps
there is something in this dream that may help
us to discover why it is you were walking in
your sleep.

la hija: i was in this house. i didn't recognize
it, but in the dream i knew it was supposed to
be my home. i was dressed in unusual
clothes. they were very fine. very expensive.
my shoes were beautiful. my hair was
beautiful. i was looking at a book of
photographs. photographs of an island made
entirely of rock. as i kept looking at the
photographs, i began to feel a pain in my
chest. i could not breathe.

and then...

she stops herself.

that's when you woke me up.

abuela, i was so scared.

she throws her arms around la abuela. la
abuela remains firm.

la abuela: control yourself, child.

it is this storm outside that has scared you.
the wind and the rain and the lighting and the
thunder. that is all.

this is nothing to get hysterical about. do you
hear me?

la hija nods.

la abuela: very good. you will come sit with
me in the kitchen. you will be very quiet
while i make you some tea. you will drink this
tea and you will see how much better you will
sleep. it is a very special recipe.

come.

la hija: abuela... i have always wondered...

la abuela: yes, child?

la hija: what is behind that door?

la abuela: what door, child?

la hija: this one over here. i have never seen it
open.

la abuela: that is because that door does not
open.

now come with me so i can make you the tea.

she points to the kitchen. la hija exits in that
direction. once she has exited, la abuela looks
towards the door.

la abuela: (to the door.) control yourself.

darkness.

end of scene.

2.

the following evening. thunder and lightning.
the wind. the same ghostly voice.

voice: (caridad/the madre)
      es imposible escapar
      los recuerdos del mar.
      es imposible dejar
      los recuerdos del mar.
      es imposible borrar
      los recuerdos del mar.

      imposible escapar
      imposible dejar
      imposible borrar
      los recurdos del mar.

      marea...
      marea...

la hija appears. she follows the sound of the
singing. she is in a trance. she follows the
sound to the mysterious door. she tries to
open the door but it does not open. she
keeps trying harder and harder. more and
more frenetically. then she notices something
slide under the door. she reaches down and
takes it in her hand. it is a razor.

la abuela enters from the kitchen.

la abuela: what are you doing, child?

la hija wakes with a start and sees the razor in her hand. she gasps and drops the razor to the floor. la abuela rushes to pick it up.

la abuela: where did you get this?

la hija: i was dreaming.

la abuela: the same dream?

la hija: it was different this time.

la abuela: different?

la hija: i was standing in the water, holding a camera. i don't know why and then a wave came and everything got dark and then a voice called to me and i... i don't remember the rest.

la abuela: to the kitchen, please. i will make you the tea again.

la hija: the voice... it was saying something. like it was calling my name. marea...

la abuela: marea?

la hija: what do you think it means?

la abuela: to the kitchen.

la hija exits to the kitchen. la abuela looks at
the razor. darkness.

                    end of scene.

3.

la abuela prepares an altar for la caridad del
cobre. this should be simple, elegant and
sincere—either she lights a candle, or puts
some flowers in a vase. perhaps she holds a
rosary.

la abuela: (singing)
        ausencia quiere decir olvido,
                (absence means forgetting)
        decir tinieblas, decir jamás;
                (means darkness, means never)
        las aves suelen volver al nido
            (birds desire to return to the nest)
        pero las almas que se han querido
            (but the souls who have been loved)
        cuando se alejan no vuelven más.
                (when they go, do not return)

la hija steps into the room and sees la abuela
kneeling before the altar.

la hija: abuela?

la abuela looks at la hija, surprised.

la hija: abuela?

la abuela looks at la hija, surprised.

la abuela: i thought you were asleep.

la hija: tell me about that song.

la abuela: what song?

la hija: the one you were just singing.

la abuela: i wasn't singing anything.

pray with me in silence or go to bed.

a moment. la hija kneels down next to la
abuela. she looks at the statue.

la hija: she's beautiful.

la abuela: in silence.

darkness.
     end of scene.

4.

later. la abuela and la hija. la abuela is laying
out a dress for la hija. it is simple and somber.

la hija slowly gets dressed and la abuela helps her, does her hair, etc.

la abuela: during my prayer, i received a vision. a word of advice.

la hija: about my dreams?

la abuela: yes, child. about your dreams.

these are nothing to be feared. that is why i have written to our spiritual director to pay us a visit. i have told him of our problems here and i have said to him that we will remain inside this house until he arrives to guide us.

la hija: when will that be?

la abuela: i do not know about these things. our spiritual director is very busy as he has many souls in greater despair to help. he will arrive when he arrives. we must be ready. we must prepare for him.

la hija: and never leave this house?

la abuela: that is correct. there is no need to leave this house. we are safe in here. we will wait until our spiritual director arrives to us and he will counsel you through prayer. you will sleep through the night again. trust in me.

la abuela notices something on la hija's leg.

la abuela: what is that?

la hija: what?

la abuela: that on your leg. is that a cut?

la hija: no. just a scratch.

la abuela: that is very deep for a scratch.

la hija: i must have scratched myself in my
sleep.

la abuela: in your sleep?

la hija: what's the matter, abuela?

la abuela: nothing. nothing's the matter.

i want us to be ready for him. he can show up
at any time. i want us to be in a state of divine
meditation and contemplation so he can see
we are good people. we love god. we don't
deserve to have maladies visit our house.

she hands la hija a copy of the lives of the
saints.

read to me from this book about the saints.
we will take turns reading and praying.

la hija: (opening the book and reading.) santa
barbara.

la abuela: santa barbara...

la abuela closes her eyes. a shift.

la hija: barbara could feel the blade. she could
sense the shiver of the sword as her father
held it to her neck. pulse against steel. the
moment, the waiting, the second he hesitated
wondering if he could do this to his own
daughter.

la abuela caresses the statue. la madre
appears. she is dressed very simply, perhaps a
white dress. her hair done as a girl of 16 or
so.

la hija: she who was so wicked to defy him.

la madre:
ausencia quiere decir olvido,
           (absence means forgetting)
decir tinieblas, decir jamás;
           (means darkness, means never)
las aves suelen volver al nido
      (birds desire to return to the nest)
pero las almas que se han querido
      (but the souls who have been loved)
cuando se alejan no vuelven más.
           (when they go, do not return)

la hija: all in the name of this man. this
imaginary god. this jesus christ.

la abuela: (singing.) no te lo dice la luz que
expira,
          (the dying light does not tell you)
sombra es ausencia, desolación.
          (absence is shadow, desolation)
si tantos sueños fueron mentiras,
          (if so many dreams were lies)
por qué te quejas cuando suspira
          (then why do you complain)
tan hondamente mi corazón.
          (when my heart sighs so deeply?)

la madre: mamá.

la madre sits at her la abuela's feet and places
her   head in her lap.

la hija: and in that second, barbara thought of
the water in the bath house her father had
built. she thought of herself naked, standing
waist deep in the water. her skin gathered in
gooseflesh as she watched the light penetrate
the three windows of the bathhouse. she had
no need for the touch of any living creature.
she had transcended beyond such ordinary
and petty things. she was ether. she was
evaporating there in the water, slowly
disappearing every day.

la madre: tengo miedo, mamá. creo que algo
terrible me ha pasado.
(mother, i am afraid. i think something
terrible has happened to me.)

la abuela: (stroking caridad's hair.) nada te
pasara. el señor te proteje.
(nothing will happen to you. the lord will
protect you.)

la hija: so she did not feel the blade. she did
not notice when her father drew his arm up,
bringing the blade down hard on her neck.
first cut. he raised his arm again, bringing it
down even harder.

la madre: tengo miedo, mamá. nadie me ha
protejido. (mother, i am afraid. no one has
protected me.)

la hija: second cut.

      la madre: nadie. (no one.)

      la abuela: (writhing in pain.)
      preciosa
          (precious.)
      querida
          (beloved.)
      purisima
          (purest.)
      mi unico tesoro
          (my only treasure.)

mi unico amor.
       (my only love.)
mi linda.
       (my lovely.)
mi hija.
       (my daughter.)
la madre: nadie.
       (no one.)

la hija: blood from the jugular stained the
blade, sprayed his tunic.

la abuela: ay!

la hija: arm raised again, bringing it down
rapidly for the third and final cut.

la madre: es tu culpa, mamá.
(it's your fault, mother.)

la hija: three blows sever the bone, the muscle,
the sinew.

la abuela: mi hija, no me dejes! (my child,
don't leave me!)

la madre disappears.

la hija: three blows for the father, the son and
the holy ghost.

thunder and lightning. the un-openable door
begins to rattle. the doorknob begins to
shake.

la abuela: that's enough child!

la hija: abuela, what's happening?

la abuela: nothing. nothing is happening. go
to your room!

la hija: the door! someone is behind it!

la hija: get those ideas out of your head. they
are fantasies!

the door rattling intensifies with the sound of
a hand banging on the door.

la hija: it's her, isn't it? the woman in my
dreams! it's her!

la hija runs to the door. trying to open it.

la hija: it's her! it's her!

la abuela: (striking la hija violently.) no! do
not touch that door! ni te atrevas!

the rattling stops. la hija is immobile on the
ground. she doesn't say a word. she does not
cry.

5.

la hija in her bedroom, thumbing through her lives of the saints. an illustration catches her eye. she holds the book away from her so she can study the illustration.

la hija: the face...

the saint's face is projected. closeup.

la abuela knocks on the door. she is holding a teacup.

la abuela: i brought you manzanilla.

la hija: i don't want any.

la abuela: i made it just how you like it... with a little bit of honey.

la hija opens the door. a moment. la abuela extends the teacup.

la abuela: take it.

a moment. la hija takes the teacup. she does not drink.

la abuela: you must understand me, child. i am trying to make sure you are better. that you have no more dreams that disturb you.

la hija: i know, abuela.

sometimes... sometimes i feel like there's a part of me that isn't quite right. like i can't ever sit still until i figure out—

la abuela:
—all you need to figure out is prayer. that will help you.

la hija: tell me about my mother.

a moment.

la abuela: you shouldn't trouble yourself with stories from the past.

la hija: do you think she thinks about me?

la abuela: your mother didn't think about anyone but herself. i don't think you should trouble yourself with someone like that.

she caresses la hija's face.

you look tired. drink your tea before it gets cold.

la hija: i'll drink it later.

la abuela: drink it now and hand me the cup.

a moment. la hija drinks the tea and silently hands the cup back to la abuela. la abuela produces a key.

la abuela: i am locking your door from the outside. i want you to stay in your room and sleep.

la hija: of course.

la abuela closes the door and locks it. la hija slumps to the floor with her book. she turns to the same illustration. it is projected again.

la hija: (singing.)
     es imposible dejar
     los recuerdos del mar ...
     imposible escapar ...
     imposible escapar ...
     imposible escapar ...

the saint's face becomes la madre's face.

la madre: marea...

la hija: mamá?

la madre: abre la puerta... (open the door)

la hija: abre... la... puerta...

she passes out. darkness. in darkness we hear
la abuela's voice.

la abuela:
quedate en tu oscuridad.   (stay in your
darkness.)
quedate en tu silencio.   (stay in your
silence.)
quedate en tu miseria.   (stay in your
misery.)
sagrado sea el dolor.   (the pain is
sacred.)
amado sea el dolor.   (the pain is
loved.)
sanctificado sea el dolor.   (the pain is
blessed.)
glorioso sea el dolor.   (the pain is
glorious.)
duermete, maria.   (go to sleep,
maria.)
duermete.   (go to sleep.)

                    end of scene.

6.

the next day. it is still raining. there is a
knock at the door. la abuela runs over to it.
she pauses before she gets there and calls out.

la abuela: who is it?

monica: (off.) it is your spiritual director, signora.

la abuela opens the door. monica is standing cold and shivering in the rain. she is wearing dark shades, a coat, and a kerchief over her head. monica speaks with a non-specific "foreign" accent...

la abuela: you?

monica: can i come in? it is... cold and it is... wet out here.

la abuela: how do i know you are really our spiritual director?

monica: i have your letter?

she hands la abuela a letter.

monica: i have come about your granddaughter. la piccola pequeña.

la abuela: she's not so pequeña any more. she is 30 years old.

lightning. thunder. la abuela crosses herself.

la abuela: please come in.

monica: thank you.

why did you just do that?

la abuela: do what?

monica: you crossed yourself.

la abuela: it is the storm. it makes me
nervous.

can i offer you something to drink? tea?

monica: oh no. i am on strict orders from the
cardinal. i must drink this holy water.

she takes out a flask.

for penance, you see.

she takes a sip.

la abuela: i see.

how is it you are the spiritual director? you
are not a priest.

monica: i have been called to god, signora. i
am a special case the holy father himself has
become aware of. god has granted me
a... sensitivity to matters such as your
granddaughter's.

la abuela: what are the matters those would be?

monica: dreams. hysteria.

la abuela: she needs prayer.

monica: does she use a discipline? a hairshirt?

la abuela: no! of course not!

monica: are you opposed to using a discipline, signora?

la abuela: no. if our spiritual dir-... sorry, if you felt it was necessary for her to use one, there would be no discussion. she would use one.

i think she's a good girl.

i have done everything i could. i have been strict. very strict.

monica: but there are matters of which you know nothing about. that is why i am here.

la abuela: you think i haven't raised her right?

monica: signora, calm yourself. don't you trust me?

la abuela: you are a woman.

monica: that's what they tell me.

she produces a small box and hands it to la abuela.

monica: a gift.

la abuela opens it. it is a rosary.

la abuela: it's beautiful.

monica: the crucifix has a relic inside of it. st. lucy.

la abuela: st. lucy!

monica: she was a true saint.

now if you excuse me, i need to use the... facilities. the how you say, the baño?

she instinctively walks towards the un-openable door.

la abuela: that door does not open.

monica: not open? how strange!

la abuela: (pointing to the bathroom.) that is the door you want.

monica: thank you.

a moment. monica enters the bathroom.

la hija comes out of her room.

la hija: is that...?

la abuela: it was.

la hija: she's... she's a... she.

la abuela: i am surprised. but she brought our letter. she came from the cardinal himself.

i know it seems strange, but there are many strange things in this world and we must put our faith in god. if he has chosen for this woman to be our spiritual director, we must obey her word.

la hija: abuela, what is a discipline?

la abuela: don't you mind about that thing, child. you listen to the spiritual director and do what she says.

thunder and lightning. monica steps out of the bathroom. for a moment the lights go out due to the storm and we see monica's silhouette in the bathroom door. the lights restore. monica walks over to la hija.

monica: hello. i'm monica.

la hija: i'm maria.

monica: how are you, maria?

la hija: nervous.

la abuela: there is no need to be nervous!

monica: (in a much calmer voice than la abuela.) no, maria, there is no need to be so nervous. we're going to be good friends, i'm sure. (to la abuela.) now, if you will excuse us, signora.

la abuela: excuse you?

monica: i would like to speak to maria alone.

la abuela: why?

monica: signora, when you go to confession you go in alone, do you not?

la abuela: but you are not a priest! this is not confession.

monica: very well. i will have my driver take me back to the cardinal. you can solve this little problem on your own.

la hija: abuela!

la abuela: i don't feel right about this.

monica walks over to la abuela.

monica: (taking la abuela's hands in hers.)
signora, remember that rosary i gave you?

la abuela: yes.

monica: it would help me and your
granddaughter if you could go into the other
room and pray several rosaries for us. like
you said, maria needs prayer. she needs your
prayers.

la abuela: i pray for her! every day!

monica: i know you do. but don't you see she
needs more? think of saint lucy and
everything she endured. think of her and find
the strength.

will you do that for me?

la abuela nods.

la abuela: she's in your hands.

thunder and lightning as la abuela exits. la hija
and monica stand at opposite ends of the
room.

la hija: can i get you something?

monica produces her flask.

monica: i'm fine thank you.

sit.

la hija sits down as monica takes a sip from her flask. monica sits down opposite la hija and lights a cigarette. she notices la hija has been staring at her intently.

monica: why are you looking at me like that?

la hija: i have never seen anyone like you before.

monica: there is nothing so special about me.

la hija: the way you dress. the way you sit. the smoke.

monica: you like the way i smoke?

she exhales... knowing she looks fabulous doing it.

well, let me assure you, maria, this... what you see... is very common out there in the world.

la hija: is it? i have always wondered.

monica: i take it you don't see much of the world, do you?

maria: my grandmother is very devout. i'm surprised she's letting you smoke.

monica: i come from the cardinal. i can do what is necessary.

people smoke out there in the world, you know. the world god made. god made this cigarette, maria, the same way he made you. and he made me.

la hija: but my grandmother would say those are temptations god has put in our way to test us.

monica: i'm very good with temptation, don't you know?

you are still staring at me.

la hija: you aren't like the other spiritual directors i've seen.

monica: well, that i will grant you. the cardinal is... progressive.

he understands that i am the best person to help you. i am not a priest, no. not even a nun. but i have been called to serve. the

cardinal asked god to give him a sign and that
night he dreamt of the holy mother.

la hija: the holy mother!

monica: he sends me out to special cases.
cases like you.

la hija: i'm special?

monica: you have these dreams. i understand
about dreams. if you learn to see them
properly they can reveal much of god's plan.
like they did with the cardinal and me. do you
understand?

la hija nods.

monica: so shall we help you get better?

la hija: that is what my grandmother wants.

monica: and what do you want?

silence.

la hija: i want to stop having these dreams.

monica: that didn't sound very convincing.

tell me what you want. tell me what i can do
for you.

la hija: i'm not so sure. i don't know why these dreams are bad.

monica: what does your grandmother say?

la hija: she doesn't say anything.

thunder. lightning.

la hija: that's some storm.

monica: it feels like it's going to start raining in here any minute. i can feel it. everything feels...

la hija: the room is waiting.

monica: waiting?

la hija: it feels like the room is waiting. to be ripped open. to be part of the storm. to be under water.

monica: (a touch patronizing.) well... before that happens why don't we talk about your dreams.

la hija: all right.

monica: (routine.) i want you to do me a favor.

close your eyes.

take deep breaths.

you are sitting in a movie theater.

la hija: a movie theater?

monica: haven't you ever seen a movie?

la hija shakes her head.

monica: well, let's see... how do i explain a movie to you? (italian.) che inocente!

la hija: (spanish.) incocente, si.

monica: (italian.) simpatica.

la hija beams.

monica: you like that, mmm?

she reaches over and pushes a stray lock of la hija's hair back behind her ear or touches la hija's cheek. a moment.

la hija: tell me about the movies.

monica: when you go to a movie, you go to a theater. which is... well, it's like a church. there's an aisle and seats on each side. and in front of you, instead of an altar is a white wall. but like the church, there is something that

occurs miraculously in this theater. imagine a
beautiful stained glass window behind you.
the sun shines through it and the light flies
over your head onto the white wall in front of
you... and you see.

la hija: what do you see?

monica: what you desire but you cannot
express. what you fear but you cannot admit.
you see yourself. you see the world.

i think... i think i've seen more angels at the
movies than i have in a church.

a moment.

la hija: are you all right?

monica: yes, of course. excuse me.

monica takes a swig from her flask.

monica: so. your dream.

close your eyes for me.

la hija closes her eyes.

good.

you are in a movie theater.

your dream flies above you in the dark and
lands on the white wall in front of you. you
see it there in every tiny detail.

what do you see, maria?

la hija: there's a woman. and i am not her.
but i feel like i am inside her. i think what she
thinks. i feel what she feels.

as la hija recounts the dream, the space shifts
so we too go into the dream with la hija.

she is walking down the street and she stops
to look in her purse for something. a tissue?
her lipstick, maybe? a shadow falls over her
and then i see his face. his eyes. they are
blue. and he is... so beautiful. she takes one
look at him and she is terrified. he smiles at
her and she cannot help but turn her eyes
away from his smile... that perfect smile. she
decides to get away from him. she continues
walking down the street on her way to the
road that runs by the water. waves are
crashing up against the wall and she's walking
right towards the water. his shadow comes
after her. he will not let her go. she gets to
the wall that separates the land from the sea
and she cannot go any further. she turns
around and faces him. she will tell him to
stop. to leave her alone. she will make him
go away. but she looks at him and she can't
say a word. he puts his hand behind her neck

and i feel like i can't breathe. he slides his
hand up her neck and pulls her head towards
his and he kisses her. my lungs burn. and i
taste his mouth. i taste the salt from the wave
that has risen up to meet them. my eyes are
stinging from the salt.

she wants to run away, but she can't.

la hija looks over to the unopenable door,
which has been glowing blue. she starts
towards it. she sings:

es imposible dejar los recuerdos del mar.
es imposible escapar.
es imposible escapar...

la hija walks over to the door. she sees that
the straight razor is sliding out slowly from
underneath. she reaches down and picks it
up. she opens it. thunder and lightning.
monica reaches over and takes the razor,
snapping her out of the dream.

monica: maria...

la hija notices the razor.

la hija: again... that razor!

monica: this has happened before?

la hija: the other night. but abuela took the
razor from me.

what do you think it means?

a moment. monica looks at the razor.

monica: (dropping the accent. in fact she
sounds a lot like claudia) maria, i've lied to
you. i'm not a spiritual director. i'm...
associated with the cardinal. he's offered me...
guidance.

la hija: what sort of guidance?

monica: let's just say when i came to him and i
was lost.

it happens. you run into too many dead ends.
too many bad situations and i don't
know... that part of you that thinks "oh well,
better luck next time" just gets smaller and
smaller. and it happened so slowly, you
know? i didn't see it creeping up on me.

the doubt. the fear. and understanding that
this was all i deserved.

i thought the cardinal would help. maybe
believe in something else. something greater.
i confessed to him. my doubt. my fear. he
said i was weak and i needed to use the
discipline... and he...

la hija: he what?

monica shakes her head. she won't answer.
but we know what he does.

monica: he's not a bad man.

i mean, he... well, he's given me work. he's
helped me out. i work in his office and i help
him with his correspondence and... i would
read these letters over and over. these people
asking him for the same sort of help i needed.
i found myself hiding these letters from him.
he's a good man, but i felt... i felt i wanted to
help them. so i tried.

and he doesn't know.

it's a sin to lie of course, but i want to see
people suffering from something real.
something large. i want to see how their faith
helps them. i lie so that i may learn something
true for me... but every time i've been
disappointed. i just end up feeling as lost as
they are.

she holds up the razor.

but this! this is something large. something
real. something i can really see.

la hija: i don't understand.

monica: you made this happen! you! not me. not your grandmother. definitely not the cardinal. this is a possibility.

she looks at the razor.

i'm not going back to him. i should tell the driver to take me to the airport. get on a plane and go to an island. anywhere.

la hija is silent.

monica: maria?

la hija: that is not a possibility. it is a... a... sign of evil. an omen. and you say i made that happen? are you saying i'm evil?

monica: (handing her back the razor.) don't you see this is a clue? it has to mean something. what do you think this is for?

la hija: i don't know! i don't anything! i live in this house and do as i'm told. i have strange dreams. i walk in my sleep. and i don't know why. i feel like i'm thirsty all the time but for what i don't know. and she doesn't tell me anything. she makes me tea but it doesn't stop my thirst. it just puts me to sleep and the dreams begin again.

there is no escape.

monica: what would you like your grandmother to tell you?

silence.

monica: maria?

la hija: i never knew my mother. or my father.

monica: are they dead?

la hija: she won't say. she won't tell me anything.

i can't look at myself in the mirror. my face disintegrates. i am no one.

she very calmly runs the blade over her arm. she bleeds. she barely reacts. monica takes a handkerchief from her purse and wipes the blood off maria's arm. a moment. she puts her lips to the cut.

la hija: is that what he does for you?

monica shakes her head again. she is silent.

monica: you and i are the same, you know. sitting in the dark. waiting for that movie to start.

you know i want to help you.

la hija: you can't.

monica: i can help you open the lock on that door.

la hija: how?

a moment. monica glances over at the door. she realizes...

monica: i bet i can pick that lock.

she goes over to the door and takes a bobby pin out of her bag and she tries to pick the lock with it.

la hija: where did you learn to do that?

monica: let's just say there was a time in my life i thought it would come in handy.

a noise.

monica: what is that?

la hija: it's abuela.

monica: she's done with the rosary.

another noise.

la hija: we must do it quickly!

monica pokes around with the bobby pin. no luck.

another noise.

la hija: open the door.

monica: this is a simple lock. i've done these in my sleep.

la hija inspects the door.

la hija: it's painted shut.

monica: oh god, it is! wait! the razor! use the razor.

maria slices the razor between the door and the jamb. the door glows bright blue. the lock gives and the door opens on its own.

a moment.

another noise.

monica: go!

la hija: i'm falling. i'm falling right through.

she steps into the door frame. thunder and lightning, then everything goes blue. the sound of water.

the blue becomes the caribbean and then
cuba.

end of scene.

7.

cuba. caridad's room. she wears a white dress
similar to lea masari's in l'avventura. in fact
she should look like ana as much as possible.
she stands with her back to us looking in a
hand mirror. we see her reflection. a small
bassinet rests on a surface nearby. we do not
see the baby inside. until indicated, the scene
is subtitled or dubbed, similar to the scenes in
part one with maria and regla.

la madre: (practicing italian phrases.)
como si chiama?   (what's your name?)
como si chiama?   (what's your name?)
mi chiamo caridad. (my name is caridad.)
mi chiamo...   (my name is)
mi chiamo...   (my name is)
ti voglio bene   (i love you very much.)
ti voglio bene, sandro...
              (i love you very much, sandro.)

the baby cries. caridad sets down the mirror
and goes over to it. she puts her hand in the
bassinet to soothe the baby.

la madre: no te pongas asi, mi amor. no...
no... shhhhh...(don't get upset, my love.)

asi... (that's it.)

asi... (that's it.)

mira a mama... (look at mommy)

mirame, marea... (look at me marea)

asi... (that's it.)

anoche tuve un sueño.
          (i had a dream last night.)
estaba en una habitación estraña.
          (i was in a strange apartment.)
y una mujer muy triste
          (and a very sad woman.)
se arrascaba la piel
          (scratched herself.)
come si le picara algo
          (like something itched.)
mucho mucho mucho
          (very very very much.)
y emepezo sangrar.
          (and she started to bleed.)
y la agarre
          (and i grabbed her.)
porque queria protejerla
          (because i wanted to protect her.)
y abrazarla
          (and hold her.)

y decirle que no se procupara.
        (and to tell her not to worry.)
pero le puse la mano en el hombro
        (i touched her shoulder.)
y me miro con una cara
        (and she gave me this look.)
de terror.
        (of terror.)
que raro.
        (how strange.)

a moment. she shakes off the thought and
looks at her watch.

caridad:
ya son las doce.
        (it's noon.)
que te parece? nos vamos?

        (what do you think? shall we go?)
si, vamonos!
        (yes, we're going.)
no te lo habia dicho.
        (i wasn't going to tell you.)
queria darte la sorpresa,
        (i wanted to surprise you,)
pero hoy vamos a ver a tu papa.
        (but today we'll see your daddy.)
a mi sandro.
        (my sandro.)
si! a tu papi! que como lo se?
        (yes! your daddy! how do i know?)
porque si!

(because i do!)
me lo dice mi corazón.
(in my heart i know!)
se que ella me esta escondiendo sus cartas.

(i know she is hiding his letters.)
yo lo se.
(i know this.)
nos deja aqui encerradas en este cuarto las
dos.

(she leaves both of us locked up.)
la muy malvada. la muy bruta. bruta no.

(she's evil. she's a brute, no...)
bruja. hechizera!
(a witch. a sorceress!)

the baby cries.

no llores, no. que hoy nos vamos!
(don't cry, no. today we leave.)
si! si!   (yes!)
asi...   (that's it.)
asi...   (that's it.)
mira que linda!   (look how pretty!)

she blows the baby a kiss. she listens at the
door. she puts on her shoes. checks her
lipstick in the mirror. she takes her purse and
puts a few things in taken from a hiding place
in the room. the lipstick? an italian
phrasebook? a dried flower? and a straight

razor. before she puts the straight razor in
her bag, she walks over to the door with it.

la madre:
lo que ella no sabe es que
            (what she doesn't know is)
yo la conozco requetebien.
                        (i know her well.)
no soy su hija por gusto.
            (it's not for nothing i'm her
daughter.
la conozco perfectamente.
            (i understand her too well.)

she slides the blade of the razor between the
door and the door jamb exactly the same way
maria did it. the door glows blue.

la madre: (smiling.) que barbara! (i'm brilliant!)

she reaches out and opens the door. la hija is
standing at the door.

la hija: mama?

sudden shift.

a moment.

la hija and la madre stand facing each other.

la hija: mama? so yo. (mama, it's me.)

sudden shift. la madre looks past la hija and out the door. thunder. lightning.

there are no subtitles/dubbing for the rest of the scene.

caridad: hay tormenta.

la hija: mama?

la madre: (to the baby.) marea...

la hija: marea...

la madre: ya es tiempo, mi amor.

la hija: it's time.

caridad puts the razor in her purse. she peers into the bassinet.

la madre: vamos a ser felices, tu y yo.

la hija: we'll be happy.

la madre: tu y yo y papa.

la hija: you, me, and daddy.

la madre: te quiero, mi tesoro.

la hija: i love you.

la abuela appears at the door.

la abuela: ¿maria, que haces? (maria, what are you doing?)

thunder and lightning. la madre knocks the bassinet over. as she does so stacks of letters and photographs spill violently on the floor. she vanishes. la hija is on the ground clutching the photos and letters to herself.

la hija: (looking at a picture.) i love you (another picture.) i love you. (another picture.) i love you.

la abuela: maria!

la hija: that is not my name!

la abuela: you should have never come in here. vamos!

she reaches over to grab la hija. la hija holds the razor out.

la hija: you stay away!

la abuela: what? do you think that scares me?

what do you think i am, eh?

la hija: i have wanted... i have wanted for so long... but i didn't even have the words... i didn't even feel i deserved to want anything...

la abuela: what? what do you want?

that woman in those pictures? you think that is your mother?

she took you out to the beach during a storm. she slashed her wrists with a razor and walked into the water. i think she meant to bring you with her, but something—alabado sea el señor!—stopped her. we found you crying, cold, bloody on the beach.

do you think that is what a mother does?

la hija: but why? why did it happen?

la abuela tends to the cut on la hija's arm.

la abuela: do you know what it is to long for something so much it makes you crazy? it makes a pain inside of you. it is a woman's right—a divine right—to make sure our memories live on in our children. but i had to beg. i had to plead. i believed in miracles then. but no matter how much i believed, la virgen didn't think i deserved what i had desired. i should have known better...

we were cursed, hija. i was thirty when i had
your mother. she was thirty when she met
this man. this italian tourist. i didn't think i
had to worry about her. she was always a
good girl. i thought she would end up being
una solterona, but i didn't care. she was a
good daughter. but then she was pregnant.
pregnant! and of course this man had no idea.
he was off in italy and she thought he would
come back, but he didn't of course.

and then you came. and then she left.

and i worried. what would happen to you?
you just turned 30. you started having these
dreams... i've tried to protect you your entire
life. i've tried to make sure the curse didn't
happen to you too.

la hija: but i felt i was... i was unable to see
anything. be anything.

la abuela: you have to sacrifice. you have to
suffer to make something of yourself in this
world. the little you suffered has not been the
same to what i have suffered.

she raises her skirt to reveal a cilice, a spiked
garter used for corporal mortification. around
the cilice, her stocking is stained with blood.

you asked me what a discipline is. well this is
it.

our spiritual director says i can only wear this for two hours a week, but i put this on every day as penance for what i have done. and i wear it so you don't have to. so don't tell me you have suffered. i have taken care of you the way she should have done.

la abuela reaches out and touches la hija.

la abuela: i am so sorry. i have tried...

la hija: (scrambling away from her.) i need to go away. i need to get away from here.

la abuela: and what good would that do? do you think you can escape all this? you will never be happy.

la hija: how do you know?

la abuela: because it is impossible. there is no happiness.

la hija: that's what you've forced yourself to believe. i need to believe in something else.

la abuela: who will keep you safe if i am not there?

la hija: (a realization.) i will.

la abuela strikes la hija. a moment.

la abuela: i'm sorry. but you must listen to
me. i know more about these things than you.

even if you run away, you will never ever leave
this house.

la hija looks at la abuela. she calmly and
resolutely walks to the door of the room. she
puts her hand on the doorknob.

la hija: goodbye, abuela.

la hija opens the door and the stage is flooded
with a title that says the end.

pause.

the projection moves backwards. cuba, the
caribbean, caridad's face, the door, thunder
and lightning, the opening credits.

darkness and immediately...

                    end of scene.

8.

maria: hand on doorknob. make it turn. leave
the room. leave the house. escape. quickly,
completely. as if i was never there. hand on
doorknob, i make it turn. but when it opens, i
step onto the rocks of the island and i see the

waves and i taste the salt. and i look down and i see her. ana. no not ana. she has my face.

and i realize...

i'm home.

we are back in maria's apartment in new york city. maria's bathroom. caridad is slumped in a corner holding herself where maria sliced with the razor.

maria: mamá... despierta... (mom, wake up.)

caridad opens her eyes. she is weak.

caridad: hija. i thought i was going to lose you again.

maria: i thought i could escape.

caridad: i told you you couldn't.

that it's impossible... i know this. i know this more than you.

he was visiting from italy. i met him on the malecón. we were looking at the sea. he said he was making a movie. a story set on an island. i know about islands i told him. and i know all about the ocean.

i was told once by una santera i would meet a man with blue eyes. and his eyes... his eyes...

i was thirty years old. i was thirty years old.

he was so beautiful and he had these eyes. i kept looking at them. i was afraid. i thought it was dangerous to look at something too much.

what else could i do?

that day... i thought about bringing you with me. i even took you with me to beach. i took you. i didn't want to be alone but i... i couldn't. i couldn't.

and i left you. i left you. i left you.

but i didn't know, hija. i thought i could destroy my flesh but i didn't know i couldn't destroy my desire for you. don't look at me that way. i'm the villain. no. i'm the victim. a victim of a curse! a curse where love means drowning. where love means suffocating. i tried... i tried!

maria holds her, trying to steady her.

la hija: mamá. it's okay. it's okay.

la madre claws at la hija.

la madre: i am not that strong. i need you. i crave you. i call out your name every night. i have to claim you as my own.

she reaches for the straight razor. maria calmly puts her hand over her mother's and stops her.

maria: no. we're going to learn a different story.

caridad: what story?

maria: havana. exterior. a woman walking down the street, holding her purse, looking for her lipstick. and then, a frigid shadow falls over her. the woman runs. gets to the ocean.

caridad: what happens then?

maria: she dives in. she cuts through the waves. and she's free.

she kisses caridad lightly on the mouth.

caridad: i'm floating...

caridad disappears.

there is a knocking on the door.

regla: maria, abre esta puerta, nos vamos!

claudia: cara... are you all right?

cara?

regla: maria!

maria: that is not my name.

she takes the razor, she closes it and puts in her pocket. she gazes at her reflection into the bathroom mirror.

maria: this is the face. my true face.

i see.

my name... mi nombre es marea.

blackout.

end of play.

LAND OF BENJAMIN FRANKLIN

BY

ANNE GARCÍA-ROMERO

About the Playwright

ANNE GARCÍA -ROMERO's plays include Earthquake Chica, Mary Peabody in Cuba, Desert Longing, Juanita's Statue and Santa Concepción. Her plays have been developed and produced most notably at the New York Shakespeare Festival/Public Theater, Arielle Tepper Productions' Summer Play Festival (Off-Broadway), The Mark Taper Forum, Hartford Stage, Borderlands Theater and South Coast Repertory. She has also written for Peninsula Films, Elysian Films and Disney Creative Entertainment. She's been a Jerome Fellow at the Playwrights Center of Minneapolis as well as a MacDowell Colony fellow. She's taught at USC, Cal Arts, UC Santa Barbara, UC Riverside, Macalester College, Loyola Marymount University and Wesleyan University. She is currently a Moreau Fellow in the Department of Film, Television and Theater at the University of Notre Dame. Her plays are published by NoPassport Press, Broadway Play Publishing and Playscripts. She holds an MFA in Playwriting from the Yale School of Drama and is an alumna of New Dramatists.

For performance rights to this play contact Susan Gurman at the Susan Gurman Agency, 245 West 99th St, 24th Flr New York, NY 10025, 212-749-4618 susan@gurmanagency.com

Land of Benjamin Franklin was a finalist in the Actors Theater of Louisville Ten Minute Play Contest, given a reading at New Georges Theater in New York City and produced and directed by Jesus Reyes at East L.A. Repertory in Los Angeles, CA as part of the Anthology series on September, 28, 2007 with the following cast:

Marta..Carla Pantoja
Joaquin..Juan Carrillo

CHARACTERS

MARTA, early 30's

JOAQUIN, mid-40's, her lover

SETTING

July, 1976. A studio apartment on the Lower
East Side of New York City.

SPOTLIGHT ON MARTA, WEARING A THIN, TIGHT DRESS, SMOKING A CIGARETTE, SITTING ON HER BED IN A SPARE STUDIO APARTMENT.

MARTA: Solar rain descends like torpedoes to the earth's surface and heats up this city until it feels like we're smoldering souls in some kind of apocalyptic garbage heap.

SPOTLIGHT OUT AS LIGHTS RISE AND JOAQUIN ENTERS, WEARING A BUSINESS SUIT, TYING HIS TIE.

JOAQUIN: In my country, this weather is mild.

MARTA LIES BACK DOWN ON THE BED.

MARTA: The solar rays are penetrating my skin, makes me want to do it again and again and again, Joe.

JOAQUIN: Joaquin.

MARTA SITS UP ON THE BED.

MARTA: Joaquin, it makes me want to suck, slurp, grunt, shriek and howl for more, more, more until the cops show up and haul us down to the station on our bare asses but we'll be sooooo satisfied we won't even...

JOAQUIN: (interrupting) Don't joke about men in authority.

MARTA: Don't place parameters on my humor.

JOAQUIN: I might not come back.

MARTA: You will. You don't have hands and lips and a tongue like this everyday, que sí?

JOAQUIN: You should learn Spanish. You're guapíssima.

MARTA: I'm gorgeous. I understand the language. Just can't really speak it.

JOAQUIN: If you could, you would increase your opportunities.

MARTA: So teach me.

JOAQUIN: Amor.

MARTA: Love. Amor.

JOAQUIN: (correcting her) More O.O. Amor.

MARTA: Amor.

JOAQUIN: Sí bien. Muerte.

MARTA: Muerte.

JOAQUIN: (correcting her) Erte. Erte. Flip the "r"

MARTA: Muerte. Death.

JOAQUIN: Sí. Mar.

MARTA: Ta. Marta. My name.

JOAQUIN: Mar.

MARTA: Mar. Sea.

JOAQUIN: Fusilamiento.

MARTA: Fusila...

JOAQUIN: (interrupting) Practice, Marta linda while I walk up Fifth Avenue and sell my fine gemstones to the man with the British accent at Tiffany's. I'll enter the carpeted palace and show him my emeralds, tourmalines, sapphires, rubies, topaz, finely cut diamonds and he will smile his toothy smile and I will be a wealthy man.

MARTA: Back here at ten for more lessons.

JOAQUIN: Sí guapíssima.

LIGHTS SHIFT. SPOTLIGHT ON MARTA.

MARTA: (quickly, desperate) Marta. Mar. Sea. Salty. Flesh. Licking. Sucking until my lips ache from exhaustion. Then streaking down Fifth Avenue. Letting everyone witness my amazing firm thighs, buttocks and breasts. Marta. Mar. Sea. I sing torch songs of love. Put on the make up, the fancy ass finery and haul my self to the Rainbow Room and wow the crowd with the sweet stylings of Marta Mar. Short for Martinez. Spanish father. American mother. Mar. Mar. Mar. Swim. Swim. Sea. (singing, nursery rhyme) Sing a song of sixpence a pocket full of rye. Four and twenty blackbirds...(changing the tune, torch song-ish) Bailamos juntos... (speaking) Breathe. Breathe. Must breathe.

LIGHTS SHIFT. SPOTLIGHT ON JOAQUIN.

JOAQUIN: (determined, cold) And they pointed the rifle at him. The barrel had a long thin knife attached to it. He said he was a good man but they shook their heads. They said, "Who are you to speak that way in a public cafe at midnight with a glass of cognac in one hand, a cigarette in the other and a smile on your face in front of a crowd of friends. You can't talk like that." Then pow, pow, pow-pow. Blood, like a tiny fountain from the top of his skull and little bits of flesh on the blue tile floor. And his spirit gone as the red liquid slowly crept across the floor in a line to my black leather shoe.

LIGHTS SHIFT. THAT EVENING. MARTA
AND JOAQUIN SIT UP IN BED.

MARTA: 1776. 1976. Big deal.

JOAQUIN: Benjamin Franklin. Betsy Ross. Thomas
Jefferson. John Quincy Adams.

MARTA: And? So?

JOAQUIN: Inventions. Freedom. Self-
determination. Self-governance.

MARTA: Why don't you sell textbooks, not
gemstones?

JOAQUIN: Your lack of appreciation is, how do
you say?, appalling.

MARTA: It's what I know, so, big deal. (seductively) Ready for more...

JOAQUIN GETS UP OUT BED.

JOAQUIN: Your lack of patriotism is really very offensive.

MARTA: I don't see how this bicentennial shit makes any difference in my day-to-day existence.

JOAQUIN: History. Self-determination. Self-rule. A limitless array of possibilities.

MARTA: Tell me more about your daughters.

JOAQUIN: I don't want to talk about them right now.

MARTA: Too painful to feel their presence while we're in here, like this. I'll bet they're niñas lindas.

JOAQUIN: (correcting her pronunciation) Lindas. Lindas. More "ee". They come running up to me when I approach the back gate of our casita, my hand on the black iron bars and I hear "Papi, Papi" and they run out of the house like angelitas.

MARTA: Little saintly spirits. And...Sol?

JOAQUIN: (seductively) I'm ready for more...

MARTA: First I want to hear more about Sol. Do you picture her here? Sol. Sun. Like a ray of sunlight shining on our "dark" deeds? I imagine my dead grandfather, Julio, sitting on that chair over there, shaking his head and saying, "Ay Martita, porque?" and I shake my head and say, "Sorry abuelo but this is my desired form of communication, connection, communion, to know I am breathing, that I can, will, do connect to another human being in this world."

JOAQUIN: I feel no guilt, sadness, shame. I travel here. We meet. We have this. I leave. I return home to my country. And Sol...my wife can't smell. Her nostrils don't function. Childhood accident. She can't smell the salt from Mar, Marta, on my skin. So I can swim to the depths of the sea and she will never, ever know.

MARTA: Come 'ere. Ven aqui.

JOAQUIN: No. (correcting her pronunciation) Aqui. Ah. Ah. Aqui.

MARTA: Ven aqui, baby.

THEY FALL INTO BED AS LIGHTS SHIFT.

DREAMLIGHTING. JOAQUIN GETS OUT OF BED, PUTS ON A PAIR OF TINY GLASSES, A GRAY COLONIAL WIG AND BECOMES

BENJAMIN FRANKLIN. MARTA GETS OUT
OF BED, PUTS ON A COLONIAL HAT,
HOLDS AN AMERICAN FLAG AND
BECOMES BETSY ROSS.

BENJAMIN: Sew me, baby.

BETSY: You like needles?

BENJAMIN: And I like leather. I like flogging. It
frees me.

BETSY: What will Thomas Jefferson and the others
say?

BENJAMIN: They won't need to know that I like
the feel of leather on my bare flesh.

BETSY: I want to rip off my bonnet, apron,
petticoat, corset and run through the cobble stone

streets covered only by my flag except...I haven't finished it yet so running naked will have to wait.

BENJAMIN: When I stood there with the kite and key in the electrical storm and felt the first jolt of lightning on my finger, I was turned on baby, pleasure and pain, electricity aroused my flabby flesh and I wanted more, more, more.

BETSY: Benjamin, your views on intimacy are revolutionary.

BENJAMIN: Betsy, when you put your fingers to cloth, holding needle and thread, I get hard.

BETSY: Benjamin, I can't hold onto this needle much longer.

BENJAMIN: We're electricity, Betsy.

BENJAMIN AND BETSY FALL INTO BED AS
LIGHTS SHIFT.

DREAMLIGHTING. JOAQUIN GETS OUT OF
BED AGAIN, PUTS ON AN OVERCOAT AND
BECOMES JULIO, MARTA'S GRANDFATHER.
MARTA GETS OUT OF BED, PUTS ON A
BATHROBE AND BECOMES SOL, JOAQUIN'S
WIFE. BOTH STAND APART LOOKING AT
THE BED.

SOL: (to "Joaquin") I look at you with her and I
blame myself.

JULIO: (to "Marta") You find in him the Latin
world you long for. He finds in you the American
world he craves.

SOL: I take care of las niñitas. I cook, clean, bake,
wait. I hear gunshots in the night. But he promises
they won't come near our casita. We're protected,
safe. I think of you here, with her. And I blame
myself.

JULIO: When my son married la gringita, I knew they would create children with two worlds split down the middle. Oil and water. Dos mundos and a wandering spirit. Martita, you have it the worst. Burning oil mixed with boiling water. Martita, Martita, porque?

SOL: You think I can't smell but I can. I tell you I was in un accidente as a young girl. It's my only defense. When you return home, I smell your shirts, socks, pants, pajamas, underthings and I know.

JULIO: "No debes. You shouldn't" I whisper to you . "Amor libre" you think. "Why don't you behave like una señorita, Martita." "This is my way, abuelo," you think. Espiritu libre. And I sit back and sigh. Burning oil. Boiling water. Ten cuidado, niña.

JULIO AND SOL SIT ON EITHER SIDE OF THE BED AS LIGHTS SHIFT.

THE NEXT MORNING. LIGHTS RISE AS
JOAQUIN AND MARTA SIT ON EITHER SIDE
OF THE BED.

MARTA: You come here. We do this. You leave.
You come back here. You come. I come. We lie
here. The rising heat sizzles our skin. Again. And
again. And again.

JOAQUIN: Martita...

MARTA: How many fine and precious gemstones
does New York City need? All those plump, rich
señoras who sit and watch my show bathed in liquid
love from head to toe must need more.

MARTA (CONT.): (singing, to the tune of Sinatra's
rendition of "Fly Me to the Moon")

Fly me to the sea,

let me swing among the fish,

let's swim you and me,

we can splish splash where we wish.

(speaking) I dream I follow you back and lie near the beach in a casita and you visit me in the afternoons as we sweat and writhe instead of taking la siesta.

JOAQUIN: You can't follow me. If you follow me, they follow me from the airport, to my back gate and they watch me. They look inside my garden at mis niñitas. They suspect everything.

They watch Sol. They watch me as I leave in the morning for work, as I walk to my car which they have worked on while I was sleeping dreaming of you and I climb into my Fiat, close the door, turn the key and then a blast of light and flame fills my body and my skeleton becomes black bone with charred flesh and mis niñitas are thrown from their beds by the explosion. (beat) Stay here and wave your flag and thank Señores Franklin, Jefferson and Washington for your libidinous liberty.

MARTA: Move.

JOAQUIN: I can't.

MARTA: I need this...daily.

JOAQUIN: I'll be back next month.

MARTA: I'll find a bigger place. I'll even move to the Upper East Side for you.

JOAQUIN: We have an agreement.

MARTA: I don't like our agreement.

JOAQUIN: We have a way of behaving that works.

MARTA: I'm tired of our way of behaving with Sol and abuelo Julio and the fucking kinky founders of this country all hovering over my tiny bed.

JOAQUIN: I have to go back to my country.

LIGHTS SHIFT.

EVENING. MARTA LIES IN BED AS
JOAQUIN STANDS NEXT TO THE BED AND
PACKS. SHE SMOKES.

MARTA: I fear death. I see it on the corner of St.
Mark's Place and Second in the eyes of decrepit
ladies begging for change with chapped, chipped
faces and hands and teeth. It fuels me though. I see
death and I run, run, run, faster, farther, better than
I've run before. It won't beat me. I won't be cut
down at fifty like mi abuelo, Julio.

JOAQUIN: Who talks to you from the dead...

MARTA: I only know him from photos and stories
my father told me. He almost got away. Valencia.

1936. And the Republican soldiers are rounding up people and they look at his hands, the delicate hands of a painter, not a worker, and they think he is a sympathizer, that they heard him speaking Italian in a cafe about his "conservative" ideas and so they decide. Then boom. To the temple. He's gone.

JOAQUIN: When mi papá was silenced, I watched him in the cafe, playing chess with his amigos. Then los militares run in. Stop. Look. Then un tiro here. Un tiro there. Pow. Pow-Pow. I will not let them repeat that with me. Never.

MARTA: In your Latin American country...

JOAQUIN: In my Latin American country.

HE CONTINUES PACKING. MARTA PEERS OVER HIS SUITCASE TO FIND A POLICEMAN'S HAT. SHE HOLDS IT UP.

MARTA: Amor. Muerte.

JOAQUIN TAKES THE HAT AND PUTS IT
BACK IN THE SUITCASE.

MARTA: Did you buy a bicentennial souvenir? You
shoulda bought the founding fathers special,
powdered wig, glasses, musket, instead you buy the
standard blue.

JOAQUIN: Time to say adios.

MARTA: What, so you'll wear that hat to show your
radical power as you bump off los militares in the
night as payback for your father? (beat) Look...I sing.
We meet. We talk. You come here. We do this. You
leave. You return. But here in this great city of
anonymity you could be anyone and so could I.

JOAQUIN: We have an arrangement.

MARTA: I'm tired of breathing in the heat of your mystery.

JOAQUIN: So, I follow orders. I come here. I sell fine gemstones so I can earn extra while I get information about los militares, their locations, their movements, their plans and I return to my city. And I wait for the next order from my compadres. But each time I return to this land of Benjamin Franklin, I'll find you.

LIGHTS SHIFT. BLACKOUT. END OF PLAY.

About the editor

Caridad Svich is a US Latina playwright, translator, lyricist and editor whose works have been presented across the US and abroad at diverse venues including Denver Center Theatre, Mixed Blood Theatre, Cincinnati Playhouse in the Park, The Women's Project, Repertorio Espanol, INTAR, 59East59, McCarren Park Pool, 7 Stages, Salvage Vanguard Theatre, Teatro Mori (Santiago, Chile), ARTheater (Cologne), and Edinburgh Fringe Festival/UK. She has been short-listed for the PEN Award in Drama three times, including in the year 2010 for her play ***Instructions for Breathing***. Among her key works: ***12 Ophelias, Alchemy of Desire/Dead-Man's Blues, Any Place But Here, Iphigenia...a rave fable, Fugitive Pieces, The House of the Spirits*** (based on Isabel Allende's novel), ***Magnificent Waste, The Tropic of X*** and the multimedia collaboration ***The Booth Variations***. She has edited several books on theatre and performance including _Trans-Global Readings_ and _Theatre in Crisis?_(both for Manchester University Press) and _Divine Fire_ (BackStage Books). She has translated nearly all of Federico Garcia Lorca's plays and some of his poems, and works by Julio Cortazar, Lope de Vega, Calderon de la Barca, Antonio Buero Vallejo and contemporary plays from Mexico, Cuba and Catalonia. Her works are published by TCG, Smith & Kraus, Playscripts, Arte Publico Press and more. She is alumna playwright of New Dramatists, founder of NoPassport theatre alliance & press, associate editor of Routledge/UK's _Contemporary Theatre Review_ and contributing editor of _TheatreForum_. She is a member of PEN American Center, The Dramatists Guild and is an entry in the _Oxford Encyclopedia of Latino History_. She trained for four years with Maria Irene Fornes, and also holds an MFA in Theatre-Playwriting from UCSD. Website: www.caridadsvich.com

NoPassport

NoPassport is a Pan-American theatre alliance & press devoted to live, virtual and print action, advocacy and change toward the fostering of cross-cultural diversity in the arts with an emphasis on the embrace of the hemispheric spirit in US Latina/o and Latin-American theatre-making.

NoPassport Press' Dreaming the Americas Series and Theatre & Performance PlayTexts Series promotes new writing for the stage, texts on theory and practice and theatrical translations.

Series Editors: Randy Gener, Jorge Huerta, Mead K. Hunter, Otis RamseyZoe, Stephen Squibb, Caridad Svich (founding editor)

Advisory Board: Daniel Banks, Amparo Garcia-Crow, Maria M. Delgado, Elana Greenfield, Christina Marin, Antonio Ocampo Guzman, Sarah Cameron Sunde, Saviana Stanescu, Tamara Underiner, Patricia Ybarra

NoPassport is a sponsored project of Fractured Atlas, a non-profit arts service organization. Contributions in behalf of [Caridad Svich & NoPassport] may be made payable to Fractured Atlas and are tax-deductible to the extent permitted by law. For online donations go directly to https://www.fracturedatlas.org/donate/2623

More titles from NoPassport Press:

Antigone Project: A Play in Five Parts by Tanya Barfield, Karen Hartman, Chiori Miyagawa, Lynn Nottage and Caridad Svich, with Preface by Lisa Schlesinger, Introduction by Marianne McDonald. ISBN 978-0-578-03150-7

Amparo Garcia-Crow: The South Texas Plays (Cocks Have Claws and Wings to Fly, Under a Western Sky, The Faraway Nearby, Esmeralda Blue) with Preface by Octavio Solis. ISBN: 978-0-578-01913-0

Migdalia Cruz: El Grito del Bronx & other plays (Salt, Yellow Eyes, El Grito del Bronx, Da Bronx rocks: a song) Introduction by Alberto Sandoval-Sanchez, afterword by Priscilla Page. ISBN: 978-0-578-04992-2

Catherine Filloux: Dog and Wolf & Killing the Boss Introduction by Cynthia E. Cohen. ISBN: 978-0-578-07898-4

Karen Hartman: Girl Under Grain Introduction by Jean Randich. ISBN: 978-0-578-04981-6

Kara Hartzler: No Roosters in the Desert Based on field work by Anna Ochoa O'Leary ISBN: 978-0-578-07047-6

John Jesurun: Deep Sleep, White Water, Black Maria – A Media Trilogy Preface by Fiona Templeton. ISBN: 978-0-578-02602-2

Carson Kreitzer: SELF DEFENSE and other Plays (Self Defense, The Love Song of J Robert Oppenheimer, 1:23,

Slither)_Preface by Mark Wing-Davey, Introduction by Mead K. Hunter. ISBN: 978-0-578-08058-1.

Lorca: Six Major Plays: (Blood Wedding, Dona Rosita, The House of Bernarda Alba, The Public, The Shoemaker's Prodigious Wife, Yerma) In new translations by Caridad Svich, Preface by James Leverett, Introduction by Amy Rogoway. ISBN: 978-0-578-00221-7

Matthew Maguire: Three Plays: (The Tower, Luscious Music, The Desert) with Preface by Naomi Wallace. ISBN: 978-0-578-00856-1

Oliver Mayer: Collected Plays: (Conjunto, Joe Louis Blues, Ragged Time) Preface by Luis Alfaro, Introduction by Jon D. Rossini. ISBN: 978-0-6151-8370-1

Chiori Miyagawa: Woman Killer introduction by Sharon Friedman, afterword by Martin Harries. ISBN: 978-0-578-05008-9

Alejandro Morales: Collected Plays: (expat/inferno, marea, Sebastian)_ISBN: 978-0-6151-8621-4

Lisa Ramirez: EXIT CUCKOO (Nanny in motherland) ISBN: 975-0-578-07520-4.

Anne Garcia-Romero: Collected Plays: (Earthquake Chica, Santa Concepcion, Mary Peabody in Cuba) Preface by Juliette Carrillo. ISBN: 978-0-6151-8888-1

Octavio Solis: The River Plays (El Otro, Dreamlandia, Bethlehem) Introduction by Douglas Langworthy._ISBN: 978-0-578-04881-9

Saviana Stanescu: The New York Plays(Waxing West, Lenin's Shoe, Aliens with Extraordinary Skills) Introduction by John Clinton Eisner. ISBN: 978-0-578-04942-7